EMMA BY THE SEA

Emma by the Sea

by

Sarah G. Levine

2025

EMMA BY THE SEA

ISBN 13: 978-1-63679-879-0

This Trade Paperback Original Is Published By
Bold Strokes Books, Inc.
P.O. Box 249
Valley Falls, NY 12185

First Edition: May 2025

Credits
Editor: Ruth Sternglantz
Production Design: Stacia Seaman
Cover Design by Inkspiral Design

Acknowledgments

To start, thank you to Sandy Lowe, Ruth Sternglantz, and everyone on the Bold Strokes Books team for welcoming me into your ranks with open arms and so much love for this book. It's a pleasure to work with you all and to be a part of your community.

An impossibly huge shout-out to Caroline Salis, Mel Whitehouse, Liza Henowitz, Rachelle Kredenster, and Goldie Flavelle for your years of friendship, support, enthusiasm, and laughter no matter the distance.

My second-grade teacher Miss Rex (whose name has changed in the last twenty-two years, I'm sure) for painstakingly teaching a frustrated and reluctant eight-year-old Sarah how to read, and for setting me on this course. To all of my English teachers and literature professors through the years for encouraging my love of books and writing. Thank you for every book you suggested I check out, for every helpful writing tip, for allowing me to dream.

To my coworkers and students at Townsend Harris High School, you all inspire me every day. Kids, please wait until you have graduated to read this book.

Of course, to my idol, Jane Austen, without whom this book wouldn't have been possible. Thank you for writing such a fun and impeccable character as Emma Woodhouse.

My family—Hannah, Zach, Liza, Harrison and Elias (also please wait, you two, until you are at least eighteen to read this). Winnie, you can't read because you're a dog, but you get acknowledged for all you do anyway.

A special thanks to my parents, Laurie and Steve, who have supported me, loved me unconditionally, and given me so many opportunities throughout this life. I am beyond lucky to have been born to you.

Lastly, to my love, Jasmine. For thinking I'm amazing every day, carrying me through when I can't stand on my own, and always reminding me that this too shall pass.

And to you, reader, for reading my words and supporting queer media, now more than ever.

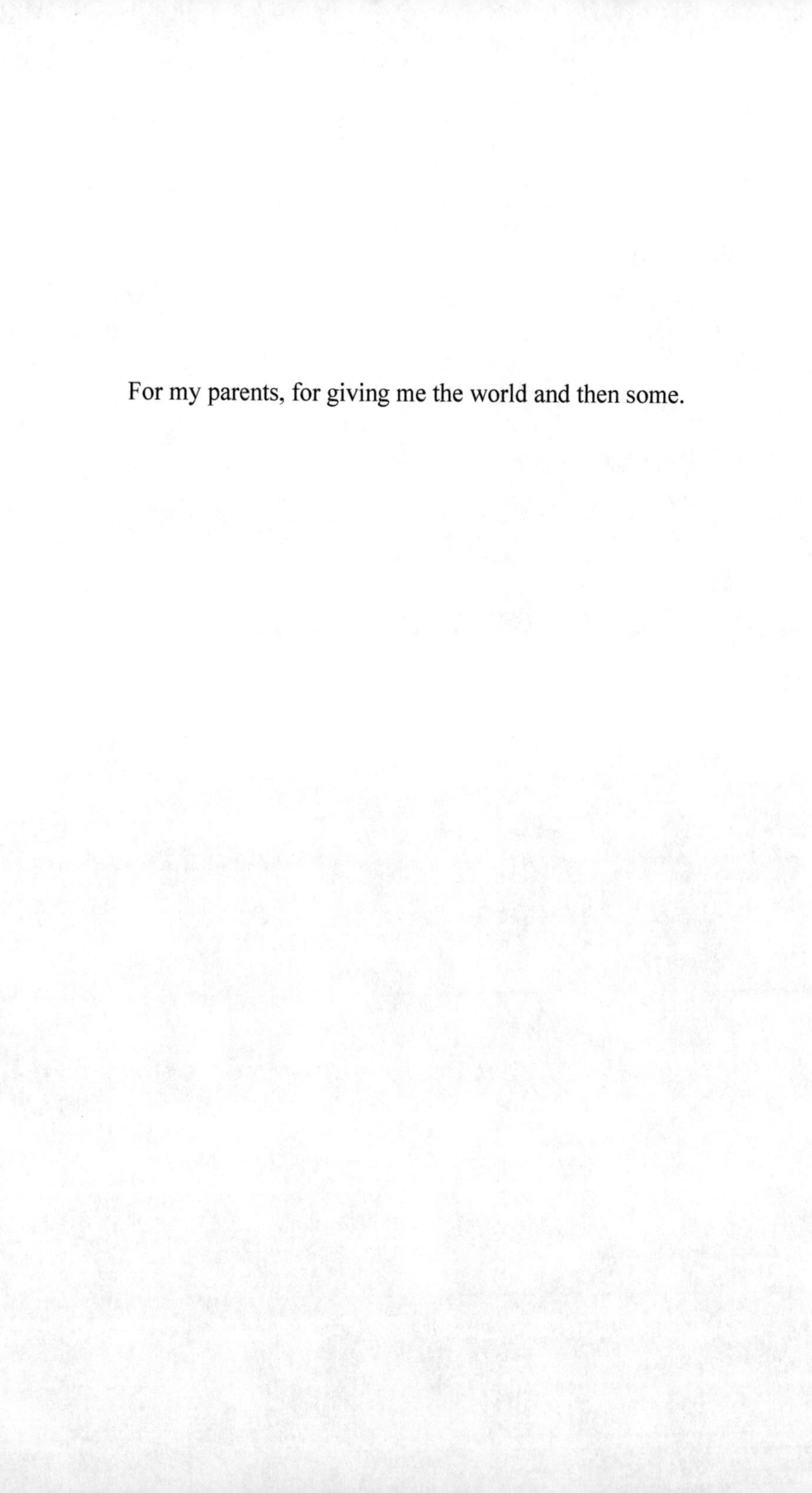

For my parents, for giving me the world and then some.

Emma by the Sea

Chapter One

From the outside, Emma Wilson—tall, blond, and the type of rich that describes itself as *comfortable* but has a yacht club membership and the forty-foot sailboat to match—had a life that seemed perfect.

She lived in a Colonial style mansion that sat high above the crashing waves of the Atlantic. A jewel-green lawn sloped down to the rocky ledge at the end of the property providing an unobstructed view of the waves from every room. The house at 50 Highbury Lane, a tiny one-way street that dead-ended at their doorstep, on the wealthy peninsula known as Marblehead Neck—home to more yacht clubs than stoplights—had belonged to her maternal great-great-grandparents once upon a time.

The house had been built as a summer home to escape the sweltering heat and stench of late nineteenth century Boston but transitioned to the family's full-time residence upon her parents' marriage thirty-three years previously. They named it Heartfield after it became their primary home—a second home on Lake Winnipesaukee in New Hampshire and a condo on St. Thomas capped off their real estate portfolio—a testament to the lasting love the high school sweethearts had shared.

Emma had lived here all her life, except for her time away at Dartmouth, and walked the halls of the house with seven bedrooms, nine bathrooms, a media room, formal and informal dining rooms, and a kitchen that had been featured in a Boston area architectural magazine a few years ago with barely a thought to the sleek styling they'd paid a pretty penny for.

To her, Heartfield and its acres of land were just home. The home where she had grown up running barefoot through the grass, chasing after the various family dogs, while her parents, holding hands, watched her indulgently. The place where, when she was twelve, her mother had died of breast cancer, the long battle finally coming to a tragic end. Where her father's heart had broken, and a decade later, his mind had started to fade.

She knew, to those who came to the Neck to walk or run or bike past the well-manicured hedges, who glimpsed the circular driveway with the stone fountain in the middle of the front lawn and the BMW SUV—hers—and Buick sedan—her father's—parked there, that their home might ooze wealth. But in a neighborhood built on old New England money, theirs was hardly the most ostentatious house in the area.

In fact, Emma thought as she ended her morning five mile run in front of the house and turned into the drive, panting and sweating in the end of June sun, the dove gray paint on the shingle facade was peeling in places and needed to be scraped. After a hard winter and a brutally hot summer, the paint had taken a beating. She'd have to look through Mom's notes to find the housepainter's number when she got the chance.

She waved hello to the landscapers trimming the plants and weeding the gardens, then turned down the shale path that cut through the lawn to the back patio where her father sat, shielded from view by an honest-to-God physical newspaper.

"Morning, Dad," she said, kissing her father's cheek.

"Morning, sweetie," he replied from behind the Metro section of the *Boston Globe*, not looking up at her.

She sank down into the teak deck chair beside her father, the breeze off the ocean ruffling strands of blond hair that had escaped from her high pony and now stuck to her sweaty neck and face. She poured herself a cup of water from the carafe that sat on the small table between the chairs, gulping it down in one long sip.

Setting the cup down and looking over at her father, she tried to judge his state of mind. You would never know that three years ago, at the ripe age of fifty-three, Henry Wilson had been diagnosed with early onset dementia. In a dark blue cotton polo, khaki shorts, and worn leather boat shoes, he looked like any fifty-six year old suburban dad, reading the paper before heading out for a round of golf with his buddies. His once mahogany-dark hair was now mostly gray but still full, his face a bit weather-beaten and lined, his body still ripcord thin from a life of summers sailing on the ocean and falls rowing on lakes and rivers.

She felt a small pang in her chest when she remembered that first time she'd gotten a call from a friend who had found him wandering around the golf club, unable to find his car. He had returned agitated, but assured her he had simply gotten turned around. She had wanted to believe him, so she did, until it became crystal clear she couldn't anymore.

She watched him now, trying to divine if it would be a bad day, a day he called her by her mother's name.

After a quiet moment, punctuated by the crinkle of newspaper as her father turned the page, the buzz of the lawn mower, and the drone of summer insects, he spoke.

"I feel you fretting over there," he said, still not looking at her.

She pulled what she hoped was an innocent look and said, "Fretting? Who, me?"

He lowered the paper so he could shoot her a skeptical glance over the top of it.

She grinned back at him.

"If I don't fret over you, who will?"

"Let's see," he said, discarding the paper on the side table and shifting to look at her full-on, lifting his hand to tick off answers, "Anne, my home health aide, who is currently doing the incredibly important activity of sorting all my pills into a days of the week holder"—he put up a finger to emphasize his point—"your aunt Isabella, who calls me every three hours to make sure I still remember her"—another finger went up—"and—"

"Good morning," came a chipper voice from the yard. Emma looked over her shoulder to see a curvy brunette in her midthirties coming toward them. She wore a pink sundress with yellow embroidery around the V-neckline that revealed a hint of cleavage, and sandals with one woven strap across her instep. They slapped against the stone of the patio as she made her way toward them, an iced coffee in a plastic cup sweating in her hand.

"Dr. Georgia Kostigiris, MD, local neurologist and neighbor," Emma's father said pointedly to Emma, raising a still dark eyebrow at her and gesturing grandly to Georgia with a sweep of his arm.

"Are we using full titles today?" Georgia asked, coming to a stop next to Emma's father's chair, resting one hand on the back and the other on her round hip, condensation dripping on the cotton of her sundress. She pushed her sunglasses up into the thick mass of her hair and looked down at them both.

"Henry Wilson, MBA and former CEO." Georgia nodded to

Emma's dad, who dipped his chin regally in acknowledgment. "Emma Wilson, BA in psychology and lady of the house," Georgia added and pulled a shallow curtsy.

Emma shot her a glare that turned into a grin when Georgia wobbled on the way up.

"Careful, old lady," Emma teased. "Watch out for your knees."

"Ha ha, so funny," Georgia deadpanned and turned back to Emma's father. "How are you doing this morning, Henry? Sleep okay?"

"You would think I'm eighty-five and a fall risk the way you both treat me," he humphed.

Emma flashed back to that horrible night two weeks ago when he'd woken at two in the morning, disoriented and screaming with no idea where he was. She'd had to soothe him back into bed before giving him a sleeping pill. She'd spent the rest of the night staring at her ceiling, heart pounding and wide-awake.

"Maybe we should get him a Life Alert," Emma quipped, pushing the memory back into a safe little box in the corner of her mind.

"We care about you, so sue us," Georgia said with a shrug, ignoring Emma's snark and slapping her dad on the back.

"Yeah, yeah, yeah," he said as he waved Georgia away, "I'm going in to see if Anne needs help with the pills."

"He just wants to get away from us and our womanly concern," Emma stage-whispered to Georgia as her father got out of his chair and turned to walk into the house. Georgia smiled at her and took her father's chair.

"How's he doing today, Em?" Georgia asked, leaning forward conspiratorially over the arm of her chair. The pendant she always wore in the shape of a compass rose swung forward with her movement, and concern tinged her voice.

Emma looked back toward the house and sighed. "I think today's an okay day. He's more annoyed than agitated, which is usually a good sign."

"No more nightmares?" Georgia asked, dropping her voice and leaning closer, her dark gray eyes staring intently into Emma's, professional and personal interests mingling in their depths. Emma could hear the question beneath the question, knew Georgia wasn't only asking about her father's mental state, but hers as well.

Emma looked out at the water, reluctant to meet the intensity of Georgia's gaze and the emotions swirling there.

"No, not like two weeks ago," she replied.

"And how are you?" Georgia reached out her hand and grasped Emma's wrist, her olive complexion standing out against Emma's paler golden skin, her touch comforting and familiar.

Emma let out a long breath.

"Right now? In desperate need of a shower."

She turned her head toward Georgia, who shot her an appraising look, not buying her deflection but not pushing it.

Emma cleared her throat. "So, did you just stop by to see Dad?"

"Actually"—Georgia sat back in her chair and let go of Emma's wrist, and Emma felt a small pang of loss at the absence of her touch—"I came here to talk to you."

Chapter Two

Came here to talk to me? What could I possibly do for the mighty Dr. Kostigiris?" Emma asked as she leaned toward Georgia from her Adirondack chair. "What's up?"

Emma's family and Georgia's had been inseparably entwined since before Emma was born. Georgia's parents, having done well for themselves, moved from their Greek enclave in Ipswich to the WASPy settlement of the Neck where the houses were bigger and the yacht clubs more plentiful, when Georgia was five. The Kostigiris family had been fast friends with the Wilsons ever since, having frequent dinner parties and vacationing together at the Wilsons' lake house in New Hampshire each summer.

According to family lore, Georgia had even held Emma only a few days after she had been born, the then thirteen-year-old Georgie terrified she'd drop the fragile little bean in her arms. She had babysat Emma from the ages of two to twelve and then sat next to Emma during her mother's funeral, holding her hand as silent tears slid down both their cheeks.

Emma was used to Georgia stopping by unannounced most days of the week. Their yards were separated only by a low white picket fence and had merged through the years into one—so much so, that after Georgia's father, drunk at the Wilsons' Fourth of July party a decade earlier, had tripped and cut his head trying to hop over the fence, they had put in a gate.

Emma had never considered Georgia a maternal figure, though, despite their age difference and Georgia's annoying tendency to lecture her. Growing up, Emma had been enamored with her, her gorgeous and wise older friend who guided her through the world of girlhood and into adulthood with a gentle, if stern, hand.

When she began dating women in high school, Georgia was who she went to for advice. And when her first girlfriend broke her heart, Georgia let her cry her eyes out in her lap while they watched cheesy 90s action movies and ate pizza. Then when Emma got too drunk at her friend's house party because her ex was there with her new girlfriend and Emma needed a ride home and someone to hold her hair back, Georgia was there to come to her rescue.

These days, with Emma's return to Heartfield and Highbury Lane, her father's sickness, and Georgia's frequent visits, their relationship had changed. They'd grown closer and more equal. And while she still received the occasional lecture, Emma felt that Georgia saw her and respected her as an adult in a way she hadn't before. It sent a little thrill of pleasure through her every time Georgia deferred to her opinion or sided with her in an argument with her father.

But in all that time, Emma couldn't remember Georgia ever asking her personally for a favor.

Emma sat back in her chair now as she toed off her running shoes and tucked her long toned legs up on the chair, resting her heels by her butt.

Georgia sat back, too, taking the scrunchie off her wrist and tying up the thick mass of her dark hair into a messy bun on the top of her head.

Emma often marveled at Georgia's long, thick, wild hair, so different from her pin-straight blond locks. She'd learned to French braid on it when she was younger and could still recall the softness of the strands as she wove them between her fingers, Georgia seated before her on the ground, patiently letting Emma twist her hair into knots.

"You know my cousin, Eleni?" Georgia asked and drew Emma's attention back to her face.

Emma nodded, familiar with the extended branches of the Kostigiris family tree still planted in Ipswich.

"Well, apparently her daughter Cora is a little boy crazy. Got caught one too many times with a boy in her bedroom late at night," Georgia said, eyebrows raised.

Emma arched her brows in response. "Okay, so Cora is a slut."

Georgia gave her a look.

"Emma, be nice," she said, her forehead crinkled in reproach.

There was a pause during which Emma caught Georgia's eye but didn't say a word.

"I mean, she *is* a little bit slutty," Georgia conceded with a shrug, and Emma laughed. "She was also ditching classes to be with this boy at the end of the year and came home drunk," Georgia continued. "Eleni makes it sound like Cora just *barely* managed to graduate from high school, but I know better. Anyway, she decided that it will be good for her to be around a *good influence*"—she used air quotes, condensation from her sweating coffee dripping down her forearm—"this summer, and for some reason she's decided that's me."

"No, really?" Emma said sarcastically. "The rich, hot doctor with her own practice, a massive house, and a 401(k)? A good influence?"

Georgia had a small neurology practice located in an office block in downtown Marblehead and treated mostly local teens with concussions and migraines and older folks with vertigo, but she had done a fellowship in degenerative diseases like Alzheimer's and dementia. She had been the first one to gently suggest to Emma, when she'd found her in tears after an uncharacteristic fight with her father where he'd called her her mother's name and smashed a lamp, that maybe they should get him evaluated.

Emma could have sworn Georgia's cheeks turned a little pink at her praise, but she also noted a small pleased smile gracing Georgia's full lips.

"So, what do you need me for?" Emma asked. She chalked up the flush in her own cheeks to the aftereffects of her run, and leaned her head back on the chair to look over at Georgia. Their eyes met for a second and held.

After a beat, Georgia looked away and swallowed before she replied, "I think you could be a good influence on her, too."

Emma scoffed, but her heart secretly swelled with pride at Georgia's words.

"I'm serious! I want you to take her under your wing this summer. Show her the ropes of what a sophisticated college graduate looks like."

"You calling me a boring prude, Kostigiris?" Emma shot back in mock outrage.

Georgia laughed. "Not boring, just…domestic?" She tried.

Georgia was a bit right that Emma wasn't exactly rolling in women or raging every night these days. Not that Emma appreciated her pointing it out.

"*Domestic* makes me sound like I'm a tradwife," Emma retorted.

She then mentally ran through her plans for the day—writing a grocery list, paying the gardeners, thinking about repainting the outside of the house—and thought maybe that description fit her a little too well.

Emma sighed, and Georgia reached out to squeeze her forearm.

"So, what does being a mentor for a troubled teen entail?" she asked.

Georgia grinned, sitting back in her Adirondack chair and shrugging.

"Just hang out with her," she said. "Show her there's more to life than making out with boys and drinking. I figure you have more time to devote to her than I do—I'm pretty swamped with my practice. And a twenty-five-year-old is way more fun than a dusty thirty-eight-year-old. Most nights I fall asleep in front of the TV with a half full glass of wine in front of me, cuddling a stack of medical files."

"You're not that old," Emma replied, punching her shoulder lightly. "And that's a very diplomatic way of saying I don't have a job."

Georgia gave her a searching look.

"Anytime you're ready to get back to work or apply to grad school, you know I would support you."

"I know, I just…not yet," Emma said, looking down. Georgia took her hand in hers and squeezed it.

"I won't push it now because I need something from you," she replied softly.

Emma snorted again.

"And maybe Cora will be a nice distraction," Georgia continued. "I told her she has to work as a receptionist at my office five days a week, but maybe you could take her out sailing or playing tennis or for lunch at the club sometime."

"Give her the full WASP treatment," Emma agreed. "Make her wear boat shoes and white pants and pearls."

"Now you're getting it." Georgia smiled. "Her mom is dropping her off tomorrow afternoon. Why don't we come over for dinner after she's settled?"

Emma bit her lip before replying, "I'll let you know how Dad is, but I think that should be okay."

Georgia smiled again and patted her thigh, then stood in a sweep of pink cotton.

"We'll see you tomorrow, Em," she said.

"Yeah, tomorrow."

Emma watched the sway of Georgia's hips as she walked back through the gate, a strange ache in her chest at Georgia's departure.

Guess I have summer plans now, she thought, the echo of Georgia saying she was a good influence playing on repeat in her mind.

If she wasn't careful, she could get used to Georgia's praise.

And her smiles.

And the way her cheeks had turned pink when Emma had called her hot.

She frowned at the thought and shook her head to clear it.

Chapter Three

It wasn't that Emma didn't want to work. It was that the pause she'd taken right after graduation had been extended by her father's worsening condition, and she now found herself shuttling him between doctors' appointments, setting up his nursing schedule, grocery shopping and cooking for him, running the house.

He'd sold his business two and a half years ago, and the money was paying for everything. That and the deep well of generational wealth they already had to draw on from his and her mother's families. Wealth that, while affording Emma endless possibilities, also embarrassed her a little. When she'd seized control of the family's finances only a few short years ago, she made sure to set up generous annual charitable donations in both their names to various Alzheimer's and cancer research and awareness organizations. The donations helped her face paying the exorbitant bills for her endless redecorating projects and her guilt when her college friends complained about student loans, of which she obviously had none.

She'd studied psychology in undergrad and once had aspirations of going to graduate school, but that had all been put on hold in the face of her father's diagnosis. Someone needed to stay on top of things, or everything around them would crumble into the sea like the side of a sand dune after a fierce winter storm.

Most days, she kept on top of paying bills, then sat with her father and Anne, his day nurse, while they chatted quietly, doing puzzles and other memory improving activities in a futile attempt to stave off the inevitable. She worked out, took him to appointments, and compared her life to her college friends' Instagram posts, not the most healthy pastime, she knew.

If she was honest, she felt aimless, adrift, wanting something more than lunch at the club, chatting about so-and-so's sister's wedding or how the pothead from high school ended up being a master hacker or was making bank in crypto.

She missed feeling smart, missed the joy of learning something new, engaging her mind. Something beyond planning menus and scheduling and reading self-help books on how to handle a relative with dementia, or mystery novels. Not that there was anything wrong with this life. It had been her mother's, and she had seemed to enjoy it.

Emma had simply never wanted it to be hers.

But whenever she contemplated taking a step forward, the fear of what might happen if she let her dad out of her sight for too long gripped her so tightly by the throat she felt like she was suffocating.

Now, as she stared forlornly out the nearly floor-to-ceiling bay windows that overlooked the sparkling blue water, gulls calling overhead as they glided through the summer sunshine, she wondered, numbly, what to serve Georgia and her cousin's slutty daughter for dinner.

And what was this Cora supposed to learn from her? She wasn't particularly polished, preferring athletic wear to nearly anything else, a habit from being a lifelong athlete. It wasn't like she was a high society lady that could help mold Cora into a mini debutante.

She had been a loud, happy child, getting only louder after her mother's death, never wanting for friends or activity, but her social circle wasn't particularly big these days. Most days she only saw Georgia, Anne, and her father. Her best friend from college, Wesley—yes, a girl's name—lived in New York, and every time they spoke she told Emma she should come down for a weekend. Emma wanted to, wanted to go to the queer bars and get drunk and dance, wanted to make out with a sexy, sweaty stranger in a dark room again, feel the energy of bodies pressed together, moving to the same rhythm that pounded through her chest.

But she couldn't leave her father, even for a night. Especially not after what had happened two weeks ago. And anyway, she didn't think Wes would get the panic that gripped her like she was drowning most days.

"Georgia's coming over for dinner tonight," Emma said, disrupting the quiet silence of the living room. Her father sat doing a crossword while Anne sat knitting on the couch across from him, her tight black coils tied up in a puff on the top of her head, her scrub shirt covered in colorful fish today, a contrast with the dark hue of her skin.

"Of course she is," her dad replied, putting his crossword down on the table. Emma noticed with faint delight that he had finished it in only twenty minutes today, a good sign. "It's Monday, isn't it?"

Emma smiled. Georgia ate dinner with her family about three times a week, when her busy schedule of doctoring allowed.

"She's bringing a guest with her."

"A new partner?" Anne asked, her Caribbean accent lilting the words.

"No, no," Emma said, a bit sharply, the idea of Georgia dating someone seriously enough to introduce to them sending a little shiver through her, part amusement, part something she couldn't quite define. Georgia was way too focused on her work to date. "Her cousin Eleni's daughter is staying with her for July."

"Oh?" her father asked, eyes quizzical. "A troublemaking teen whose mom is hoping serious Dr. Georgia will scare her straight?"

"Something like that," Emma said, picking at a loose thread in the arm of her chair. "I think Georgia is actually hoping *I'll* take her under my wing. Teach her to be responsible or something."

Her father cast a look at Anne.

"What?" Emma objected. "I'm responsible."

"You left the freezer open two weeks ago, and Hattie had to throw away a week's worth of meat," he answered. Hattie was their housekeeper.

Emma held her tongue. She had left the freezer open because she had been so tired after her father's middle of the night outburst that she had fallen asleep eating a bowl of ice cream at three in the morning and had barely been able to drag herself up to bed. She tried to keep the worst of the way her father's condition affected her hidden from him so as not to add to his stress.

Anne cast her a sympathetic look. Emma just rolled her eyes and shrugged. "I get a bit snacky at night sometimes."

"Well, anyway, it will do you some good to have something to do other than just hang around here waiting for me to deteriorate," he said, a sad note entering his voice.

Emma made a face, then leaned forward to squeeze his hand. She didn't know what to say to comfort him when he got like this.

Her father had been an active man for most of his life. He and her mother had loved to go out dancing, to host big dinner parties with their friends, Georgia's parents always in attendance. Emma had often sat bored in a corner in a scratchy outfit her mother had forced her into during these parties. She'd watched her parents as they laughed with their friends and danced together, her mother elegant and willowy, her father the picture of an adoring spouse.

Her parents would take long hikes together when they went up to their lake house, leaving Emma behind with the nanny when she was small, or to hang out with Georgia if she was staying with them when she was older.

He had been a boisterous presence throughout her life, always loud, always the first to crack a joke or laugh, never one to sit still. Emma took after him in that regard. He'd been a titan of industry, a businessman wining and dining clients and making deals.

Now, though, there were days he forgot what year it was, forgot where he was, got disoriented and angry. Emma had heard him crying softly to himself late at night on more than one occasion.

God bless Anne, Emma thought as she watched the older woman knitting. She took the brunt of his agitation when Emma wasn't around and could talk him down when Emma wasn't getting through, her presence steady and calm like the surface of a lake.

"Is that for your son, Frankie?" Emma asked her, nodding to her needles.

Anne smiled softly. "Oh yes, his daughter is due in six weeks."

Anne's son lived in Atlanta with his wife, and Emma knew she missed him something fierce.

She returned Anne's smile, feeling that old ache that her mother would never get a chance to meet her child, if she ever had one.

Right now, that future seemed impossible. How was she supposed to meet someone to have a kid with, or care for a kid, when she was too preoccupied with her father to really care for herself? And she would most likely be taking care of her father for years yet.

Sure, she could hire more help, get a night nurse for when Anne left. If she was honest with him about the nightmares, that's what he would suggest.

But she cherished the good nights, when it was just her and her father, maybe Georgia, too, and they would curl up in their usual places on the couch after dinner, bickering over what to watch like they'd done nearly every night she was home since her mother died.

Emma would glance at him from her spot, a bowl of ice cream settled in his lap, his familiar face bathed in the blue light from their massive TV, and she could pretend, if only for a moment, that everything was alright. That fear and anxiety didn't dictate her every moment, that she didn't worry the last best day was already behind them. That if she let him go, just an inch, just for one fraction of a second, he'd slip between her fingers and disappear.

Sometimes, it felt like she was already grieving him even though he sat right there.

Chapter Four

Emma could only sit so long in that room, especially on such a gorgeous day. If she stayed still for too long, her entire body began to vibrate with the need to move, to stretch, to lose herself in the sweet oblivion of burning muscles and harsh breathing and the salt of sweat. And even though she'd already run this morning, that familiar itch was tickling the back of her mind.

So she took her bike out of the garage and set off for the local small grocery store to pick out some things for dinner. Despite her weekly Friday meetings with Hattie where they planned the groceries for the week, she wasn't satisfied with what she'd found in the fridge.

She'd settled on having Hattie whip up a simple meal of maple roasted salmon with asparagus and rice pilaf. She wasn't sure what type of food Cora would enjoy, but salmon was a pretty neutral food.

She rode across the causeway that separated the enclave of the Neck from the rest of Marblehead, passing families with toddlers unloading cars full of chairs and towels and beach toys at the public beach, and teen girls perched on the seawall, swinging their legs in their jean shorts and bikini tops, not a care in the world.

Colonial houses with white picket fences lined with granite boulders and orange lilies of the valley blurred past her as she pedaled through town. She stopped at the small grocery manned by bored college kids home for the summer, then pedaled on to the fish store in a tiny harbor with its stack of lobster traps and dinghies, the tank of lobsters bubbling in the corner and oysters and clams and mussels on ice by the register when she picked out her hank of fish, pointing through the glass, for the older woman with weather-beaten skin to cut and size for her.

This town was as familiar to her as her own face, the mirror that reflected her life back to her. The little beaches only revealed by low tide where she used to search for sea glass and pretty pebbles with her mother, the winding one way streets lined with three-hundred-year-old houses she'd been running through since she was fourteen.

She loved it, truly. She just never thought she'd be living here again this early in her life.

"Morning, Hattie," she called as she came into the kitchen, sweeping her helmet-sweaty hair into her habitual high pony after she dropped the shopping bag on the counter.

"Hey, sugar," Hattie said, looking up from her phone. Hattie was a white woman in her early sixties who had been their housekeeper since Emma was eight, as much a member of the family as Georgia. She was tiny, barely five feet tall, and plump with gray hair she kept short and neat, tucked up under a red bandana most days. She favored leggings and tie-dyed tunics and those plastic clogs made for gardening.

When she hugged Emma, who was six feet tall, the top of her head barely came up to Emma's sternum. The flesh of Hattie's forearms hung like crepe from her bones, and she jangled musically as she unpacked the shopping, thanks to the multitude of slim beaten silver and bronze bangles that slid up and down with her movements. Her neck was weighed down by at least three necklaces with large crystal pendants, and small studs lined the perimeters of both ears.

"There's four for dinner tonight," Emma told her, leaning her forearms against the marble top of the large center island in their open-plan kitchen. The room, which Emma had overseen the renovation of one summer in college, was clean and classic and elegant—top of the line ovens, a Sub-Zero fridge, a large gas range with a brass hood. Brass fixtures complemented the white of the cabinets and the dark marble of the counters that ran along the window-lined wall. A deep walk-in pantry, its shelves lined with Hattie's preserves and ingredients labeled and sorted in glass jars, was directly opposite the kitchen island where Emma sat on a metal stool.

"Georgia bringing a date, then?" Hattie replied as she placed the fish in the giant fridge and pulled out a glass container of cut up melon, placing it before Emma for her to pick at.

Emma took a piece of melon from the bowl. Its cold sweetness burst in her mouth when she bit down. "Why does everyone keep assuming that? Georgia dates as much as I do."

Hattie gave her a pointed look.

"Georgia's a grown woman. We don't know everything that goes on in her life," Hattie said to her, an almost scolding note in her voice, like Emma was still a naughty child who'd tracked mud into the house.

Emma glared at her, popping another piece of melon in her mouth and trying to pretend the thought of Georgia with a partner didn't disturb her for some reason.

"*I'm* a grown woman," she said, pouting.

"And you, too, could have a secret girlfriend we don't know about," Hattie said, patting her arm patronizingly. "Maybe all those runs you go on are actually hookups. Maybe nights we think Georgia is working late, she's actually out getting laid."

"Gross, Hattie," Emma said, shivering and trying not to picture some stranger's mouth on Georgia's graceful neck, their hands dipping into the neckline of her ample cleavage, their thigh pressed between Georgia's own luscious legs as Georgia's hips ground against it, soft moans echoing from her full, parted lips. Emma shook her head and attempted to dispel the images, her insides squirming with discomfort.

But Hattie had a point. It had been…a while for Emma. Two years. The last date she had gone on she'd had to cut short because she'd gotten a call from Anne that her father was frantically looking for her. The woman, just some dating app match she'd chatted with for a week, had been understanding, even asked to reschedule. But Emma had decided it just wasn't worth it.

Besides, she could channel her sexual energy into exercising. Nothing curbed your libido like the sheer exhaustion of a grueling ten mile run after three hours of restless, anxiety laced sleep. And if she still felt horny, she could take care of herself.

"I've got too much going on to date," Emma retorted, and Hattie arched her eyebrow as if to say *oh, really?* "Besides, it's not like I could bring someone back here, with Dad and all."

"Yes, but other people have their own homes," Hattie said, no sympathy in her voice. She took the melon away from Emma, covered it with cling wrap, and put it back in the fridge, as if Emma didn't deserve it.

Emma rolled her eyes at her as Hattie shooed her elbows off the marble so she could wipe down the condensation from the melon bowl and Emma's drying sweat.

"I'm just saying, doll, you're too young and beautiful to be wasting away, locked up in this house with us old fogies day after day," Hattie said as she rested her jangling hand on her round hip.

"You sound like Georgia," Emma said and stood from her stool. "She's always telling me I should be getting out more, apply to some jobs, read more books, yada yada yada."

"Our Georgia is a smart woman," Hattie said with an approving nod.

"Sure, sure, whatever," Emma said with a dismissive wave of her hand.

Feeling ganged up on by Hattie and the spirit of Georgia, Emma got up and turned to head out the door. "Dinner at seven," she called over her shoulder, and she heard Hattie's sound of acknowledgment.

She passed her father and Anne, now doing a puzzle in the sunroom, but felt no desire to return to them. She went into what used to be her mother's study, the cherrywood desk and soft blue walls the same as they had been since her mother's death, the one room she couldn't bring herself to contemplate renovating.

She sat by the window that looked out onto the driveway and the blooming blue hydrangea bushes and roses the size of salad plates that lined it as she aimlessly scrolled and clicked on her laptop. She nestled herself in the upholstered roll-back armchair that had been one of her mother's favorite reading spots because it was bathed in shafting rays of sunlight for most of the day.

She stared out the window for a while, brain blissfully blank, laptop sitting unopened on her thighs. Then her phone vibrated against her leg and she looked down at the screen.

Just a spam email from J.Crew.

Above it, the clock read eleven thirty.

Chapter Five

At six fifty-five, Emma walked into the kitchen to check on dinner, dressed in ankle length slim-fitting white jeans and a knitted oatmeal sleeveless sweater, small diamond studs in her ears, her long blond hair blown out and sleek. Hattie had left for the day, and dinner sat plated on the marble island. She leaned down and opened the twelve bottle wine fridge at the base of the island, pulled out a chilled chardonnay, and poured herself a large glass.

She walked out onto the patio where she had set place settings on the round teak outdoor table, citronella candles burning in a cluster in the middle. She took a seat at one of the deck chairs to the right of the dining area and contemplated if it was cool enough to bring out the Solo Stove.

Taking a long swig of the buttery, oaky wine, Emma let out a long sigh.

"What do you have to be so forlorn about?" a low female voice asked off to her right.

Emma turned her head to see Georgia walking toward her from the gate between their backyards. She was dressed in summery light blue high-waisted wide leg jeans that clung to her lush hips and thighs and a billowy white blouse with ruffled short sleeves and bright embroidery around the neck. Gold hoops the size of quarters dangled from her ears, and her dark hair hung loose and waving thickly around her soft, oval face.

Something in Emma's chest loosened at the sight of her, and a smile spread across her lips before she could help herself. Georgia smiled back at her, her gray eyes crinkling at the corners.

Then Emma glanced past her shoulder and saw the teen girl skulking behind her.

"Em, this is Cora," Georgia said and gestured at the girl by her side.

Cora was a pretty seventeen-year-old with thick chestnut hair currently tied up in a bun at the top of her head, amber eyes and the same olive skin as Georgia, tanned deeply already by the sun. She was dressed in a gray T-shirt, baggy ripped jeans, and chunky white sneakers, with a number of silver rings on her fingers and chipped blue polish on her nails. A small stud glinted in her right nostril, and thick swoops of eyeliner lined her upper lids.

She was, quite frankly, much cooler than Emma had been at that age. Emma hadn't been a loser in high school. She'd been the captain of the lacrosse and field hockey teams—yes, she was a lesbian stereotype—and had her fair share of party invites. But she also tried incredibly hard to blend in, to match everyone's style, to belong to her teammates. The town was socially liberal, but it was small enough that she'd been one of the only queer girls, and she dreaded being known as The Lesbian.

"Hi Cora, I'm Emma," she said now, standing from her deck chair and extending her hand not holding the wineglass to the teen to shake. Cora stared at her hand for a second like Emma was offering her a dead fish to hold, then took it in hers.

"Um, hi," Cora said. Her eyes met Emma's, and Emma swore she could see a hint of defiance in them. "You must be my babysitter for the summer."

Georgia rolled her eyes behind Cora's back and Emma stifled a smile.

"Let's think of it as you're being forced to hang out with me rather than me watching you," she said, looking at Georgia, whose eyes sparkled at her with amusement.

"Whatever," Cora said, in the grand tradition of moody teen girls through the ages. She took her hand back after the weakest handshake Emma had ever experienced. "Why are your hands so rough? Aren't you, like, wicked rich?"

Georgia covered her eyes with her hand. Emma tucked her hair behind her ear and willed herself not to blush. Her hands were ruined from crew, a mess of tough calluses and old blister scars, and new ones from using the erg and rowing on the harbor.

"I row," Emma said, quickly clarifying at Cora's blank look, "you know, like, in a boat. I did crew in college, and I still row."

Cora just nodded at her.

They all stood looking at each other for an awkward moment and then Emma cleared her throat. "Can I get you guys something to drink?"

"Wine would be amazing, Em," Georgia said. She practically sagged with relief and turned to follow Emma over to the outdoor kitchen part of the patio.

"Oh yeah, I'll have some, too," Cora chirped.

Emma and Georgia turned to give her skeptical looks.

"Nice try, Cor," Georgia said, accepting the chilled glass of white from Emma gratefully.

"We've got seltzer or lemon water," Emma offered.

"Polar?" Cora asked.

"Is there any other kind?" Emma quipped and Cora smiled.

"There's a fridge full of seltzer in the pantry. Go through that door and take a left and you'll see it," Emma said.

"A seltzer fridge? Dude, why don't you have one of those?" Cora asked Georgia.

"Guess I'm just not as cool as Emma," Georgia said and gave Emma a wink. Emma felt her chest ease further and the strange edge that had been there since her conversation with Hattie dissipated.

Cora went into the house to get a seltzer and also, Emma suspected, to snoop around.

She watched Georgia take a long sip of her wine, her throat working as she swallowed, and then asked, "How was drop-off?"

Georgia sighed, running her hand through her thick waves.

"That bad?" Emma said. She knew Georgia well enough to interpret what she wasn't saying.

"She and Eleni pulled up in the middle of a big fight about how Cora had been out all night the night before with her boyfriend, Martin, who's nineteen and a community college dropout," Georgia told her.

Emma winced.

"Yeah"—Georgia nodded—"he apparently has a small place in Gloucester with a couple of buddies, and Cora fell asleep there and didn't come home until, like, five. Eleni told me, in no uncertain terms, that Martin is not allowed to see her this summer. If he shows up, I'm supposed to, I don't know, turn off all the lights and pretend we're not home."

Emma laughed. "Wow, Georgie, you've gotten yourself into some deep fucking drama."

"I know." She sighed again, taking another sip of her wine and looking into the house after the human hormone tornado that had just moved into her home for a month. "Why do I have to be so nice and selfless all the time?"

"Because you love your family, and being able to take care of them and help them brings you great joy," Emma replied, squeezing Georgia's soft upper arm affectionately.

"I need to be meaner to everyone," Georgia grumbled, leaning a bit into Emma's touch, and Emma smiled. She rested her head on Georgia's shoulder and wrapped her arm loosely around Georgia's waist, breathing in her comforting scent. Georgia smelled like summer sunshine and the lavender and eucalyptus shampoo she used.

"It's what I get for being the rich cousin," Georgia said.

"If it helps, you can be extra mean to me," Emma said and squeezed her hip. "And at least *your* hands are the appropriate softness for your socioeconomic class."

"Hey, I like your horse hoof hands," Georgia replied, looking down at Emma who still rested her head on Georgia's shoulder. They shared a glance, Georgia's eyes roving gently over her face, and Emma felt her cheeks warm. She lifted her head from Georgia's shoulder, took a sip of her own wine, and stepped away from her.

"How was your day, Em?" Georgia asked as she took her usual seat, across from where Emma sat. Emma's father always sat between them, Anne sometimes across from them when she stayed for dinner.

"Oh, you know," Emma responded, putting the salad on the table next to the rolls and butter, "as exhilarating and jam-packed as ever. Went for a run, sat in the living room with Dad and Anne while they bickered about crossword answers, went grocery shopping, sat and stared into the abyss for several hours."

"You know you *could* change that anytime you wanted," Georgia reminded her, her voice practically finger wagging. Emma sighed, the ease in her chest tightening again. This was old ground they covered almost weekly, Emma's insistence on putting her life on hold for her father and Georgia's objections to it.

Emma was spared reopening this can of worms by Cora's entrance to the patio with her father in tow.

"I found a stray rooting around our seltzer fridge," her father said. He greeted Georgia with a kiss on her plump cheek and took his usual spot at the table. Cora settled into the remaining chair, can of cranberry lime seltzer in hand.

"This is my cousin, Cora Legaros," Georgia said.

"Remember, Dad? She's staying with Georgia for the summer," Emma said, scooping salad onto salad plates and handing them around the table.

Her father glared at her. "Yes, I remember, Emma darling. My brain isn't Swiss cheese yet."

Emma plastered what she hoped was a friendly smile on her face and held her tongue. She felt Georgia's eyes on her but resisted meeting her gaze.

"So, Cora, what did you do to get you exiled to Highbury Lane?" Her father launched in with no preamble. "Drugs? Drinking? Steal your mom's car and drive to New Hampshire without telling her and then get pulled over for speeding?"

"That was one time," Emma said and Georgia grinned. She had been the one Emma called to cry to about the whole thing.

"My mom thinks I'm too obsessed with my boyfriend," Cora said with a shrug, poking at the watermelon and feta salad with mint leaves on her plate. "She thought some space might be good for us."

"Ah, young love." Her father sighed dramatically and Emma pulled a face. "I had a girlfriend in high school I thought I was going to marry. Her name was Alicia Marcus, and she gave the best blow jobs in the whole school."

He smiled fondly at the memory.

"Ugh, we didn't need to know that, Dad." Emma coughed, nearly choking on her wine. Georgia laughed, and Cora stared at him like he had eight heads before smiling broadly. He had started doing this, sharing a bit too much with people, as if he forgot who he was talking to in the middle of speaking.

"She was a great girl, too, funny, smart, the whole package." He ignored Emma and continued his memory.

"So, what happened?" Cora asked as she took a bite of watermelon.

He shrugged.

"I met Emma's mother, Giselle, on the first day of senior year, and it was over. She was the most amazing woman I ever knew."

"She was pretty great," Georgia added with a smile.

"Wasn't she? Driven and intelligent and sweet. Emma's a lot like her," he said, patting Emma's hand.

Even though her mother had been dead for thirteen years, it was still painful for Emma to think of her, her own memories growing a bit dim with age. She could remember her mother's smile, a faint echo of her scent from the perfume bottle she kept under her bed, but she couldn't hear her laugh anymore, couldn't remember whether she liked her coffee black or with milk, the sound of her footsteps as she came down into the kitchen in the morning. It ached to think about, particularly now she knew she was slowly losing her father, too.

She felt a tap on her foot underneath the table and looked up to see Georgia giving her a gentle expression. Emma tapped her toes back and watched her answering smile.

"How'd you meet Giselle?" Cora asked.

"Oh God, don't get him started," Emma groaned.

A beatific smile spread across her father's suntanned face, making him look years younger.

"Our senior year, she gave me a black eye with a dodgeball in gym class and felt so bad about it, she told me I could ask any favor of her, within reason, and she'd do it," he recounted.

"And the favor was going out with you?" Cora supplied.

"If only," Emma answered as she got up to clear the salad plates and refill wineglasses, "instead he did something weirder."

"I asked her to be my pitching coach," he said dreamily, and Cora laughed. "That's how we fell in love."

"That's a great story," Cora said, taking a sip of her seltzer.

Her father nodded vaguely, lost in his memories, in a world of his own.

Emma brought out the salmon and served it as her father asked Cora what she wanted to study at college in the fall, which turned out to be environmental science.

"I'm really interested in conservancy," Cora said, the sullen teen now animated by the topic, "particularly salt marshes. Their ecosystem is such a delicate balance, and they provide a great refuge for, like, migrating birds and other animals, and with rising sea levels they're getting flooded more often. It's throwing that balance all out of whack. I want to study how the ecosystem is adapting and what we can do to help protect it."

Emma thought the passion in Cora's voice suited her and wondered absently if her deadbeat boyfriend could appreciate this side of her. She noted the pride shining on Georgia's face as her younger cousin talked, her hands folded under her chin, elbows resting on the table, and eyes intent on Cora's face. It reminded Emma of the way Georgia used to look at her when she talked about her future when she was in college, the research she was assisting with, the professors she admired. It had been a long time since anyone looked at her that way.

Of course, Georgia still looked at her these days, though the emotion behind her eyes was a bit harder to decipher.

She's really not such a bad kid, Emma thought as she listened to the conversation swirl around her. A bit less eyeliner, a bit less time spent on a couch watching a nineteen-year-old play video games or whatever she and Martin did in his—as Emma imagined it—dingy apartment with no sheets on the bed and only one pillow, and she might turn out okay.

Maybe Emma could even introduce her to a boy at the club. Chris Elton, back from his first year at BU, might be her speed. Emma didn't know much about him beyond that he was a boy about Cora's age who was cute in a WASPy way, lots of Brooks Brothers and Vineyard Vines clothes and fleece lined vests.

She glanced back at Georgia to see that Georgia was already peering at her, an unreadable expression on her face, a glint in her eye.

Dinner wrapped up, and everyone brought their plates into the kitchen. Her father retreated to his study, and Cora went back outside to the patio, typing on her phone the whole time, no doubt texting her boyfriend.

"That wasn't too painful," Georgia sighed as she leaned against the counter and watched Emma rinse the dishes and load the dishwasher. Emma straightened up, saw Georgia scrubbing the plate the salmon had been on, and frowned.

"You don't have to help clean up," Emma said as she rested her wrists on her hips so she didn't get oil or soap on her white pants.

Georgia raised her eyebrows at her and kept scrubbing, and Emma just shook her head as she turned back to loading the dishwasher.

"Cora seems like she's actually a pretty cool kid," Emma remarked as she bent over to place plates on the rack.

"Hmm?" Georgia said distractedly.

Emma straightened up and looked over her shoulder at her. Georgia's gaze flicked up to meet hers, and Emma brushed the back of her leg to see if there was something on it since Georgia had been looking there, but her hand only encountered white denim.

"Oh yeah, she's really pretty smart. Going to UMass Amherst in the fall on a full scholarship," Georgia said, drying the dish and putting it on the marble counter. "I just wish her mom was a bit easier on her. But teen girls and their moms, you know."

"I don't, actually," Emma muttered softly as she focused on the plate she was transferring to the dishwasher.

She felt a hand resting on the small of her back, warm and steady, and looked up to see Georgia gazing at her, eyes apologetic.

"Sorry, Em, that was thoughtless of me," she said softly, voice full of remorse.

Georgia rubbed her hand lightly in a soothing circle, and warmth spread through Emma to chase away the chill of grief. Emma gave her a small smile in return.

"It's fine, really," she said, equally softly, as she stood. Georgia's hand slipped from her back as she moved to cork the bottle of wine and return it to the fridge.

She took a breath to steady herself in the glow of the fridge.

"What are you going to do with her?" Emma asked as she turned to face Georgia and leaned against the marble countertop with her left hip, crossing her arms over her chest.

"Well, I taught her the appointment software today, so she's going to be my new receptionist," Georgia said and frowned out the window at Cora. "She doesn't have any work appropriate clothes, though. Think I can send her over tomorrow after work and she can borrow some of yours?"

Emma shrugged. "Sure, they're not really getting any use now."

"They could be," Georgia said, a singsong note to her voice.

Emma shoved her.

"Go take your ward and go home," she grumbled.

Georgia laughed, wrapping her in a hug, quick but tight. Emma's lean body pressed into her soft one, Georgia's head reaching Emma's shoulder and resting against it, her hair soft as lavender scented silk against Emma's skin. Emma let herself be held for exactly three seconds before she pushed away.

"Thanks for dinner, Em, and for helping me with Cora," Georgia said, patting her cheek in farewell.

"Anything for you, Georgie," Emma said teasingly, but meaning it.

CHAPTER SIX

The next day was the same.

Run in the morning, followed by a quick dip in the ocean, the days becoming hot all of a sudden in that way they did in a New England summer, the weather turning from cool and rainy one day to sunny and humid the next.

Emma found her father on the patio with Anne, a good morning, and gave him a kiss on the cheek. She showered, paid some of their bills—electric, water, medical, insurance—and then looked up to find it was only noon. She sighed and went to take out Johnny, Georgia's golden retriever, who she often cared for when Georgia didn't take him into the office.

Johnny was thrilled to see her, as always, and they spent a pleasant hour walking around the neighborhood, Johnny lumbering along, Emma listening to a podcast about the wellness industry.

She walked him by the yacht club and saw a group of women lunching on the deck, eating enormous bowls of salad and drinking iced tea.

"Emma Wilson, is that you?" One of the women, dressed head to toe in tennis whites, her hair a perfectly crafted soft blond in its neat low pony, waved to her.

"Hi, Connie," Emma said brightly and pulled out her sunshiniest smile. Connie had been close friends with her mother—they'd played tennis doubles together and staffed the PTA at Emma's middle school. Emma liked her not so much for her personality, which tended toward gossipy, but for the reminder of her mother seeing Connie always gave her.

Connie came over to the railing of the deck and called down to Emma, "We haven't seen you at the club in ages, honey. Where have you been? We could use you for our twenties and thirties pickleball league!"

Emma opened her mouth to respond, but Connie was on a roll.

"Oh my God, did you hear about what happened with Rachel Whiteman's wedding? Turns out that her fiancé had been screwing her roommate for months, the roommate who was supposedly gay!" Connie gave her a knowing look. She had loved reporting anything remotely queer to Emma ever since she'd come out when she was fifteen.

"Anyway, Charlotte was telling me that poor Rachel can't get the money back from the caterers because the wedding was supposed to be in two weeks, can you imagine?" She punctuated this sentence with a dramatic flip of her hand and then laughed.

One of her friends called to her from their table, and Connie turned.

"I better get back to my girls, honey, but let's do dinner soon, okay? I feel like it's been forever since I saw you and your father."

Emma smiled. "Absolutely, we're pretty free, so just text me."

"It's so wonderful to see you, Emma dear. You look so much like Giselle these days," Connie said. Connie gazed at her a second longer, a bit misty-eyed, before she turned back to her friends.

A memory surfaced of her mother saying, "That Connie Brightley, mouth like a freight train, but a more upbeat person you'll never meet."

Emma felt her chest warm at the memory and walked Johnny back home.

Five thirty saw Emma seated on the back patio pretending to read a book but really just staring aimlessly at the ocean when Georgia and Cora appeared at the gate between their yards.

"What's up, Doc?" Emma called in greeting.

Georgia was dressed in summer business casual, black linen pants and a pale pink silk blouse, her hair tucked back in a low bun, small drop pearls dangling from her ears. She looked elegant but effortless, the high waist of the pants accentuating her hourglass figure. She'd evidently taken off her shoes when she'd gotten home and now strolled barefoot through the grass over to Emma, coral tipped toes flashing up from the green with each step. Cora was dressed in a simple black shirtdress and flip-flops, her long hair braided over one shoulder today, eyeliner still thickly lining her lashes.

"How'd the first day go?" Emma asked as they reached her. Georgia flopped dramatically into the deck chair next to her. Cora took a chaise lounge Emma had dragged out earlier.

"One of her patients asked me what was wrong with my eyes," Cora said.

Georgia laughed. "You are wearing, like, a ton of eyeliner, Cor. They're not used to being greeted by a surly teen in stage makeup."

Cora rolled her eyes and shot back, "This is how everyone on TikTok wears it."

"My office is not TikTok," Georgia retorted, and Emma could tell by the weary note in her voice that this argument had been going on all day.

Deciding to defuse the tension, Emma cut in, "You wanted to borrow some of my old business casual stuff, right?"

"I guess," Cora said, a definite lack of enthusiasm notable in her voice.

"She did," Georgia said firmly. It was fascinating watching Georgia in a parental role. She was good at it, maybe from her years of herding nieces and nephews and younger cousins around.

Emma sometimes wondered if Georgia wanted a partner, a husband or wife to come home to every night, who'd be excited to see her at the end of the day. Kids, family vacations, the whole nine yards. A part of her, the smallest, most selfish part, hoped Georgia never married, so she wouldn't ever lose Georgia to another.

Not that Georgia was *hers* to lose anyway, not really.

"Alright, let the makeover commence," Emma said, hopping out of her chair and clapping her hands together. This was the most excitement she'd had in weeks.

"Wait, who said anything about a makeover—I thought I was just gonna pick up some, like, pencil skirts or something," Cora said, a look of horror crossing her face.

Emma made a face back at her. She wasn't the most fashionable of people, she preferred athletic clothes to almost anything else—case in point, she was currently wearing bike shorts and an old T-shirt from a regatta from college—but even she knew no one wore pencil skirts anymore.

"Cora, no one's worn a pencil skirt in, like, twenty years," she replied.

Georgia sighed.

Emma led Cora and Georgia up to her room. It was at the back of the house on the second floor, with a view of the water and the lawn rolling down to it. The hardwood floors were covered in a soft white rug with a yellow pattern of geometric designs on it that complemented the pale blue walls. Her queen size bed with its white wooden bed frame and mountain of throw pillows sat facing the windows, matching nightstands bracketing it. She'd had it redone when she'd officially moved back home and had been entirely satisfied with the results then.

Now, though, it almost struck her as a child's idea of an adult's bedroom. Something about that made her sad.

"Closet's over there," she said and gestured to the double doors of her walk-in closet on the far side of the room.

Cora threw open the doors and gaped, saying, "Bro, *this* is your closet?"

One side had shelving for her leggings and sweatshirts and multiple pairs of sneakers. There was a rack for her non-athletic shoes as well as boxes for her sweaters and other storage. On the back wall hung her fancy clothes, dresses for galas and weddings and other events she'd attended with her father when he still had his business. On the right side lived her more casual hanging clothes, her jeans and tops and jackets.

"This is the size of my bedroom at home," Cora said as she ran her hands over Emma's clothes and frowned a bit. "You have a lot of workout clothes."

"Former college athlete, remember," Emma said. She took a seat on her bed and watched Cora flip through her clothes. They were about the same size, although Cora's body was a bit curvier than Emma's. She had a waist and hips, and breasts that required a bra, where Emma was more long, straight lines, flat chested, and muscular, although Emma had a good four or five inches on Cora.

"Em, do you mind if I leave her here with you?" Georgia asked quietly. She rested her hand on Emma's shoulder, the warmth seeping in through the cotton of Emma's T-shirt. "I've got some insurance paperwork I need to finish before tomorrow."

"Of course," Emma said and looked up, for once, at Georgia where she stood next to where Emma sat on the bed. Georgia smiled down at her and kissed her cheek, Georgia's lips soft against her skin.

She felt a shiver run through her at the contact, the wave of sweet smell coming from Georgia, eucalyptus and lavender and something harder to describe, and chalked it up to the fact that it had been forever since someone had touched her like that.

"You're the best," Georgia said, breath puffing against her temple. Emma resisted the urge to bite her own lip and turned back to Cora, giving herself a mental shake.

"Hey, Cor, I'm going to leave you in Emma's capable hands," Georgia called to her cousin. "I've got to work tonight, but you can order a pizza or something when you get home."

"She can stay here for dinner," Emma said before she knew she was going to say it. "Do you like ravioli?"

Cora shrugged and held a sheer blouse up to the light like she was inspecting it to uncover its hidden purpose.

"Okay," Georgia said, "I'll see you both later."

And then Georgia left Emma with the seventeen-year-old menace now eyeing down her formal wear.

Chapter Seven

"So," Emma said as she walked over to Cora in her closet, "how do you like working at Georgia's office?"

Cora shrugged again. It seemed to be her main form of communication.

"It's fine, I guess. Beats working at a clam shack like my friend Maddie does. She always comes home smelling like fried grease and seafood. We make her jump in the ocean before she can hang out."

Emma crinkled her nose at the thought. Her summers growing up had been spent at camps—field hockey, rowing, educational—and in internships, padding her college résumé. No summer jobs in seafood shacks for her.

"How did you meet Martin?" Emma asked as she pulled down her box of business wear, untouched for three years since her last internship in school.

"He was in my math class junior year," Cora said. She pulled out a shimmering strapless black gown Emma had last worn the year before to a black tie event at the yacht club.

"Isn't he nineteen?" Emma inquired when she put the plastic bin on the ground and rooted through the contents.

She pulled out a pair of slim cut navy cotton dress pants she had worn at least once a week during her internship senior year where she had spent hours in front of a computer recording surveys about the happiness male students felt in their friendships. It had been tedious work and she had loved it, each data point a new insight into the psyche of another human being.

"Yeah, he failed that class the first time, so he had to repeat it to graduate," Cora replied, coming to sit on the closet floor next to Emma, her long braid swinging forward as she peered into the contents of the box.

"Sounds like a great guy," Emma muttered under her breath.

"Lots of people are bad at math," Cora shot back with a glare, and Emma held her hands up in surrender. "He's just not really a school person."

But you are, Emma thought to herself. Even after only a few hours in Cora's presence, that much was clear to her.

"Why do you have all these clothes? Don't you, like, not need to work?" Cora asked while sifting through Emma's old work wear.

"From internships in college," Emma said and pulled out a black wrap dress she'd worn to the sports banquet her senior year, when she'd been awarded Most Spirited Senior from her coach and then Sam, her college girlfriend, had unwrapped her in her apartment after. She glanced from the dress to where the plaque was tucked into a memento box in her nightstand. "Try these."

She gave Cora the navy pants and a flowy white blouse. She immediately stripped down to her underwear and put the clothes on. Emma admired her confidence. This was a girl who knew herself, who felt not an inch of shame in her body or any urge to tone herself down. For all her extroversion, Emma's driving impulse had always been to fit in. To be a version of herself that was palatable to others.

Cora, not so much.

Cora tried on the outfit and looked at herself this way and that in the full-length mirror inside the closet while Emma laid out outfit after outfit for her.

"I guess this isn't too horrible," Cora concluded. The pants were a bit long on her, but they generally fit well overall.

They went through several more outfits, and Cora ended up with enough clothes to keep Georgia happy.

While they were cleaning up the rest of the box, Cora got a text and looked down at her phone. Emma could tell from the smile that it was from Martin.

"So, you and Martin have been together for a year?" Emma pried.

"No," Cora said, not looking up from her phone as her thumbs flew with impressive speed over the screen, "I dated his friend Matt for a bit in the fall, but he had a small penis and liked EDM too much, so I dumped him."

Emma stared at her, mind still trying to absorb the small penis comment, as Cora happily continued relaying her and Martin's dating saga.

"I started dating Martin maybe, like, a week later? They all live together, so I had been seeing a lot of Martin while Matt and I hung out." Cora looked up to see Emma staring at her. "What?"

"I…You started dating your ex's roommate a week after you broke up with him?"

She wasn't going to touch the small penis comment.

"I mean, dated I think is a strong word? We, like, hooked up for most of last summer, but I was also hooking up with this guy Louis from my English class at the same time, so it wasn't, like, *serious* serious, you know?"

Emma raised her eyebrows and Cora rolled her eyes.

"You look like my mom. She's all like, *Cora, if you keep this up you're going to end up pregnant and stuck in this shitty town. Don't you want to be like Georgie?* She thinks Georgia is, like, the epitome of success and that I should be more like her."

She's not wrong, Emma thought, a small bubble of warmth forming in her chest.

"You're pretty lucky to have someone like Georgia around," Emma agreed.

Cora gave her an assessing look for a second and then said, "Are you fucking her?"

If Emma had been drinking water, she would have done a spit take. The question threw her so off guard.

"What?" she spluttered.

"Are you fucking my cousin?" Cora repeated.

"Oh my God, no," Emma said, feeling her cheeks going red and pressing her palms to their heating surface. "She's, like, my best friend and mentor and kind of bossy older cousin. She's known me literally since I was born. Plus, she's, like, thirteen years older than me."

Cora shrugged. "You guys are just, like, really close and physically affectionate. I was trying to figure out why you'd be willing to help me out so much if you weren't hooking up with her."

"Because I love her!" Emma blurted out, "I mean, you know, like she's family. She's a very important person to me and has helped me out a ton over the years, and I'd do anything for her."

"So, you guys have never even kissed? You've never even thought about it?" Cora seemed perplexed.

"No! God, no," Emma said. Her heart was suddenly hammering in her chest. She rested her hand against it, the words tasting like a lie.

"Seems like a waste to me," Cora said, turning back to folding clothes. "You're both hot and you clearly like each other, why not make out?"

Emma stared at her, dumbfounded. She'd forgotten how horny teenagers were all the time.

"Because that's not how adult relationships work," she replied. "You can't just go around making out with whoever you think is hot. Besides, what Georgia and I have is too precious to mess with."

"So, you *have* thought about messing with it," Cora said, and she crossed her arms and smirked knowingly.

"Oh my God, you are so fucking annoying," Emma said, desperate to move the conversation way from this topic. "No, I haven't thought about messing with it."

Cora shrugged.

"Seems like a waste to me, but okay," she said and turned to replace the clothing box on the shelf.

"Hey, Martin is having a party on Friday night. Could you get me, like, a handle of vodka to bring?" Cora asked over her shoulder as she left the closet.

"One hundred percent no to that," Emma said flatly. She flopped onto her back on the bed and tried to calm her racing heart, as exhausted as if she'd just competed in a 2,000-meter sprint.

After a moment she got to her feet and followed this wrecking ball of a girl out of the room.

"And I'm also not going to tell Georgia you asked me to do that," she said.

"Ugh, you're so boring," Cora said, rolling her eyes as they walked down the carpeted hallway that led to the stairs.

Cora left after having dinner with Emma and her father, ravioli in Hattie's homemade marinara with sautéed broccoli rabe. She, for all her questionable life decisions, was a charming dinner guest. She made Emma's father laugh with her impressions of an eighty-year-old patient trying to find her insurance card in her purse and dumping out what looked like an entire diner's worth of jam packets on the front desk to locate it.

Emma watched TV with her dad and told him she'd run into Connie at the club. He seemed appropriately scandalized by her gossip about Rachel Whiteman's cheating fiancé and agreed they should have Connie and her husband over for dinner soon.

"You know what your mom used to say about her?" he started. "*That Connie, mouth like a freight train—*"

"*But a more upbeat person you'll never meet,*" Emma finished, and they shared a bittersweet grin. She rested her head on his shoulder as he flipped to the Red Sox game.

Later, though, when she had seen her father up the stairs, given him his medicine with a cup of water and made sure he took it, gotten herself ready for bed and lay staring at the ceiling, she thought back to her conversation with Cora.

She had lied to her.

She *had* thought about kissing Georgia, of course she had. As a hormonal teenage lesbian, she'd inevitably had a huge crush on her when she was younger, before Georgia was an everyday fixture in her life and just the gorgeous older neighbor who thought of her as the annoying kid she'd babysat.

She'd seen her as terribly mature and wise and the pinnacle of womanhood, someone to aspire to be like, to emulate in her life choices. Not to mention incredibly beautiful, with her lush curves and trim waist, her long, thick, dark wavy hair and gray eyes, luminous and framed with long black lashes. Emma had woken more than once from a dream about Georgia with a pounding ache between her thighs. There had never been a doubt in her mind that Georgia would never return these feelings, but the yearning for her had helped Emma understand her sexuality all the same.

She had gone to Georgia for advice on dating and life choices growing up. When she'd been deciding between Dartmouth and Brown, Georgia had been the one she'd bounced ideas off, who'd made the pros and cons list with her.

As she'd gotten older and had real life romantic and sexual experiences with women to replace her childish fantasy of Georgia, she had become less out of reach, still older and wiser and more mature, sure, but her friend, too, her most important friend now these last three years. A day didn't go by where they didn't see each other, didn't talk or text.

Emma was afraid to admit it, but she needed Georgia in her life in a big, nearly overwhelming way.

As she lay in bed staring at the moon's reflection on her ceiling and picked restlessly at her summer weight duvet, listening to the lapping of the waves, she pictured Georgia's smiling face, the way her kiss felt on her cheek this afternoon.

Deep inside her, a small voice whispered that she might even still *want* her, just a little, too.

Chapter Eight

The rest of the week went by uneventfully. Emma ran and swam and biked to the store. She finished her book and scheduled the gardeners and thought of ideas for redesigning her bedroom. She went over the shopping for next week and gossiped with Hattie, sharing the news Connie had told her about Rachel Whiteman's wedding, which Hattie thought was salacious.

She did puzzles with Anne and her father and ran through the memory exercises his doctor suggested could be helpful. Thursday he was a bit agitated, forgetting who Anne was briefly and, once, asking when Giselle would be back from the store, something that never got easier for Emma.

Friday night, Cora and Georgia came over for dinner again. Emma bickered with Georgia about whether or not she should be spreading the Rachel Whiteman news around town. Georgia thought it was probably hard enough for the poor woman without everyone else whispering behind her back. Emma figured it was already out in the ether, so why should she pretend to not know about it?

She was actively trying not to think about kissing Georgia, but the muscle memory of her teenage crush seemed to have seeped back into her. She couldn't deny that Georgia was a beautiful woman, even more so now. She practically glowed in the golden summer light, the rich blue of the flowing high-necked sundress she wore setting off the tan just starting to settle on her olive skin. Emma caught herself staring at her several times during dinner and looked over to see a smirk on Cora's face. She glowered at her in return and tried to flip her off with her eyes, but Cora just smirked harder.

What a menace, for putting these ideas back in my brain, Emma mused moodily.

Saturday, she woke early. She liked to go for longer runs on weekends and preferred to get out before the sun was fully up and hot. She did her usual loop around the Neck, up past the lighthouse, down past the yacht clubs getting ready for the day, out across the causeway just as the clock struck eight and all the clubs shot off their cannons and hoisted their flags up the masts.

She ran through downtown Marblehead, the shops shuttered, people just starting to stir, taking their dogs and babies in strollers for walks. Down through Old Town, the Colonial houses with their plaques crowded around the winding one-way streets, all the way to Fort Sewall at the other end of the entrance to the harbor. She paused there for a minute, caught her breath and watched the sailboats, kayakers, and early morning paddleboarders glide through the boats moored in the harbor, the water sparkling like a thousand diamonds in the sunlight.

It was mornings like this, perfect summer mornings, mornings that belonged on a postcard or in a painting, that made her glad she lived here. The endless warm promise of a New England summer day, the eternal beauty it held. She closed her eyes, breathed in the salt air, and felt the heating sun on her face before she continued with her run.

By the time she reached the Neck again, people were drinking coffee on their porches or headed down to the beach loaded with umbrellas and beach chairs, calling for their kids to stay on the sidewalk.

Georgia and Johnny were outside when she got back home. Emma was covered in sweat and gasped for breath as she slowed to a walk. Georgia was in her pajamas—shorts and a baggy T-shirt—her hair tossed up in a bun and glasses on. Emma couldn't help but notice it made her look younger and softer. A frisson of self-consciousness zipped through her at the sweaty state she was in.

"Morning, Em," Georgia called as Emma walked past her front gate, and she waved Emma over. Johnny wagged his fluffy tail as Emma approached the fence that lined Georgia's property. Although their yards bordered, Heartfield and Georgia's home sat across Highbury Lane from each other. "How was your run?"

"Fine," Emma gasped as she caught her breath. "Went up to the fort. Water looks gorgeous this morning."

Georgia hummed her agreement, taking a sip of her coffee. Emma reached over the fence and bent down to pat Johnny's flat head, scratching him under the chin until he closed his eyes, a doggy smile on his snout.

"Your hand is going to be covered in fur," Georgia noted.

"Worth it," Emma replied, and they shared a smile as she straightened up, and Johnny walked off to go sniff another corner of his lawn.

Emma's hand was indeed covered in fur, but she wiped it on her running shorts and then used her T-shirt to mop some sweat off her face. When she lowered the shirt, she thought she saw Georgia's eyes flit away from her flat stomach.

"Cora's still sleeping?"

"Oh yeah," Georgia replied with a flippant wave of her hand, "I don't expect her to surface until noon. Eleni says she sleeps like the dead on weekends."

"She's got some…interesting ideas about life," Emma remarked. She rested her hands on her hips and remembered her conversation about Cora's love life from a few days ago.

Georgia shook her head ruefully and chuckled.

She said, "She takes after her mom. As much as she'd hate to admit it, Eleni was similar when we were growing up. Had a different boyfriend every few months until she met her husband, Ryan, when they were twenty."

"Probably why she's so hard on her," Emma said. "Sees too much of herself in her kid."

Georgia smiled at her and said, "There's that psych degree."

Emma rolled her eyes at her and changed the subject. "Hey, beach in a bit? I'm going to rinse off and wake Dad, but maybe around eleven thirty, want to head down?"

"Sure, I've got some work stuff to do before, but we'll meet you down there," Georgia said.

Emma left Georgia and Johnny to their morning sniff. As she walked across the street, Emma whipped off her shirt as she went and used it to mop up more of her sweat.

She entered the house through the back way—Hattie was always yelling at her for tracking dirt in through the foyer—and poured herself a big glass of water from the fridge. She checked the oven clock—it read nine oh five—and set up a pot of coffee to brew. She decided that if her dad wasn't up by nine thirty, she'd check on him.

Her dad used to be up with the sun. He'd take these long winding runs with her on the weekends when she was home, but his meds made him sleepy now, and the risk of him getting lost on a run, forgetting where he was and how to get home, had become too great in the last year. She missed those times when their breathing and strides would sync up, the feeling of connection bonding her to her father without either of them having to speak.

These days, she felt like she could feel him slipping through her fingers every minute, like sand through an hourglass.

She took her coffee and breakfast of yogurt, granola, and protein powder out to the patio and sat down, scrolling aimlessly through her phone between sips. Her old friends posted about brunches and parties and work achievements. A few older girls she knew from the crew team posted engagement photos, their left hands conspicuously visible on their fiancés' buff chests, all their faces shining with picture-perfect happiness through the screen. She knew comparing herself to others was the devil's way, but it was hard not to see her stagnation in harsh relief when she saw those pictures. Hard not to resent her father, just a little.

He joined her at nine forty, to her relief, and they enjoyed a mostly silent leisurely morning together, making comments about the news and the goings on of the town occasionally.

At eleven, Emma saw a very tousled Cora emerge into Georgia's yard, coffee mug in hand. She gave Emma a sleepy wave before settling on her own ocean facing chair, Johnny curled at her feet.

For a moment, everything felt peaceful and normal. Emma leaned back in her chair, lowered her eyelids, and stared into the red depths behind them. She could almost pretend in her mind that she was visiting for a summer weekend from her life in Boston or New York or somewhere else, that her father's mind wasn't fading. Even that her mother was in the kitchen, just about to emerge to scold them for being lazy on a beach day.

Her mom had been ravenous for beach season. She'd spent every second possible soaking up the sand and surf while she could in the brief span between cold and rainy seasons. If Emma could just keep her eyes closed for a moment longer, she might be able to inhabit this space for the rest of time.

Then Johnny barked at some noise in the distance, and the illusion was ruined.

She was disoriented by a wave of sadness that dragged her under for a moment before a familiar, soothing voice said, "Hey."

Emma looked over, and there was Georgia with a smile on her full lips as she leaned against the fence in her white linen beach tunic, the hint of her pink and orange color-blocked one piece just visible through the fabric and a wide-brimmed straw hat perched on her head.

Emma returned her smile, head still resting against her chair as she squinted at the sun shining in her eyes.

"Hey," she replied.

"Are you going to lounge there all day, or are we going to the beach?" Georgia scolded good-naturedly.

Chapter Nine

It took another hour for Emma to change, get her dad moving, gather up the beach snacks—cold grapes from the fridge, some sliced melon courtesy of Hattie, popcorn and Cape Cod chips, and a cooler of water—and load it all up into the beach wagon with their chairs and towels. Then it was a ten-minute walk to the beach across the causeway, the one with rocky sand but plenty of space to spread out. Georgia and Cora were already down there due to the fact that they'd brought only themselves and their chairs, towels, and books.

Cora was in the water with a group of teen girls in brightly colored bikinis, wading up to their waists and chatting. Even from the beach Emma could see that the backs of her shoulders were already pink from the sun.

Georgia waved to them when she saw Emma step onto the beach. She was easy to spot, Emma knew, her six-foot frame readily visible in her green Dartmouth baseball cap and yet another baggy regatta T-shirt and jean shorts.

She pulled the wagon over to their spot and parked it.

"I don't know why you packed a picnic for six," Georgia snarked as Emma unloaded her gear.

"You make fun, but just see if I share my melon with you in an hour when you're hot and cranky," Emma shot back as she continued to unload.

Georgia flicked her foot at Emma, toes painted a coral pink that almost matched the color of the V-neck top of her bathing suit. Sand landed on Emma's neatly laid out beach blanket.

"Ah, watch it!" Emma cried.

She caught Georgia's ankle in her hand before Georgia got more sand on her clean towel and gave it a playful yank, trying to ignore the smooth curve of her calf. Georgia's head lay on the pillow attached to her chair, and her body glistened with a fine sheen of sweat mixed with sunscreen as she peered down her body at where Emma fussily brushed sand from her towel and still held Georgia's foot out of the way. Georgia laughed at her and tugged her foot out of Emma's grasp. Her toes grazed Emma's neck as she pulled them back, and Emma shivered.

Georgia crossed her thighs and shifted in her chair before she teased, "You're too easy to rile, Em."

Emma tried not to sweep her eyes up Georgia's legs—rounded calves, plump thighs, wide curving hips that sloped alluringly to her waist—and above them the deep slice of tanned cleavage revealed by the low-cut top of her bathing suit, her compass rose necklace sticking to her sternum.

Tried and failed miserably.

Emma felt her mouth go dry just looking at her and quickly turned away. She busied herself with taking off her clothes and rubbed her pale, freckled arms and legs with sunscreen. When she was done, she realized she needed someone to do her back.

She glanced around, but her dad was deep in conversation with a golfing buddy who had stopped by on a stroll, and Cora was now playing a game of chicken in the freezing water with the teens she'd been chatting with. That just left…

"Need your back done?" Georgia asked as she leaned forward in her chair and picked up the sunscreen from the blanket before Emma could respond.

Emma swallowed and replied, "Y-yes."

Her suit was a plain navy one piece with a halter top, the back dipping just below the barely perceptible curve of her waist. She couldn't see Georgia's eyes behind the reflective coating of her round sunglasses, but she could have sworn that Georgia froze on her way up from the blanket at the sight of Emma. Thought she saw Georgia's gaze sweep up the length of her body before she seemed to remember herself and sit up fully. Georgia shifted in her chair, pressed her thighs together, and looked down at the bottle in her hands, fiddling with the lid.

She's being weird, Emma thought. Fuck, could she tell I didn't want her to put sunscreen on me and now is feeling awkward about it?

No, she reasoned with herself, maybe she just got a crick in her back. She was in her thirties, after all.

Emma kneeled on her beach towel, her back to Georgia, and took a deep breath to brace herself for the feel of Georgia's hands on her skin.

Calm down, calm down, calm down, Emma chanted internally as Georgia started rubbing the lotion into the skin of her back, and every single nerve ending she possessed jerked alive at once.

The slide of Georgia's smooth hands against the skin of her back sent a shiver through her, particularly when her fingers dipped into the low back of her bathing suit to spread sunscreen just beneath the edge of the cloth. Georgia's fingers then dipped into the sides beneath the suit and grazed her ribs, touching the skin tantalizingly close to Emma's breasts, doing a thorough job of protecting Emma from the sun.

She thought she heard Georgia's breath hitch, felt the gust of it, a tad quicker than it should be, on the back of her neck, and balled her hands into fists. Her fingernails bit into her palms, and the pain grounded her and stopped her from letting out a whimper as Georgia traced the bottoms of her shoulder blades, trailed her fingers lightly up Emma's spine, her touch nearly teasing.

She clenched every muscle to keep herself from moving as Georgia smoothed her hands over the tops of her shoulder blades, up her traps and the back of her neck, and rubbed the top nub of her spine slightly.

It felt unbelievably good to have Georgia's hands on her skin like this. They were soft and supple and warm, and her body thrilled at every pass.

She wanted Georgia to slide her hand up higher and cup the back of her head, bury her fingers in Emma's hair. Wanted to turn her face to Georgia and lick the taste of her iced coffee from her mouth.

Be fucking cool. It's just because it's been years since someone else touched you skin to skin, Emma reasoned with herself. That's why this felt this good.

Still, that didn't stop Emma from arching her neck a bit to encourage Georgia to keep rubbing her. A little thrill shot through her when she heard Georgia's hum of amusement at her action. Georgia dug in with her thumbs and rubbed a moment longer before she moved on and smoothed down the sides of Emma's neck and over the tops of her shoulders, touch that light brush again. If Emma didn't know better, she'd think Georgia was exploring her. That she was mapping the play of her muscles as they shifted under her hands.

Emma felt her nipples peak and dug her nails into her palms harder.

Fucking. Cora.

Cora, who put these ideas in her head and reawakened the vestiges of her long dead crush. Cora, who reminded her that she'd once fantasized about Georgia's fingers on her with even less clothing on.

Georgia did a few last swipes of sunscreen over the tops of her arms. Her fingers still trailed almost hypnotically along Emma's skin, up over her collarbones, under the strap of her bathing suit, and out to her shoulders.

"So strong," Georgia murmured as she squeezed at Emma's shoulders. Her breath tickled the back of Emma's neck like she had scooted all the way forward in her chair to reach Emma. Like her lips were only mere inches from Emma's skin.

Emma felt her muscles tense at the thought and Georgia's grip tighten in response.

Just then, there was a loud crash of waves followed by a child's shriek of joy. Emma jumped and felt Georgia's hands leave her body, Georgia's breath disappearing from her skin suddenly, leaving her cold despite the heat of the day.

Emma probably imagined the slight husk to Georgia's words when she said, "You're all set, Em," because when she turned to settle in her own chair, she found Georgia looking at the water and sipping at her iced coffee coolly, as unruffled as ever.

She tried to pretend her insides weren't positively quaking as she rose to take her chair under the umbrella she'd set up next to Georgia. Unlike her Greek companions, Emma's Puritan ancestry meant that she turned bright red like a lobster in a pot first before tanning.

They sat in companionable quiet for a while, Emma leafing through the local design magazine she'd brought with her, reading her book idly, or just people watching.

The beach was a great place to see and be seen. She watched her neighbors chase their little kids as they toddled too close to the water's edge. Watched blankets full of teen girls in tiny bikinis and one pieces that barely covered their asses giggle with each other, egging each other on to go talk to the cute lifeguards or the boys riding wakeboards in the surf, one or two casting furtive, appreciative looks at each other.

Couples, young and old, strolled hand in hand along the shore, and older women in skirted bathing suits waded into the water only up to their ankles or calves and stayed to chat.

"Does Cora know those girls?" Emma asked when she came back to her seat after a quick dip in the ice-cold ocean and gestured to where Cora was seated on a blanket with a group of four girls who looked to be her age.

"Oh yeah, a couple of her friends from home came out to see her," Georgia replied, following Emma's line of sight. "She did a good job at the office this week, so I figured she'd earned a reward."

Georgia frowned as a group of boys swooped in next to the girls, put their own blankets and chairs down, and formed a circle. Emma noticed that the girls' body language immediately changed. They angled toward the boys, sucked in their stomachs, and stuck out their chests.

"Any sign of Martin?" Emma inquired.

"Nope," Georgia said as she looked back at her book, "those are all high school boys. And they better stay that way."

After a second she closed her book and stood up, saying, "I'm going for a dip, want to join me?"

Emma shook her head.

"Still thawing from my last one," she replied.

She tracked Georgia's progress to the water from behind her shades, trying and failing not to stare at the sway of her hips, how good the firm cheeks of her ass looked in her bathing suit. Despite the glacial chill from the water still dripping from her body, Emma felt herself heat up. She felt like a horny teenage boy, unable to stop ogling her friend.

She took a deep breath and looked over at her dad, who was now snoring with his book spread across his chest.

Maybe it was too much sun scrambling her brain? Or she was dehydrated?

Yeah, horniness was definitely a sign of dehydration. She'd surely read that somewhere, once.

She took out the watermelon from the cooler and plopped a still chilled chunk into her mouth, letting the cool sweetness of the juices take the edge off.

It worked, a little.

Until Georgia walked back to them, hair slicked back and stuck to her body. Water sluiced off her with every step, and she somehow looked impossibly hotter.

Unfair, unfair, unfair, Emma's brain bleated at her in alarm as Georgia took her seat and leaned back so the water droplets that slid down her chest caught the sun. Emma's stomach clenched at the sight.

"Can I have some of that?" Georgia asked.

"W-what?" Emma stammered.

"Can I have some of that melon?" Georgia repeated, pointing to the container in Emma's lap.

Emma swallowed and thought the only way out of this was to be a brat.

"Oh, look who wants a part of my picnic for six now," Emma snarked. "Too bad these snacks are only for people who appreciate preparedness."

Georgia grinned evilly at her for a second before she leaned over and wrung her hair out on Emma's shoulder, cold water splashing over her bare skin.

"What the fuck, Georgia, are you, like, twelve?" Emma squeaked. Georgia exploited her distraction to snatch the melon container out of her lap, and her fingers grazed against the top of Emma's bare thighs in the process.

She settled back in her seat, a smug smile on her lips as she winked at Emma and took a bite of melon, juice running down her lips.

"That's what you get for sassing me," Georgia quipped, wiping her mouth on the back of her hand as she finished her melon.

Emma was struck briefly speechless, all her focus caught on the bead of melon juice that dripped down Georgia's chin, and gripped the arms of her chair to stop herself from leaning forward to wipe it off with her mouth.

God, what was wrong with her?

Before Emma could respond, a voice called out her name, and then Connie Brightley was before her in a beige knitted caftan and a wide-brimmed beach hat.

"Emma! Georgia! Hey, ladies! Enjoying this amazing beach weather, I see," Connie said enthusiastically, and she came to stand before them and blocked out the sun.

"Hi, Connie," Georgia said while she put the lid on the melon container and handed it back to Emma. Since both Georgia and Connie belonged to the same yacht club and were personal friends of the Wilsons, they were often in proximity and knew each other well.

"What's this I hear about you having a houseguest this summer, Georgia? Elizabeth McNeely was telling me that she went to see you this week about her tension headaches and there was a teen girl with the most…interesting eye makeup at reception."

She said *interesting* like she was talking about a slug she'd found in her pristine organic vegetable garden.

"Anyway," she continued before Georgia could say a word, "Elizabeth was telling me that the girl told her she was your cousin and that she was there as some sort of punishment for *slutty behavior*—her words, not mine."

She made scare quotes when she said the phrase *slutty behavior* and grimaced like the words tasted bad.

Georgia grimaced back at her.

"She's my cousin's daughter," Georgia replied. "My cousin thought living out here and working for a little while might help her get ready for college in the fall."

"Oh, so she *is* going to college," Connie said and nodded, like that fact might be in doubt.

"Yup, UMass Amherst, full ride," Cora said as she came up behind Connie and rested her hands on her hips.

"Congratulations!" Connie cried and swatted her on the shoulder with her French tips.

"Cora, this Connie Brightley, Connie, this is my cousin Cora," Georgia said, politely making introductions.

Cora waved at Connie and then turned to Georgia.

"Can me and my friends go back to the house and use your pool for a while?" she asked.

Georgia gave her an appraising look.

"Just you and your *female* friends?" she said, arching a well-groomed brow.

Cora rolled her eyes and crossed her arms over her triangle bikini top. Connie shot Emma a look with raised eyebrows, and Emma grinned back.

"*All* of my friends," Cora said, gesturing behind her to the blanket where the boys and girls were now mingled as they laughed and ate chips out of the same giant bag. "It's just Jonah and Brett and Marcus, they're all, like, brothers to us anyway."

"Fine," Georgia said and gave her a firm look. "But you know the rules. No—"

"No Martin," Cora finished, eyebrows lowered in annoyance, and turned to stomp moodily back to her friends.

"Who's Martin," Connie asked, "a troublemaker?"

"Cora's older boyfriend who her mom doesn't want her to see," Emma answered.

"Ah," Connie said knowingly, "the cause of the slutty behavior."

"More or less," Georgia replied as she warily watched the group of teens gather up their beach gear and head to her house. "You think I just made a mistake?"

Emma reached over and squeezed her forearm comfortingly.

She said, "I think that Cora will appreciate you trusting her."

Georgia looked at her and smiled gratefully as she rested her hand on Emma's hand still on her arm and squeezed back.

"Or you'll come home to an orgy," Connie interjected, and then she and Emma laughed as Georgia groaned and dug her nails just a bit into Emma's skin, sending a tingle of sensation up her arm that had her hips shifting in her chair.

"I don't know the first thing about parenting a teen," Georgia complained. She slumped back in her beach chair and tossed her hands up into the air in frustration.

Connie gave her a sympathetic smile.

"At least you're only doing it for a summer. Imagine having to do it for ten years," she said with a shudder.

"How are your sons?" Emma asked, and that sent Connie on a ten-minute spiel about her three sons, Matthew, John, and Paul, all born two years apart, all graduates of the same private Catholic school, and all, in Emma's opinion, assholes.

She smiled and nodded along as Connie detailed her sons' various jobs—computer science major, investment banker, consultant—and where they were living and the girls they were dating, three women so similarly brunette and thin and basic they might have been the same girl.

"What about you, Emma? Been a while since we met that college girl of yours. What was her name, Tyler? Jamie? Something unisex like that," Connie asked with a vague wave of her hand.

"Sam," Emma supplied.

"Sam, yes, that's it. Have you been dating anyone since Sam?" Connie inquired, peering at Emma over the top of her designer sunglasses.

"Um, no, not really," Emma said. She felt her cheeks flush and hoped that it just looked like she was hot. "Been a little too preoccupied with life to date."

Connie made a humming sound of understanding and gave a not so subtle glance to Emma's father, who still slept in his chair.

"Well, I better get back, or Gerald will think I floated out to sea," Connie said with a laugh. "Tell your father I stopped by. We'll see you Monday at the club for the fireworks?"

"Absolutely." Emma smiled, and Connie waved good-bye.

"Why aren't you dating, Emma?" Georgia asked, after a beat.

"Ugh, not you, too," she groaned. "You know why."

They both looked back at her father, who had woken up and was rubbing sand out of his eyes.

"I know you worry about him," Georgia said. She dropped her voice and leaned toward Emma so Emma had an excellent view down her bathing suit, not that Emma took advantage of the angle. "But that doesn't mean you need to put your whole life on hold—"

"I think I've had enough sun for one day," Emma said as she stood to gather her things, not feeling like being lectured by Georgia right now.

"Em, come on," Georgia said, and she grabbed her wrist to keep her from walking away. "I just think you should think about it. You're clearly bored out of your mind sitting around the house all day—"

"Georgie, please," Emma said, turning back to her, but not taking her hand out of Georgia's grip. She looked down into her open face and felt anger and sadness mixing in her chest like water and sodium, waiting to ignite. "We were having such a nice day—can we please not argue about this right now."

"I just want what's best for you, what's going to make you the happiest," Georgia said quietly, hand slipping from her wrist to her palm, giving it a squeeze.

Emma sighed, the wind going out of the sails of her anger instantly. "I know you do."

Georgia smiled up at her and gave her hand another squeeze and then a yank.

"Come sit back down next to me and scold me for not bringing snacks to the beach," Georgia said, a peace offering.

"I mean," Emma said, and she put up no resistance as she settled back into her chair and knocked her knee into Georgia's, "if you took just a *little* more time to plan before coming down, you might have cold grapes to eat right now. But since you were in such a hurry, it looks like I have to just eat them all by myself."

"Might not be the smartest move on your part, there aren't any bathrooms close by," Georgia said while she retrieved the melon container from the cooler.

"Gross, Georgie," Emma said with a laugh and dug into the grapes, resigned to share her snacks.

As she settled back into her chair, she tried not to replay the peek she'd taken at Georgia's truly spectacular breasts in her bathing suit. They looked so soft and deliciously heavy, like they'd feel incredible in her hands and—

No! she screamed internally to herself. You are not fantasizing about Georgia's breasts when she's sitting right next to you.

She gave herself a mental shake and picked up her book to use as a shield while she gathered herself.

They spent another hour or so on the beach, squabbling about this and that, her dad joining in on teasing Emma about her overpreparedness, and then headed home as the light began to slant and the daytime crowd made way for the sparser dinner crew.

They walked the ten minutes home in a sun-drunk silence, sandals slapping against the asphalt. Emma's calves burned from her longer run that morning as she tugged the wagon behind her.

When they turned down the lane, there were two extra cars parked in front of Georgia's house.

"Oh, I think I've fucked up," Georgia groaned and Emma's father barked a laugh.

"Good luck, Georgie girl," he said and patted her shoulder good-naturedly.

Before opening her gate, Georgia took a deep breath and squared her shoulders.

"Remember," Emma said, coming up behind Georgia to grip her tense shoulders bracingly, "they're just kids, they can't hurt you."

Georgia glared at her over her shoulder, and Emma leaned in and kissed her cheek affectionately.

Mistake! she thought immediately as she drew back and took Georgia's scent with her, beach roses and cedar smoke and salt, a combination that curled down into her center and sparked in her stomach.

"Let me know if you need reinforcements," Emma threw over her shoulder as she walked to her door.

"If you don't hear from me in an hour, come do a wellness check," Georgia called back.

Emma found her father standing at the back door, gazing at it as if it mystified him.

"Dad?" she asked softly and put her hand on his shoulder to let him know she was there.

He hummed, as if coming out of a moment of deep contemplation.

"The door's open, you can go inside once you rinse off your feet," she added softly.

She caught the grateful glint in his eye, as if he had forgotten the order of operations for how to get into the house and needed her to guide him. He rinsed his feet and sandals off, just as he always had whenever they'd come back from the beach, and hung up his towel on the drying rack by the grill.

How could she ever devote even a fraction of her attention elsewhere, she wondered as she watched him through the kitchen window as he poured himself a glass of water, drank it, and then headed upstairs to shower.

She sighed to herself, and she set about unpacking from the beach, putting chairs away in the garage, composting what was left of the fruit, sealing up the open bags of chips and popcorn before she stowed them in their proper places in the pantry.

Her phone buzzed from its position on the counter, and when she glanced at it, she saw it was a text from Georgia.

Georgia: *So far, so good. All teens present and accounted for in the pool area. No orgies in process.*

Emma smiled and heart reacted to the message.

She was about to put the phone down when a new text from Georgia came in.

Georgia: *Oh God. Am I supposed to feed them???*

Emma: *Just order some pizzas and call it a day.*

Georgia: *Ok, phew, looks like they ordered pizzas themselves.*

Emma: *Some of them ARE legal adults with jobs, they can figure out how to feed themselves.*

Georgia: *I remember a certain eighteen-year-old frantically texting me from Hanover asking if you need to put water in the Mac & Cheese bowl before you microwave it.*

Emma rolled her eyes. She'd never live that down.

Emma: *It's not my fault Hattie is too good at her job and never taught me life skills.*

Georgia sent her a GIF of Mr. Krabs playing a tiny violin, and Emma snorted.

She looked out the kitchen window. She couldn't quite see Georgia's pool from here, some trees and shrubs stood in the way, but she could imagine her, glass of wine in hand, long dark hair now wound in a bun on the top of her head as she stood in her kitchen window and watched Cora and her friends splash in her pool.

Emma: *Glad someone's making use of that money pit.*

Georgia: *You could come over and use it anytime.*

Emma: **Screaming emoji* And give you reason to feel good about owning it? Never.*

Georgia: *I will never understand your aversion to pools.*

Emma: *We live by the LITERAL ocean, why would you need a pool?*

Georgia: *Yeah, but you can do cool flips into a pool.*

She must be on her second glass of wine, Emma thought. She gets sillier the more she drinks.

Emma: **Eye roll emoji**

Emma: *I dare you to go do a flip in front of the teens, see how well they react to it*

Georgia: *Do you want Cora to never respect me again?*

Emma heard tires on the road and then an engine cut off.

Emma: *Let the ravenous hordes know their pizza is here. AND remind them to tip.*

Georgia: *Always a stickler for etiquette *heart emoji**

Emma put her phone down on the counter, a smile on her cheeks.

She and her dad had a quiet evening. They ordered their own pizza and ate it in front of a movie before heading up to their rooms. Georgia texted Emma a steady stream of commentary about the strange teenage creatures in her backyard all the while.

Emma didn't often feel their age difference that acutely these days. What was thirteen years when you had known each other for twenty-five? But tonight, she was reminded that Georgia hadn't been a teen for twenty years, that she hadn't really been around them since Emma was one.

It didn't make Georgia feel different, though. She was just Georgia, the girl who had taught her to roller skate and then bandaged her knees after she fell, making her laugh to dry her tears. And anyway, Emma felt like she was about eighty most days now.

Besides, Georgia didn't look like she was close to forty, Emma thought as she lay in bed.

Unbidden, an image of Georgia lounging in her beach chair

postswim popped into her head, her hair wet and plastered to her back and chest, those little beads of water dripping down her large breasts, disappearing below the dip of the vee.

Emma ran her hands down her own small breasts over her sleep shirt, palms rubbing light circles over her nipples as her heart rate picked up, breath becoming a bit ragged. Her mental gaze tracked down to Georgia's soft stomach, her cinched waist, the flare of her wide hips and ass, and those lusciously thick thighs.

One hand slipped down her flat stomach to gently rub between her legs, the other dived under her shirt and pinched at her nipple, as she imagined kneeling and running her hands slowly up Georgia's legs, fingers digging into her thighs. She pictured herself leaning up and placing nipping kisses on Georgia's neck, following the neckline of her bathing suit, burying her face in the valley of her ample cleavage, mouthing her nipple through her bathing suit as her fingers reached between Georgia's thighs, touching softly. She wondered what Georgia's face would look like flung back in pleasure and flushed, her hips rocking under Emma's touch, little needy sounds falling from her lips.

She did to herself what she imagined doing to Georgia, fingers flying over her slickness until her stomach clenched and she bit her lip to muffle her moan, head thrown back on the pillow.

She caught her breath. Her hair now hung messily around her face and her stomach and thighs quivered with aftershocks.

"Fuck," she muttered to herself.

CHAPTER TEN

Despite lying in bed staring at her ceiling for hours the night before, Emma went for another extra long run the next morning, fueled by adrenaline, lingering lust, and the need to sort out her thoughts.

It was just because she was lonely, she was horny, she needed to have sex. It was just because Georgia was the only queer woman she knew, who happened to be right next door and *so fucking hot*.

No, no, that part wasn't helpful to think about.

Emma put on a burst of speed, practically sprinting mile five. She was nowhere near the shape she had been in when she'd been a college athlete, waking up at five in the morning to row on the misty Connecticut river, weight lifting in the afternoon, and conditioning practices in between, but she could still run a six minute mile when pushed. Today, she let the familiar burn in her muscles burn the bullshit in her brain away.

Okay, yes, she was attracted to Georgia. She'd been attracted to Georgia since she hit puberty, that was nothing new. She had been good at putting it in the background, though, these past few years, letting their friendship precede any sort of lust she felt. She could master herself again, push those feelings down again.

Touching herself to thoughts of Georgia in a swimsuit was not something she needed to be doing right now, an added complication to her life that she just didn't have the energy to deal with.

She focused instead on the annoying parts of Georgia. Her need to always butt into Emma's problems and voice an opinion. The way she wanted to push Emma out of Heartfield. The way she always brought up Emma's psych degree and the dreams she'd once had. How she loved to boss Emma around. How she sometimes made little noises when she chewed.

The way she smiled after she made Emma laugh, like she was proud of it.

The way she'd licked the melon juice off her lips yesterday at the beach.

Yeah, okay, nope. Definitely *not* helping.

The run did help her tame her lust, downgrading it from raging wildfire to a hearty hearth blaze. Still, she was a bit relieved that Georgia and Johnny weren't out in the yard this morning. She didn't see Georgia the rest of the day, which she kept having to remind herself was good. Some space right now would help her cram her crush back into the little box it had lived in for years.

Instead, she and her dad went to the farmers' market, and she played hostess to a group of his old golfing buddies that came by a couple of times a month to drink beers or scotch and talk sports or old rounds. It always amused Emma how they gossiped as much as the women did about the goings on in their small town.

They had dinner at the club, and her father, exhausted from the day, went to bed early.

Emma, still feeling restless and wanting to crawl out of her skin, drank an extra glass of wine or two and, around eleven, went outside to smoke a joint. She didn't smoke that frequently, but desperate times called for instant calming.

She was just taking her third drag on the joint when she heard a car pull up in front of Georgia's house. Curious, she peered around a bush and saw Cora, fully dressed in jean shorts and a crop top, thick eyeliner wings in place and a purse big enough to be an overnight bag swinging from her shoulder, open the front door and sneak out, headed for a beat up old Honda Civic.

"Whatcha doing over there?" Emma called as she snuffed out her joint and walked out of the shadows.

"Shit! Emma, you scared me," Cora exclaimed, resting her hand on her chest in surprise. She still carried on slinging her bag into the back seat of what Emma assumed was Martin's car.

"This must be the infamous Martin." Emma bent down to see the scrawny looking boy with dark brown hair and scruff lining his jaw in the driver's seat and felt thoroughly unimpressed.

"Hey," Martin said. He lowered his window and stuck his hand out for a shake, a move that struck Emma as surprisingly polite. Emma stared at it for a second. Feeling obligated, she took it and shook, calloused palm meeting calloused palm.

"Hey," she replied. "I'm Emma."

"Emma is Georgia's neighbor," Cora said as she opened the side door of the car. "One who *won't* tell Georgia you came to pick me up tonight."

Emma crossed her arms.

"What makes you think that?" she huffed.

"Because, if you don't, I won't tell Georgia how you're lusting after her," Cora said, an evil glint in her eye.

Emma's heart dropped and she stared at her.

"Excuse me?"

The nerve of this girl.

"I saw the way you were practically drooling over her at the beach yesterday," Cora said.

"I have literally zero idea what you're talking about," Emma said haughtily, feeling her buzz fading as panic pounded through her body. "Where is Georgia, by the way?"

"On a date," Cora said and then burst out laughing. "You should see your face right now, dude. Nah, bro, she's just sleeping. Went to bed at, like, nine thirty like the old lady she is."

Emma noted the tone of affection in the teasing and leaped on it.

"She's really trying her best, you know. Wants you to trust her," Emma said, deciding to go for the guilting tactic. "I know you guys are in love or whatever, but going with Martin tonight is going to fuck up that trust she's put in you so far. I know you wouldn't want to hurt her."

"Touché," Cora grumbled. She narrowed her eyes at Emma and seemed to hesitate, looking down at Martin and then back at the house.

"Babe," Martin said, "maybe you should listen to her. If you're good, maybe Georgia will let me visit legally. From what you've told me, she seems wicked cool and chill."

"She is, mostly," Emma agreed.

Cora sighed.

"Fine," she relented, "I won't sneak out of the house, even though you look *so* cute I could kiss your face off right now."

Cora pinched Martin's cheeks through the driver's side window.

"Don't watch, Emma. I wouldn't want you to be arrested for child pornography," she said, leaning into the car to give Martin a long, sloppy kiss.

Emma averted her eyes and exasperatedly stated, "You're both legal adults."

"Bye, Emma, it was nice to meet you. Georgia is lucky to have such a loyal neighbor," Martin said when Cora had relinquished his mouth.

"Um, thanks?" Emma said. She had to admit, she felt a bit confused by the nice boy driving the car.

"Thanks for cockblocking me, Em," Cora said, humphing loudly as she crossed her arms over her chest and watched Martin pull away, pouting like a toddler.

"Cockblocking," Emma muttered to herself, "yuck."

Then she started giggling.

"Are you high right now?" Cora asked her, peering at her curiously. Emma just kept on giggling. "Wow, some role model you are."

"Never claimed to be one," Emma said as she tried to catch her breath. "Although I do think you can do better than sneaking out to meet some boy."

Cora looked at her one last time, rolled her eyes, then headed back toward Georgia's house.

"He's not just some boy," she called over her shoulder as she went. "He's the love of my life."

She slammed the door dramatically behind her.

This set off another round of giggles in Emma, and she decided it was probably time to go to bed.

Figuring she should let Georgia know about Martin's drive-by, she picked up her phone and texted her.

Emma: *Martin came by to pick up Cora tonight. She tried to sneak out but I caught her.*

She wasn't expecting a message, but her phone buzzed almost as soon as she put it down on the nightstand.

Georgia: *Thanks for that. How did you get her to stay?*

Emma: *Told her how you sleep with a big knife under your pillow and have a tendency to stab first and ask questions later.*

Georgia: *Seriously, Em. What did you say?*

Emma: *Just that you were putting a lot of trust in her and that going with Martin would break your trust and hurt her. Seemed to work. Weirdly, Martin was on my side.*

There was a pause as Georgia's three dots bounced and disappeared twice before her message came through.

Georgia: *Didn't think that would work.*

Emma: *She looks up to you like crazy. Even I can see that. Why wouldn't she, you're amazing.*

Emma squinted at the text after she sent it and wondered, vaguely, if it was too much.

Georgia: *Go to bed Emma, you're high. Don't think I didn't see you smoking out in the backyard.*

Emma smiled, imagining Georgia sitting in her bedroom, watching the smoke from Emma's joint curve over the gate that separated their yards.

She really must be high if she found that image romantic.

She put her phone down and tucked herself into bed.

The last image behind her eyelids as she drifted off to sleep was Georgia's smile.

Chapter Eleven

After two gorgeous beach days, Monday the Fourth of July dawned cloudy and gray and only got worse from there, sheets of rain pounding down and washing away the patriotic cheer.

Emma spent the day cozied up on Georgia's couch with her, Johnny, and Cora. They watched movies, Emma only feeling comfortable to unwind because she knew Anne was with her dad. She felt bad that Anne wasn't spending the day with her own family, even though Anne insisted they didn't do much, but Emma had resolved to give her a big holiday bonus regardless.

The fireworks, Emma's favorite part of the holiday celebration, were canceled, but she didn't even mind that much as she spent the evening laughing with Cora and Georgia at old rom-coms. Georgia was nostalgic for her youth, but Cora insisted on dissecting all the toxic masculinity, lack of consent, and massive holes in the plot lines.

"I mean, she lied to everyone, made the teacher think he was committing pedophilia, and *still* thinks he'll meet her at home base? Seems highly suss," Cora said, outraged.

"It's romantic," Georgia insisted.

"Um, no. As the only one currently *in* a romantic relationship, I decide what's romantic, and that is *so* not romantic," Cora said, and she chucked some popcorn at the big screen in Georgia's den. The three of them were sprawled on opposite sides of the giant mushy brown sectional Georgia's parents had bought a decade ago. Its cushions were now perfectly broken in and molded to Emma's body, so they cradled her as she watched the cousins bicker.

"Emma, weigh in here," Georgia implored.

"I have to agree with Cora," Emma said, scrunching up her face apologetically. "The whole teacher plotline is a bit skeevy, now I think about it."

"Betrayal!" Georgia declared dramatically.

Georgia tossed some popcorn Emma's way, and Emma ducked. Johnny padded over and happily gobbled up the kernels.

They had ice cream sundaes for dinner, and Emma went home, stomach full and aching, proud of herself for not fantasizing about licking whipped cream off Georgia's lips, even a little bit.

She fell asleep without the aid of a substance for the first time in a long time.

She couldn't be quite sure what it was that woke her around one in the morning. There was something about the house that just didn't feel right, some sort of disturbance in the air. She got out of bed, thinking maybe she just needed some water. Barefoot, she headed down the stairs but stopped when she saw that the front door was wide open.

It took her a second to fully understand what she was seeing, and then panic gripped her tight as an iron fist. She sprinted up the stairs and to her father's room. This door, too, was flung wide open, his covers tossed wildly about.

"No, no, no, no, no," Emma chanted frantically and hoped that if she said it often enough it would be a magic spell that would bring her dad back to his bed.

She ran out the front door, thinking that maybe he was just sitting out in their front yard, or in Georgia's, but no such luck. Her heart galloped in her chest now.

This was one of her worst fears, the reason she triple-checked that the front door was locked before she went to bed each night.

Emma did the only thing she could think to do, run over to Georgia's house and bang on the door. After two minutes that felt like an eternity, a bleary eyed Georgia appeared at the front door and squinted through her glasses.

"Emma? Em, sweetheart, what's wrong?" Georgia asked, her face paling at the sight of Emma. It was then that Emma realized that she must be crying.

"My…my dad," she stuttered through sobs, "he…he wasn't in his bed. I don't know where he could have gone."

Understanding flashed across Georgia's face at once, and all traces of sleep vanished. Here was Georgia Kostigiris, MD, capable, calm in a crisis. She gripped Emma's shoulders.

"Okay, okay, Em, let's put some shoes on, and then we'll go look for him," she said, voice measured and even. She gave Emma a pair of her flip-flops, only one and a half sizes too small, and pushed her feet into her sneakers. Then they took off, Emma practically vibrating with worry.

"What if he gets confused and ends up stuck in a ditch with a broken leg?" Emma panted through her tears, powerless to stop them from falling.

"There are very few ditches around here, Em," Georgia said as she gripped Emma's hand in hers, grounding her in her panic. "He's lived here practically his whole life—muscle memory alone will get him somewhere safe."

Emma couldn't process her reasonable tone right now, though. She raced blindly through the dark streets. The storm had finally blown over to reveal a full moon that cast shadows that played tricks on her stressed mind, made her see limp broken bodies in the branches and rocks.

"Hey, hey, Em, look at me," Georgia said, yanking on her wrist to make her stop and face her. "I need you to breathe with me, can you do that? In and out, just like that, honey. That's it."

Emma knew she was on the verge of a panic attack. She hadn't had one since the months after her mother died, but she could feel that familiar squeezing around her lungs, that sense that she needed to *run run run* to escape this reality at any cost.

She took a deep breath, mirrored Georgia's long slow inhales and exhales, and shoved the panic to the back of her mind.

She dragged air into her lungs once, twice, and her chest loosened enough for her to think.

"Can you think where he might have gone? Anywhere at all?" Georgia asked.

Emma thought for a second and then said with certainty, "The lighthouse."

Georgia nodded, and no questions asked, they headed there. Georgia never let go of her hold on Emma, even though Emma knew she must be hurting Georgia with the pressure her own hand exerted back.

Sure enough, when they reached the lighthouse, there was the outline of her father as he stared up at the moon, perched on a rock. Emma sprinted the last few yards to him as a relief so pure flooded through her whole body it felt like she was flying.

"Daddy," Emma gasped as she knelt down in front of him and reached for his wrists, her head dropping as a sob racked her body.

"Giselle, what's wrong?" he asked, a tender smile gracing his face as he gazed at Emma. "I woke up and you weren't in bed and I went to look for you, but I knew you'd turn up here. You always do."

Emma rested her head on her father's knee, gripped his hands, and swallowed.

"Hey, Henry, why don't we get you and Giselle home," Georgia said softly as she rested her hand on the nape of Emma's bent neck, rubbing back and forth soothingly.

"Demetria, what are you doing here?" her father said, looking at Georgia.

"I was out for a walk with Giselle," Georgia said. She didn't miss a beat as he called her her mother's name. "We forgot to leave you a note. I'm sorry we confused or worried you."

"It's okay. I'm glad my wife has such a good friend like you," her father said, and he patted Emma's hand.

Emma's heart clenched painfully.

"Let's go home now, Henry," Georgia said.

She wrapped an arm around his shoulders and guided him back down the street, leaving Emma to collect herself enough to follow.

They got him home and tucked back into bed without incident. Emma checked and checked and rechecked the locks on all the doors about a thousand times while Georgia sat with her father as he fell asleep.

After her last check, she sank to the cold tile of the foyer and let the panic she had pushed down finally take over. Georgia found her there, shaking, arms wrapped around her knees in a tight ball. Georgia sat down on the floor beside her, not touching her, but lending her support by proximity.

A few minutes later, tears began to leak out of the corners of Emma's eyes and slide down her cheeks.

"Hey, hey, hey," Georgia chanted as she knelt and wrapped her arms around Emma this side of too tightly. She squeezed her and warmed Emma's suddenly frozen body with hers.

"Shh, Em love, just breathe," Georgia whispered and ran her hand soothingly over Emma's hair as Emma sobbed out the panic on her shoulder. Georgia's arms tightened around Emma, providing a deep pressure.

"You did so good, honey. He's safe, and you knew exactly where he would be," Georgia cooed in her ear, rocking her back and forth. "You did everything perfectly, and he's safe. He's safe and home with you."

Georgia's soft words lulled her, and the tears started to slow, the shaking in her limbs easing as the tide of panic receded back to that low hum that had lived in her skull since the day they'd learned her father's diagnosis.

Georgia kept rubbing soothing circles on her back and rocking her gently, her arms loosening their hold bit by bit until they lightly rested around Emma.

Emma laid her head on Georgia's shoulder for one second more before she pulled back and gazed up into her face. With her hair thrown up into a messy bun, in her pajamas and glasses, Georgia had never looked more beautiful to Emma than at that moment.

So strong and sturdy and calm under pressure, talking Emma off the ledge, talking her dad into coming home and getting back into bed.

Emma wanted to thank her, to show her her appreciation for all she was, but speech had left her for the moment.

Before she could even process what she was going to do, could even think about it for one second more, she surged up and kissed her.

CHAPTER TWELVE

For a second, nothing happened, and Emma knew that if she drew back, she could blame it on a surge of emotions, the late hour, her panic scrambled brain, and they would forget all about this. But then Georgia's soft lips pressed back against her own, and her hand came up to tangle in Emma's hair, and she pressed Emma's face farther into her own and urged Emma to kiss her deeper, and all Emma could think was *yes, God, yes.*

She leaned fully into Georgia, let Georgia take over control of the kiss, let her angle Emma's head so her tongue could sweep into Emma's mouth, bringing her sweet taste with her.

Emma's mind was too blank to have any thoughts beyond flashes of sensation. The scrape of Georgia's teeth on her bottom lip, the press of her chest against Emma's, the zing of pleasure as their nipples slid against each other. The soft cotton of her T-shirt under Emma's gripping fingers. The low moan Georgia made when Emma kissed below her jaw, when she slid her hands under Georgia's shirt and cupped her heavy breasts in her calloused palms.

"Emma, Emma…" Georgia breathed into her ear and grasped at her wrists to halt her motions. For one horrifying second, Emma thought she was going to pull away and tell her to stop.

"Let me touch you, let me just touch you and make you feel good, please," Georgia said instead, nearly begged, as she pressed open-mouthed kisses down Emma's cheek to the collar of her shirt, hands sliding down to grip her hips under the hem, fingers against bare skin.

"Fuck," Emma rasped. She wanted to touch Georgia so badly, but how could she say no to that desperate tone in her voice? She nodded frantically and said, "Mm-hmm, sure, yes."

Georgia slid Emma's shirt up and ghosted her fingers over every inch of Emma's skin that was revealed along the way. Emma bit her lip to contain her moans at the feeling of Georgia's fingers, electric sparks of sensation that shot directly between her legs.

Georgia pulled away far enough to whip Emma's shirt off over her head, looking down to take in Emma's strong chest, her small breasts seated atop defined pecs, and flat abs illuminated by the light of the full moon shining through the windows. They both watched her hand slide up over Emma's stomach and ribs, tracing the underside of her breast. Emma closed her eyes and shivered and then groaned when she felt Georgia's lips close around her nipple, when she opened her lips wider and took Emma's small breast whole into her mouth, sucking lightly.

Her hands urged Emma to climb into her lap, and Emma happily complied, straddling Georgia's plush thighs with her own long and lean ones. Georgia's knees bent to form a seat for her as her mouth still sucked and nibbled at Emma's breasts. Emma's fingers tangled in Georgia's hair and pulled her closer to her chest, urged her on, hips beginning to shift restlessly against Georgia's stomach.

"God, Emma," Georgia breathed against her chest, looking up at her from underneath long thick lashes. She trailed her fingers down Emma's stomach, up her ribs. "So, so beautiful."

Speechlessly, Emma looked down at her, Georgia's eyes open and sincere and shining with a rich emotion Emma couldn't even begin to name. They stared at each other for a long moment. Moonlight and streetlamp light streamed in through the glass panes and outlined Georgia's plump lips, her dark hair. Emma raised her hands to frame Georgia's cheeks, wanting to tell her how gorgeous she was, but unable to get the words past her lips.

Instead, she lunged for Georgia's mouth, gripped her hips with her thighs for stability as she crushed their lips together. The intensity of this kiss seared through her, all the way down to her toes, which curled against the wood of the floor. She felt Georgia's arm wrap around her back, supporting her, crushing her bare chest to her still T-shirt clad one, her soft breasts and belly molded around the spare hardness of Emma's torso. Georgia's other hand slid down Emma's lower stomach, dived, sure and steady, into her sleep shorts.

Georgia pulled back to get approval, fingers running through Emma's pubic hair, tugging lightly.

Emma nodded frantically again.

"Please," she whispered against Georgia's lips before she sucked Georgia's lower one into her mouth and grazed it with her teeth.

At the first touch of Georgia's fingers against her, Emma saw stars behind her squeezed shut eyelids and moaned. She felt Georgia pull back again, felt the weight of her gaze on her flushed face.

"Like that?" Georgia whispered, fingers pressing and touching and exploring Emma confidently. Emma bit her lip to keep herself from being too loud when she hit the right angle, the right pressure.

"Look at me," Georgia rasped softly and squeezed Emma's slim hip for emphasis with her free hand.

Her eyes met Georgia's as Georgia stared at her, rapt. Gray eyes flicked around her face, greedy for every tiny expression. She was the picture of absolute desire in Emma's view, pink lips open and breaths panting as she continued to coil Emma's pleasure tighter.

Emma looked down and felt her whole body tighten at the sight of Georgia's wrist where it disappeared beneath her shorts. The pressure and pleasure in her body grew stronger and stronger until she couldn't hold herself back anymore, and she grabbed Georgia's face and brought their mouths together in a sloppy, panting kiss.

It was fast after that.

Their kisses turned more to hot ragged breath against lips. Emma's hips twisted and lifted in Georgia's lap, fingers gripped on Georgia's shoulder and hair so hard she would have worried about ripping it out if she could have formed a single thought. Purer pleasure than she'd ever known coursed through her bloodstream like a sugar rush as Georgia's fingers kept touching and touching and touching her. Emma threw her head back, and Georgia's lips fastened to her neck, teeth scraping a sharp shock of pain that added to her ecstasy.

Her brain kept stuttering over the fact that it was Georgia, *Georgia*, who touched her like this, made her body sing like this. That fact alone amplified everything a hundredfold.

She buried her head against Georgia's shoulder, muffled her noises against the fabric of her T-shirt as her body finally shook and shook and broke like the surf against Georgia's rocky shore.

Release left Emma wrung out and limp, draped over Georgia's body, limbs as shaky as a newborn fawn's. Georgia's arm wrapped around Emma's back was the only thing that kept her upright as Georgia pressed gentle kisses to her hot face, rubbed soothing strokes against the bare, sweat-damp skin of her back.

"My Emma," Georgia murmured when Emma could move her limbs again and started to pull away. "Not yet."

Emma leaned down and rested her forehead against Georgia's.

Their breaths synced, her heart rate slowed, and her body went quiet and loose.

"What was *that*?" Emma asked softly into the quiet between them when she could speak again, her blond hair hanging like a curtain around them.

Georgia swallowed and said on a shaky breath, "I-I don't know."

Emma went to pull back, and this time Georgia let her. They knelt on the cold tiles of the foyer, staring at each other, their still harsh breaths echoing in the quiet.

Then it all hit her, the whole emotional ordeal.

Waking up to discover her father missing, the relief of finding him, her panic attack, kissing Georgia, touching Georgia, Georgia touching *her*. It was too much, too much to process, too much to deal with at two in the morning.

She started to laugh slowly, and the sound built until she quaked with near silent peals of hysterical giggles. She knelt topless on the cool tile of the floor and her shoulders shook.

Georgia stared at her for a second before she reached out and tucked Emma's hair behind her ear. She gripped Emma's chin and made her turn to face her.

Emma saw an unsure smile spread slowly across Georgia's face as she leaned forward to rest her forehead against Emma's.

"You okay, Em?" she asked tenderly as Emma continued to hiccup laughter into the air between them.

"I'm honestly not sure?" Emma said, voice lilting up at the end.

"That, ah, seems about right," Georgia replied, as she let out her own disbelieving huff of laughter. "Let's get you to bed, okay? It's been a…long night."

Emma's laughter died down, and she looked up. Their eyes met, and Emma bit her lip, saw Georgia's eyes drop to her mouth, saw lust simmer in Georgia's gray eyes.

"You want to get me to bed, huh?" Emma said with a mischievous grin.

"Oh my God, you absolute brat," Georgia groaned and then tugged Emma forward by the chin, kissing her. Emma, still in a state of shock, buried her hands in Georgia's hair the way she'd dreamed of doing. She knocked Georgia's bun out and let the strands tumble loose around her shoulders, digging her fingers indulgently into the thickly waving strands.

Georgia groaned again in frustration and released her hold on Emma's face. She ran her hands through her own hair before tying it back up again, her pajamas askew from Emma's frenzied search for skin to touch, to kiss, lips red and swollen.

She looked rumpled and punishingly gorgeous, and Emma wanted to devour her piece by piece like a chocolate bar.

Emma buried her face in her hands to block out the sight of Georgia before she did something foolish like tackle her to the ground, yank her clothes off, and taste every inch of her in the foyer.

She made herself find her shirt and pull it on. Then she turned to find Georgia, hands balled up into fists on her thighs where she still knelt on the tiled floor, like she needed a second to master herself or else she would grab for Emma again.

Emma turned toward the stairs, tripped on an uneven tile, and her chest fell into Georgia's as she stood. One second she looked down into Georgia's face, and the next they were kissing again, this time soft and slow. Emma bent at the shoulders to meet Georgia, Georgia craned her neck up to reach Emma. Emma's hands cupped Georgia's skull like water, Georgia's fisted Emma's baggy shirt to pull their bodies flush together as their lips met and parted and met again.

Emma felt something in her chest settle at the gentle brush of Georgia's mouth, the warmth of Georgia's body pressed to hers, not in lust but in comfort.

They pulled apart and gazed at each other for a heartbeat.

"Yeah, okay, bed now for you, alone," Georgia said and cleared her throat. "Before we do something like fuck on the floor of your foyer. Again."

The shock of hearing the phrase *fuck on the floor* come out of Georgia's mouth and be applied to the two of them had Emma dissolving into giggles again, her brain and body just too damn tired to do anything else in response.

"Shut *up*," Georgia whined and dropped her head against Emma's collarbone.

"You just fucked me on the floor of the foyer," Emma gasped out.

Georgia slapped her hand over Emma's mouth.

"I'm perfectly aware of what I did," Georgia said, a slight edge to her tone that sobered Emma up.

"Georgie…" Emma said after she'd peeled Georgia's hand from her mouth and tangled her own fingers with Georgia's.

"Yeah, Em?" she said, the edge softening from her voice.

"Will you tuck me into bed?" Emma asked and felt a blush come into her cheeks.

Georgia smiled. "Of course."

They walked up the stairs hand in hand, and Georgia tucked her in, smoothing Emma's hair back and pressing a kiss to Emma's forehead before she left.

"Georgie?" Emma whispered to her when she was still a few inches away.

"Yeah?" Georgia answered, matching Emma's quiet voice.

"Thank you for answering the door, for coming to my rescue, for being so…you," Emma replied.

Georgia was illuminated by the moonlight that came in through the window, a gentle expression on her face.

"Anything for you, Em," she murmured in response.

"Can you check—"

"He's still in bed, his door closed, all safe and sleeping," Georgia said calmly before Emma could voice the thought.

She swallowed, letting out a long, long breath.

"Sleep, Em," Georgia said quietly, tenderly, as she turned toward the door of Emma's bedroom.

Emma's eyes were shut, her mind drifting even before she heard the door fully close.

Chapter Thirteen

The next morning, Emma was convinced it had all been a dream.

There was no way, *no way*, it had happened. It was probably just a panicked hallucination brought on by sleep deprivation and stress. It had to be.

There was no way Georgia, the same Georgia who had teased her mercilessly and bossed her around since she was a child, had kissed her and touched her to orgasm in her front hall.

It was improbable, inconceivable, a whole bunch of other words that start with *in* and meant basically that Emma's brain had briefly glitched.

And even if it *had* happened, even if somehow she hadn't been hallucinating, it must have just been some trauma response, a stress valve they both needed to press with the closest living woman they could find.

But Georgia hadn't gotten off, and Emma couldn't get the sound of her begging, *begging*, to touch her out of her head. Like all she wanted was to make Emma feel good, feel wanted and loved and held.

Maybe it was the only thing she could think of to comfort Emma, to distract her from what had happened with her dad.

She was just being a good friend.

Emma lay in bed and remembered the feel of Georgia's tongue in her mouth, on her breasts, the way her fingers had felt as they slid against her.

Fuck, she couldn't think about this right now. She needed coffee.

She stumbled down the stairs, determined to take some space from Georgia and Georgia-shaped thoughts today.

"Hey, sugar," Hattie called from her habitual spot by the center island counter. "You're up late, rough night?"

Emma was relieved to find it was just Hattie in the kitchen, a steaming mug of coffee placed on the gleaming marble countertop before her.

"Yeah, something like that," Emma said, gratefully accepting her own mug of coffee from Hattie, milky with a teaspoon of brown sugar, just the way she liked it.

She opened her mouth to spill the whole story to her when a voice from the kitchen table said, "I told her about your dad's little late night walking adventure."

Emma whirled around to find Georgia, dressed in a short sleeved orange cotton shirtdress with a tie around the waist, her hair half pulled back from her face in a claw clip and tassel earrings dangling from her ears that accentuated the elegant swoop of her neck, sitting in her kitchen with her steaming mug in front of her like she hadn't fingered Emma not twenty yards from where they were, five hours ago.

They locked eyes and a spark seemed to pass between them.

"What are you doing here?" Emma blurted before she could master herself.

Georgia took a careful sip of her coffee. Emma glanced at her mouth, and the memory of kissing her, hot and desperate, flashed through her head.

Her gaze darted away.

"I came to check on how you were doing before I left for the office. Last night was…intense," she said, putting her mug back on the table with a clink. Her gaze was steady on Emma, and Emma knew that if she never brought up what they'd done last night again, Georgia would follow her lead.

Emma looked down into her own mug and leaned a hip on the kitchen island across from where Hattie, who now glanced between them in fascination, stood.

Did Emma want to pretend it had never happened?

The part of her that was absolutely *screaming* to find out how the coffee tasted from Georgia's lips wanted to bring it up this instant and demand an explanation, maybe demand more kisses as well.

But the rational part, the part that was focused on how her dad was doing, that mentally checked the date to figure out when his next doctor's appointment was and assessed the level of pills in the bottles in the cabinet, disagreed. Knew it would be too complicated, mess up the delicate equilibrium they had established. Knew it was too scary to push for more.

"Yeah," Emma croaked, her mouth suddenly dry. She cleared her throat, took a sip of coffee, started over. "Yeah, it was pretty scary. I feel like I have an adrenaline hangover."

Hattie reached over and patted her hand, saying, "From what Georgia was telling me, though, you handled it like a champ."

"Only because she was there to give me a hand," Emma added, internally cringing at her choice of words, and thought she saw a blush creep across Georgia's round cheek as well.

"I was glad I could help," Georgia replied. She shot Emma a piercing look, like she meant it about more than just her father. She pushed back her chair and grabbed up her work tote, slides slapping against the kitchen tiles. "Okay, I need to head out. Cora is opening the office for me today, and I need to make sure she hasn't antagonized any patients away from the practice already."

Emma and Hattie both laughed, the spell of tension broken.

Georgia came over and gave Emma a hug. Although it was quick, Emma felt her body melt into the feel of her, her warmth and smell, the softness of her pressed against her.

"Your dad is doing much better this morning," Georgia said when she pulled back, grasping Emma's hands and squeezing them.

Had they always been this physical with each other? Emma wondered.

"I checked him out before you came downstairs," Georgia continued. "He doesn't remember the episode, which isn't unusual. It's not a cause for alarm, but I'll still send a note to Dr. Tobin later."

Dr. Tobin was her father's memory specialist at Massachusetts General Hospital in Boston.

"Thank you," Emma said softly.

Georgia patted her cheek, her hand lingering for a moment. There was a second before they separated where Emma saw Georgia's eyes flit to her lips. The tip of Georgia's tongue darted out to flick at the corner of her own glossy pink mouth, and the urge to kiss pulsed between them like a heartbeat. But then Georgia pulled away, turned to say good-bye to Hattie, and headed out the back door. Emma watched her go, feeling an ache in her chest she couldn't quite explain.

"What the hell happened there?" Hattie exclaimed. She leaned the back of her wrist against her ample hip and shifted her weight, the motion swaying her cotton tie-dye dress, bangles clinking.

"What do you mean?" Emma hedged, sipping her coffee and picking up a banana.

"I'm talking about the ungodly amount of sexual tension that was just filling my kitchen," Hattie said. She pointed between Emma and the back door.

Emma didn't want to tell her, but she needed to say the words out loud to someone to make it real for herself. Normally, she'd talk to Georgia about this, but that obviously wasn't an option. She could call Wes, but she wouldn't understand all the implications, and Emma didn't really feel like getting into the details of the true extent of her father's condition. Cora would just shrug and say I told you so, and besides, she didn't want to confide in someone who couldn't legally drink.

"Georgia and I had sex last night," Emma said in a rush, unable to keep those words inside any longer.

Hattie stared at her dumbfounded, mouth agape in shock.

"Before or after you had to hunt down Henry?" she asked.

Emma swallowed and said, "After. I was kind of panicking after we got him home, and Georgia was trying to calm me down—"

"By seducing you?" Hattie interrupted.

Emma made a face at her and tucked one long leg up on the seat of the chair. God, she was still in the same pajamas, still in the shirt Georgia had tossed over her shoulder unseeingly, eyes glued to her naked chest. Still in the little shorts she had put her hand down. Emma felt goose bumps race up and down her arms at the thought.

"No, it was more kind of after I was calm? She was rubbing my back, and I kissed her, and it just kind of spiraled from there," Emma said, her face heating at Hattie's raised eyebrows.

"Where were you?"

"You want details?" Emma said, shocked. She raised her eyebrows at Hattie who rolled her eyes back.

"Oh, no way, I just want to know what part of the house I need to scrub extra thoroughly today," Hattie said, laughing.

Emma flipped her off.

"So, what now, kid?" Hattie asked.

Emma scrunched up her face and replied, "What do you mean?"

"I mean, how do you feel about it? Did you like it? Do you want it to happen again?" Hattie raised a finger for each question, her metallic blue nail polish winking in the sunlight.

Emma scratched at the wood grain of the farmhouse table they were sitting at.

"I mean," she said reluctantly, "I've…thought about her in that way before."

"How could you not—she's gorgeous and in your space all the time and you have eyes," Hattie said and laid her hand over Emma's.

Emma met her gaze and opened the floodgates to her whirring mind.

She said, "But I have no idea why she did it, what it meant to her, if it meant anything to her at all. I mean, what happens if I say, okay, yes, let's kiss again, and she says no and then it's awkward between us and my dad and I have to move?"

The sound of Georgia begging to touch her flitted through Emma's mind again, but that could have just been the heat of the moment.

Hattie waved her hand as if swatting all those thoughts away.

"Sure, sure," she said dismissively, "but how do *you* feel? Forget Georgia. Forget other people. What do *you* want?"

Immediately, Emma's mind supplied: I want to kiss her again. I want to kiss her again like she's water and I just ran a marathon.

But what if Georgia didn't want that? And worse, what if she did, but Emma couldn't give Georgia all of what she wanted, what she needed, because of her dad?

It would be too much to have a taste of that with Georgia and then watch her live her life with someone else. Because really, what last night proved to her was that all Emma could offer was a taste.

And maybe Georgia didn't even want that, anyway.

"I-I don't know," Emma stammered.

"Uh-huh. That was a lot of thinking for just an *I don't know*," Hattie replied, giving her the I-know-you're-bullshitting-me eye.

"I need to go erg about this," Emma said. She put her banana peel in the silver compost bucket by the sink and turned to leave the kitchen.

"Spoken like a true meathead," Hattie called after her.

Emma put on some old bike shorts and a sports bra and her gym shoes and went to the basement where she had a home gym with her own water erg. She put on her most upbeat playlist and strapped her feet in.

She did a quick warm-up and settled in for a nice long row. Running helped her empty her mind, but rowing helped her order it. The repetitive motion, the pull and release, pull and release, the stretch and burn of her muscles, the rhythmic whoosh of the water as it turned in the wheel of the erg helped to focus her.

She set up a moderate pace, chose a stroke she could maintain without too much difficulty, and began.

She started by sorting through her memories of the night before, taking it moment by moment. She allowed herself to truly know, truly feel that her father, safely ensconced in the living room with Anne where she attempted to teach him to knit, was fine.

She hadn't experienced terror like she had last night since her mother's cancer treatments, when she'd wake sobbing in the middle of the night, convinced something horrible had happened. Every shadow, every tree branch, every stray cat had transformed into a menacing omen of danger.

She drew in a deep breath on an off stroke, then released it as she pushed off the footboard of the erg, using the power of her legs and abs to pull the handle up to her chest, her body stretched out long, the emotion releasing with the coiled tension in her muscles.

How many more nights or mornings or moments like that are coming, she wondered.

How much more panic and relief, how many more slaps of grief when he called her Giselle or spoke to her like a stranger would she have to endure before the father she loved so fiercely was gone for good and a different person wore his skin?

The thought put a burst of power in her arms and legs, her core, the burn in her muscles intensifying, the meters per stroke number inching up on the stats of the little green backed screen of the erg, meters getting eaten up. She barely heard her music over the pounding of her heart, the slosh of the water in the wheel of the erg.

She wished she had a team at her back, other women to rely on, a coxswain calling directions for her to follow, beats for her to match. She missed that feeling of belonging, of a shared victory or defeat, a huddle of arms to fall into no matter what.

She thought of the feeling of Georgia's arm wrapped around her back as it grounded her, held her securely, let her know it was safe to lean on her, to let go, if only for a moment.

She slowed her strokes to an easy beat, let her breathing and her heart rate climb down, and felt herself settle more firmly in her body.

One thing was for certain: She could never leave her father, not while he was still well enough to live at home.

CHAPTER FOURTEEN

So what exactly is a yacht club?" Cora asked as she walked down the road with Emma that Friday afternoon. "Like, what is the point of it?"

"It's part social club, part restaurant, part event space with a harbor launch, outdoor pool, and tennis courts thrown in," Emma said, smoothing a hand down her French braid and adjusting the strap of the canvas tote bag that hung from her shoulder.

Georgia was meeting some friends for dinner in Salem, so Emma had taken charge of Cora for the evening. She'd decided to take her to a pool party at the club.

She hadn't seen much of Georgia since Tuesday morning, just the usual morning hello and a text or two throughout the day. They still hadn't talked about what had happened between them, and Emma was starting to think they never would. That it had been just a weird middle of the night blip in their timeline that they'd laugh about in years to come.

"Oh hey," she'd turn to Georgia and say, probably several glasses of wine deep, "remember that time my dad got out and wandered to the lighthouse looking for my decades-dead mom and then we made out in my foyer half naked? Ha ha ha, good times."

"So, it's, like, a rich people thing? Everything you do needs to be exclusive and also you pay for your friends?" Cora asked, her plastic flip-flops slapping against the asphalt.

She was wearing her usual nonwork uniform of high-waisted cutoff denim shorts with fraying hems and a cropped T-shirt, long chestnut hair thrown up in a messy bun, eyeliner wings sharp and thick on her upper lids.

Emma wasn't sure where the sense of wearing makeup to a pool party was, but then she'd never really been a makeup kind of girl.

"Ha, yeah, I guess. Speaking of friends, I haven't seen any late-night visitors pulling up to Georgia's house recently," Emma remarked.

Cora crossed her arms.

"Martin is being all annoying and respectful. He says that as long as I'm staying with Georgia, we should honor her rules," she replied, clearly unhappy with her boyfriend's moral code.

"Seems like a change of heart from the school year," Emma commented.

"Nah, not really. I was always the one that pushed curfew or fell asleep at his place by accident. Martin was reminding me to text my mom if we were running late. And he always made sure I did my homework before we hooked up or anything."

"How…responsible of him," Emma said, trying to keep the surprise from her voice.

She still had her doubts about Martin, though, mainly based on his lack of formal higher education and his willingness to date a minor.

"There'll be some other teens there tonight," Emma said. "I think you met some of them at the beach last weekend before your friends came."

"Oh yeah, they were cool," Cora said neutrally. "I don't fully understand why we're going to another pool when Georgia has a perfectly good pool in her backyard that no one really uses."

"Don't get me started on Georgia's pool," Emma said with a dismissive flick of her hand.

"If you hate pools so much, why are we going to a pool party?" Cora shot back.

"Look, I don't hate all pools. I just don't think Georgia should waste her money caring for something she can only use for, like, ten weeks a year when we have a perfectly good ocean to swim in a hundred feet away," Emma said.

"You guys are, like, wicked codependent," Cora replied.

Emma snorted. "Do you even know what that means?"

They reached the club, a sprawling blue-gray building that looked like a two-story mansion with a big wraparound porch and a green lawn that sprawled down to the harbor. The pool was next to the tennis courts on the far side of the building, and the party was in full swing, teens lounging on the pool deck and laughing with their friends who were swimming. Little kids splashed in the shallow end, their parents keeping one eye on them as they sipped rosé or beer or dark and stormies, and snacked on burgers and dogs from the grill while the staff, mostly college-aged kids in polos and khaki pants, picked up trash and delivered food and drinks on black plastic trays.

Emma glanced at Cora and saw her looking around apprehensively at the scene, warily eyeing the waitstaff and the older kids in the pool.

"Emma!"

She looked over to see Connie waving at her from her tennis group.

"I'm going to go say hi," Emma said to Cora. "Want to come?"

"I think I'll grab some food first," she said and headed toward the buffet table set up by the grill.

Emma chatted with Connie and her friends for a while, now and then glancing over to see Cora with the same group of teens from the beach, her feet dipped in the pool. Emma noted that Cora was laughing at something Chris Elton was saying and smiled into her glass of rosé.

"Oh, Emma, have you met Bridget, the new tennis instructor?" Connie said, calling Emma's attention back to her and waving over a woman in her early twenties with curly hair to come join them.

"Emma, this is Bridget," Connie said when the woman had joined their little circle. "She's got a mean backhand and just recently broke up with her girlfriend."

Connie gave Emma a meaningful look that she was sure half the pool caught. Bridget was very cute, Emma couldn't deny. Tall, although not quite as tall as Emma, with a willowy frame that filled out the black one-piece and white wrap skirt she wore nicely. Her coppery hair hung in ringlets past her shoulders and framed a face dotted with red-tinged freckles.

"It's nice to meet you," Emma said. She shook Bridget's hand and noted that it, too, was covered in coppery freckles, stark against her pale skin. She had a warm, firm grip that revealed the sculpted muscles of her forearms and biceps, and her green eyes danced with mischief.

"And sorry about your breakup," Emma added.

Bridget laughed.

She had a nice laugh that seemed to come from her chest, boisterous and earnest.

"I take it from that intro that you, too, played a lot of women's sports growing up?" Bridget said, cocking an eyebrow, as Connie turned back to her friends.

Emma laughed back and replied, "Yup, and college, too."

"I haven't seen you around the courts, though," Bridget said and shot Emma an appraising look. "I'd have noticed."

Emma felt herself blush a bit and shrugged. This girl certainly had charm.

"I'm not much for tennis. More of a team sport girl," she said.

"Let me guess…" Bridget took a step back, eyeing up Emma head to toe, eyes lingering on her bare legs revealed by the oatmeal linen shorts set she wore over her bathing suit. "Basketball?"

"Close, crew." Emma smiled, feeling her chest warm at Bridget obviously checking her out. There was nothing wrong with a little harmless flirting, was there?

"Mmm"—Bridget nodded—"you do have the legs for it. Where did you go to school?"

They exchanged the usual getting to know you chatter, colleges and majors and hometowns. Emma learned that she was from the area originally but had moved when she was in elementary school. She graduated from college in May and was starting law school in the fall in Philly.

"I'm staying with my aunt for the summer. Do you know Ocean Street? It's about half a mile from here? We're the big green house on the left," Bridget said, gesturing over her shoulder with her thumb.

Emma knew the house she was talking about and secretly thought it was ugly, too modern and geometric for her taste.

"What about you? Home for the summer?" Bridget asked her, gesturing at her with her glass of wine.

"I live at home currently," she said and left it at that. She didn't need to get into her whole sob story with this cute stranger, minutes after meeting.

"Who wouldn't want to be here in the summer?" Bridget replied, taking her short answer good-naturedly, gesturing to the setting sun lighting up the water.

"I know." Emma smiled, surveying the pinks and purples of the sky. "You ever been up to the lighthouse to see the sunset?"

Bridget shook her head.

"People make a whole thing of it, bring picnics and set up chairs and watch it like it's a performance. It's really beautiful," Emma added.

Her mother used to make them go watch the sunset almost every day in summer and early autumn, when the weather was clear, people cheering and clapping for the sun as she did her slow slide to the horizon.

She smiled at the memory.

"I'll take you sometime," Emma found herself saying, to her surprise.

She wasn't sure why she said it, but she liked Bridget. It felt good to talk to someone her own age, someone who wasn't worried about her or burdened by her family's tragedies.

Bridget grinned back at her and tilted her head. "That would be great. I could use someone to show me around town. Here, let me give you my number."

Bridget fished her phone out of the pocket of her skirt and handed it to Emma, their fingers brushing. Emma noticed Bridget's lingered a bit when she handed hers back.

They talked more about what Bridget thought about working at the club, Emma laughing at her impressions of the kids missing the ball wildly. Bridget rested her hand on Emma's knee or touched her arm throughout their conversation, casual contact that reminded Emma what it was to be young and carefree.

It had been a long time since someone had flirted with her, especially someone as cute and charming as Bridget. She basically glowed with the vitality and lightness of the unburdened, and Emma felt a bit lighter herself just by proximity.

Around eight thirty, she decided she'd had enough. Plus Anne was off at nine—she'd stayed longer so Emma and Cora could go out—and Emma wanted to be prompt in relieving her.

"I'm going to head out," she said to Bridget, "but I'm glad Connie introduced us."

"Me too," Bridget replied, leaning in to hug Emma good-bye, pressing just a tad too close, lingering a breath too long.

"I'm holding you to that sunset invite," Bridget said when she pulled away.

"Sure thing. You have my number, just let me know what night you're free," Emma said, smiling widely.

They parted ways, and Emma craned her neck to find Cora. She was seated with Chris Elton and his friends in a corner, and Emma wove her way through the crowd to them.

She tapped Cora on the shoulder when she reached them, and Cora looked up at her.

"Hey, I'm heading home. You want to come?" Emma asked.

"Um, I think I'm going to stay a bit longer if that's okay," Cora said.

Emma noticed how close Chris was sitting to her, their thighs practically touching, and felt a flutter of apprehension.

"That's fine, I guess," Emma replied. "Just make sure you let Georgia know where you are."

"Okay, Mom," Cora said sarcastically. Some of the kids around her snickered, and Emma decided that was her cue.

"Whatever," she said eloquently in response and made her way out of the party.

She walked home through the last of the evening light, the sky darkening now the sun had set, the streets quiet and empty away from the harbor side of the peninsula.

When she turned down Highbury Lane, she automatically glanced over at Georgia's house, the rooms dark, the driveway empty. A small pang she didn't feel like exploring went through her chest at the knowledge that Georgia wasn't in her house, wasn't waiting for Emma to knock on the door.

"Hey, Dad, hey, Anne," she called when she entered the house, through the front door for once, and kicked off her sandals.

"Hi, honey. How was the pool party?" her dad asked.

"Look at you, remembering where I was," Emma said, flopping down in her usual chair in the living room across from her dad and Anne, who were both knitting—Anne, an adorable pair of baby booties with a complex pattern of whorls, her dad, what looked like a long thin snake.

Her dad humphed and then turned to Anne, saying, "Why does it look like this?"

He gestured to the increasing thickness at the top of his snake.

"You keep adding stitches, Henry. Remember to count them as you go through a row," Anne said in her lilting accent.

Emma watched them go back and forth, Anne unraveling her father's stitches to his dismay. Anne swatted his hands away gently when he tried to interfere.

She thought of what her friends from college might be doing tonight. Going out to bars, renting houses for the weekend on the Vineyard or down the Cape or in the Hamptons. Going on dates, getting drunk, and hooking up.

She thought, really, if she had a choice, she'd probably choose being here anyway. Watching her father and Anne bicker good-naturedly, the summer warmth and salt air still blowing in through the open window.

On instinct, she turned to look to her left, to the chair Georgia usually occupied, to tell her her thoughts.

But the chair was empty.

"I'm going to get some ice cream from the kitchen," Emma announced, needing to get up and move. "Anne, do you want some before you hit the road?"

Anne was now demonstrating to her father the proper way to hold the needles.

"No, sweetheart, I better get going. Frankie worries when I drive after dark," Anne said, looking up from her demonstration. "Have a good weekend, Henry. I'll see you Monday morning."

She stood and balled her knitting up into a large tote bag she had at her side, tugged down her scrub shirt, today a soft pastel purple, and headed for the door.

Emma walked with her. "How was he tonight?"

Anne patted her shoulder. "Oh, he was fine, dear."

"Good, that's good," Emma said, wringing her hands nervously.

Anne rested her warm dry hands on Emma's anxious ones.

"I know he scared you the other night. Georgia told me," she added, at Emma's questioning look. "Did you tell him about it?"

"No, I thought it would stress him out too much," Emma answered, not meeting Anne's eye. "And his doctor says stress is bad for him."

Anne squeezed her hands and said, "Stress is bad for everyone. It's a tremendous burden for one person to carry alone. Be kind to yourself and remember that you can't take care of others if you aren't taking care of yourself."

Emma felt tears prick her eyes at those words.

"Thank you," she said quietly.

Anne gave her a parting smile, patting her hands one last time before letting go and leaving.

Ten minutes later found Emma seated and talking with her dad over bowls of mint chocolate chip ice cream when her phone buzzed.

Bridget: *It was great meeting you tonight, probably the best part of the whole party* :)

Despite the obvious line, Emma still felt her cheeks split into a grin.

"What's making you smile down at your phone like that?" her dad asked.

"Nothing," Emma said, typing out a response to Bridget and feeling a blush creep across her cheeks. "Just a text from someone I met at the pool party."

Emma: *Not the rubbery hot dogs?*

"At the club pool party?" he echoed skeptically.

"Yeah, there's a new tennis instructor for the summer named Bridget," Emma replied, then took a bite of her ice cream.

"Ah yes, I've heard of Bridget," her dad said with a smirk. "My buddies have been talking about her."

"Gross," Emma said with a shudder. "I don't want to hear what your council of horny old men have to say about her."

"They just say that she's a very nice looking young woman with a mean backhand," he replied with a shrug. "And judging from your blushing over there, you think so, too."

"Can't remember where he put his shoes, but he remembers what the guys say about the hot new tennis instructor," Emma grumbled, and her dad laughed.

"She's hot, now, is she?" he teased.

Emma ate the rest of her ice cream in silence until her phone vibrated again.

Bridget: *It was a close call, but I think you just edged out the hot dogs *tongue out emoji**

Emma caught herself smiling, again.

CHAPTER FIFTEEN

Later that night, Emma was reading in bed when she heard a car driving down their usually silent street.

Georgia had returned from her night out around ten, not that Emma had been waiting or anything, so the sound of an engine intrigued her.

Double-checking that her dad was asleep in his bed and the front door was firmly locked behind her, she quietly went out to the street.

To her surprise she discovered Cora fumbling around in her purse for her keys, barely able to stand up straight. Emma looked down the street and saw the taillights of a silver car, much too fancy to be Martin's, streaking out of sight.

"Cora?" Emma called, walking across the street and letting herself into Georgia's front yard.

"Emma!" Cora boomed, her voice loud and slurring in the still of the night air. "Emmsy-bemsy," she hiccuped, "you look so pretty under the streetlights. Did you know that your hair is just *so*"—she drew out the syllable—"blond? Like, really when you think of the word *blond*, that's what your hair looks like. It's unreal. Do you dye it, or it's just genes?"

"Are you…drunk?" Emma asked her warily, hoping against hope she was wrong.

"No, silly." Cora giggled drunkenly, tripping over her own feet and nearly dropping her purse. "I just can't find my keys. This bag got deeper, I swear."

Emma took the purse from her and located the keys in two seconds flat, dangling them from her fingers before Cora's face.

"Wow, you're, like, a witch or something. Did you use a summoning spell?" Cora said, glazed eyes going wide.

Emma sighed and let her into the darkened house.

"Shhh, I don't want Georgia to find me," Cora whispered loudly and flopped onto the bottom stair of the staircase directly in front of the entrance. She kicked off her shoes wildly so they went flying, "Because then my mom will be mad at me and I won't be able to see Martin for forever and ever. And Georgia will get that disappointed little crinkle between her eyes, you know the one."

She dug her nail in between her brows so hard it left a mark.

"Oh, I'm familiar," Emma said, surveying the lump of underage girl before her, hands on her hips. She debated if it was worth it to try to help her climb the stairs or if she should just hoist her over her shoulder and carry her up. "And I thought you weren't drunk."

Cora put her index finger against her lips and giggled again. She then leaned her head against the banister railing and closed her eyes, her hair falling around her face in limp hanks.

"I bet you probably think it's cute," Cora mumbled drowsily, "when she's all grumpy. *Emmmmaaaa*, can you make the staircase stop spinning?"

"Stay right here," Emma said. She made sure Cora wasn't moving before she went to the kitchen to get her a glass of water.

"Hey, Cora?" she said when she returned a minute later with the glass, lightly slapping her face to wake her up. "Drink this."

Cora grumbled and swiped her hands away. Emma, ignoring her refusal, thrust the glass of water into her hand again and watched Cora take a sip before she slumped back against the stairs.

Emma debated just dumping her in the guest room bed and letting Cora sort out this mess for herself, but her loyalty to Georgia won out. She walked up the stairs to Georgia's bedroom, her stomach clenching with dread.

She knocked on her bedroom door, and Georgia said, "Come in," in a soft, sleepy voice.

Emma, heart hammering, took a deep breath and opened the door to find Georgia sitting up in bed, her dark hair tied back in a loose braid and glasses on, reading a paperback.

"Em," she said, sitting up straight in surprise, putting her book face down on the bedspread. She pushed back the covers, revealing her bare legs in her sleep shorts, and Emma willed herself not to react to the sight of them. Georgia was wearing a matching set tonight with a pattern of little daisies on black pima cotton, the shorts hitting high on her curvy thighs, the buttons straining a bit across her cleavage. "Is everything okay? Is your dad okay?"

"What?" Emma said, a bit distractedly. She had to pry her eyes away from the way the fabric pulled across Georgia's chest. "Oh, uh, no, everything's fine," Emma said in a rush, fighting against the rising flush in her face. "Well, not everything. It's…Cora's downstairs. Drunk."

"She's drunk," Georgia repeated, blank faced.

Emma swallowed and nodded. "Yeah."

"And how did she get drunk?" Georgia asked, a steely note entering her voice, eyes going hard, as she got out of bed and crossed the room to stand in front of Emma, arms folded across her chest and one thick brow arched.

"I haven't gotten that out of her yet. I came outside because I heard a noise and thought it might have been…well, you know, and I found her fumbling for her keys in her purse. I left her at the pool party hanging out with Chris Elton and that gang and came home so Anne could head out," Emma said in a rush.

She nervously tucked a stray strand of hair behind her ear and smoothed her hand over her ponytail. The force of Georgia's gaze steadily on her, that dreaded crinkle forming as she spoke, caused nervous energy to spike in her veins.

Cora was wrong. Emma didn't find that crinkle cute.

"You took her to a party at the club and left her there alone, with kids you don't really know," Georgia said. It wasn't a question, her tone flat and angry.

Emma felt her heart drop. "You think this is *my* fault?" she asked indignantly, pressing a hand to her chest.

Georgia just shook her head and sighed, arms falling to her sides resignedly, brow furrowed.

"Where is she?" Georgia asked sternly, striding out of the room with purpose.

"I left her with some water at the bottom of the stairs," Emma said as she followed Georgia out of her bedroom. "I thought about carrying her up, but she seemed happy there, and I thought I should get you first."

Georgia simply nodded, apparently too focused on getting eyes on Cora to comment on Emma's actions.

"Hey, girl," Georgia said, voice gentle now as she crouched at the bottom of the stairs and lightly shook Cora awake, "let's get you up to bed."

"Georgie!" Cora cried blearily, rubbing at her heavy-lidded eyes with a fist. "You came to join the party!"

Emma was suddenly struck by how young Cora looked, her hair falling in long loose waves around her shoulders, her resemblance to Georgia in that moment striking.

"I did," Georgia replied steadily, taking Cora's hands in hers and helping her stand. "How about we take this party upstairs?"

"*Ooooh*," Cora cooed, nearly wistful, "yes, bed please, now."

Emma watched them together, Georgia's arms wrapped around her younger cousin as she helped her walk up the steps to the second floor, the tenderness in Georgia's movements clear.

"How was your dinner, Geo?" Cora asked as Georgia nearly carried her up the stairs.

"It was fine," Georgia replied. "Mostly other doctors and their spouses. They talked about their kids the whole time."

"*Pshh*," Cora slurred, swatting at the air in front of her face, "you don't need any of that. You're a strong independent lady. I mean, look at you, you're carrying me up the stairs even though Emma is, like, wicked strong and could probably do this one-handed. Right, Em?"

Emma, who had been trailing the cousins up the stairs holding Cora's water, replied sheepishly, "Maybe not one-handed."

"Emma met someone hot tonight," Cora said, out of the blue. Georgia's shoulders tensed as they reached the landing and turned right toward the guest room that was serving as Cora's room for the summer, Emma hot on their heels. "Didn't you? I saw you flirting with that girl."

"I…I mean…" Emma said.

"She was clearly into you," Cora continued as Georgia set her down on the bed and pulled back the covers so Cora could slip in and curl on her side. "She kept touching your arm and playing with her hair." Cora demonstrated by fiddling with a lock of her hair, twirling it exaggeratedly around her finger. Georgia pushed her shoulder gently to get her to lie down.

"Chris was saying how it would be cool if you guys hooked up, like, such a classic meet cute. Thanks for introducing me to Chris, by the way, Emma," Cora mumbled sleepily as she nestled into the sheets. Georgia pulled the covers over her and Emma put the glass of water on the nightstand. "He and his friends were wicked cool. We went down to the beach and had a bonfire, and Chris broke out this handle of vodka his older brother had scored him, and we all shared it. He tried to kiss me, but I won't hold that against him."

Cora finished her sentence on a yawn, closing her eyes.

"That's nice of you," Emma said as Georgia plumped the pillows behind her.

"You should ask out the tennis girl, so you don't die a lonely virgin spinster," Cora said on another yawn.

Emma scoffed, but Cora had already drifted off, breath deep and even.

Georgia put a bottle of Advil next to the water on the nightstand and gestured for Emma to follow her. She closed the door softly behind her.

They walked silently down the stairs, Emma's shoulders creeping up to her ears as she braced for the storm sure to follow.

"Chris fucking Elton," Georgia began, anger jumping into her voice like sparks crackling from a fire as soon as they reached the living room. She crossed her arms and paced over the carpet, her long braid swaying like an angry snake down her back with the movement.

"I'm going to call his mom and tell her how her underage son got a girl drunk and tried to take advantage of her, the little yuppie scumbag piece of shit," Georgia stormed.

"That is pretty skeevy," Emma agreed.

This was, apparently, the wrong thing to say because Georgia whirled around and pointed an accusatory finger at her.

"You thought because they were yacht club kids, she'd be fine," Georgia said, her gray eyes bright. "Didn't you? You thought because they all went to fancy private schools and are going to private colleges in the fall that she'd be fine, more trustworthy than the public school trash she hangs out with regularly."

Emma held up her hands to defend herself from Georgia's judgment, the venom in her voice stinging, making her wince because that *had* been what she was thinking.

"Em, if something happened to her, that would have been on me," Georgia said, slapping her coral-tipped fingers against her chest, the color incongruously cheery. "Her mom trusted me to keep her safe and curb her behavior, not let her wander around getting drunk with rich brats," she spat. "And God forbid something worse than getting drunk had happened to her. What if Chris hadn't taken no for an answer, huh? What if he hadn't just tried to kiss her?"

Emma felt her heart sink into her stomach at the idea of something like that happening to Cora. Of Cora vulnerable and alone with strangers that Emma had left her with.

"I know, I know, and I'm so sorry I left her," Emma said, each of Georgia's rebukes hitting her like a tiny shard of glass lodging in her heart, "but—"

"But you had to get back to your dad," Georgia finished. She sighed deeply and looked to the ceiling, resting her interlocked hands on the back of her head, elbows spread wide.

She closed her eyes and took a long breath in, letting it out before dropping her arms and looking at Emma.

"Cora is my main responsibility right now, Em. My cousin trusted me to keep her safe, and you jeopardized that tonight. Sometimes it feels like all you can see is Henry, and that makes you oblivious to everything else going on around you," she said in a tired, resigned voice.

"That's not fair," Emma said defensively, her shoulders curving in and her arms crossing against her chest. "I know this time maybe I was a bit distracted, but Anne had been with him all day, and I genuinely thought Cora would just hang out with them for, like, maybe half an hour more and then come right home. How was I supposed to know she was going to go off and drink strange boys' alcohol on the beach?" She tossed up her arms frustratedly at the end.

Georgia scoffed.

"Have you met her? That's completely in character for her. Maybe if you thought about it for more than, like, five seconds, you'd remember that her mom sent her out here because she's been partying with Martin and being generally boy-crazy the past year."

Emma thought that was an unfair characterization of Cora. Although she had caught her sneaking out to go to a party with Martin not long ago, so maybe not the time to press the issue.

"And I guess you weren't so *totally* focused on your dad tonight that you apparently couldn't flirt with hot women," Georgia added, her tone suddenly frosty.

That brought Emma up short.

"What?" she said, confused.

"You know, the hot tennis girl Cora said you were chatting up," Georgia replied, crossing her arms and sitting into her right hip. "Maybe if you weren't so busy making eyes at her, you might have noticed

Chris Elton hitting on Cora and being a douche, and you might have had more sense about leaving her there."

"Excuse me?" Emma shot back indignantly. "For your information, I was not making eyes at Bridget, I was making polite yacht club small talk after Connie introduced us. You make it sound like I was groping her by the side of the pool."

"Well, did you want to be?" Georgia asked aggressively.

Emma just gaped at her.

"What the fuck, Georgia? No! I literally *just* met her. And aren't you the one always telling me to go out and meet people? Have a life beyond my dad? And here I am doing that, and you bite my head off," Emma retorted, her own anger flaring up.

Georgia just glared at her, arms crossed tightly under her breasts.

"And it *was* nice to talk to another young queer person for a change," Emma added with a shrug.

"Oh, because I'm *so* old," Georgia huffed indignantly, rolling her eyes. The similarity between the cousins had never been stronger.

"I mean, you are thirteen years older than I am," Emma shot back, frustration mounting.

"That's right, I am," Georgia said, matching Emma's tone, taking a step toward her, gaze latched to Emma's now. "And I know things you don't."

"What does that even mean?" Emma nearly shouted, throwing up her hands.

Rather than replying, Georgia grabbed her wrists and pulled her toward her.

Abruptly, Emma realized they were standing toe to toe, breathing heavily in each other's faces. She stared Georgia down for another second, then the eye contact became too much and she shut her eyes tightly.

But she could still feel her, the gust of Georgia's breath like fingers faintly trailing over her cheek.

And then she realized there *were* fingers running over her cheek, Georgia's fingers. They were ghosting across her chin, down her throat, and around to her jaw, angling her mouth down.

She opened her eyes just as Georgia looked up from her lips, and the tension between them pulled taut. One second passed and then it was like a trip wire had been pulled, and they exploded into action.

Emma grasped Georgia's hips and hauled her body against her

own at the same moment Georgia wrapped her arms around Emma's neck, their lips meeting in the middle.

It was like the other night, desperate and shocking and nearly dreamlike as the frustration and confusion pounding through Emma's body gave way to a heady desire.

This can't really be happening again, Emma thought as she tangled one hand in Georgia's braid, the other trailing up and down and over the deep sloping curve of her waist, the lush softness of her breasts pushing against her own small ones, the taste of Georgia's mouth, mint toothpaste and heat, flicking in with her tongue.

Georgia was on her tiptoes, yanking at Emma's neck to get her mouth closer to hers. Emma knew her neck would twinge later, but she didn't care. Couldn't care as Georgia nipped at her lower lip and made her gasp into her mouth.

She felt frenzied, the need to feel all of Georgia, to touch every part of this infuriating woman who she cared so deeply for washing over her and sucking her under like a riptide.

Gripping the soft cotton of Georgia's pajama top, she backed her up to the nearest wall, pressing her body against Georgia's heat. She bent her knees to bridge the gap in their heights as she leaned down to suck at Georgia's neck. Georgia's hands flew to tug at Emma's ponytail, sending her hair cascading down her shoulders before Georgia buried her fingers in it and tugged slightly as Emma's teeth grazed her neck below her ear.

"Fuck, Em," she whimpered, and Emma felt it low in her stomach, the breathy way she said her name. Georgia trailed her fingers up the backs of Emma's thighs, her touch tickling the hair there and sending chills throughout her body, before sliding up her shorts and stroking the bare skin of her ass.

Emma heard herself let out a little whining sound at the contact, causing Georgia's fingers to grip her firmly.

She could feel Georgia push back against her, into her, as she trailed her hand up Georgia's top. She felt the curve of Georgia's round stomach, the flare of her hips before they narrowed to Georgia's waist, the heavy weight of Georgia's breasts in her hands, her skin hot and silky smooth.

Had it been like this the last time, hot and intoxicating and so, so good?

Last time, she'd been panic drunk and addled and half awake, unable to really take it all in. Her body had only been able to process

Georgia and fingers and skin and lips and *pleasure pleasure pleasure* zinging up her spine before it was over.

Now, though, she felt wide awake and clearheaded, her brain storing every detail in high definition.

The little sound Georgia made when she guided Emma to slip her thigh between her legs. The way Georgia pressed into it, grinding herself against Emma's muscles, hips circling slowly, using her hold on Emma's ass for stability.

The way she bit her lip when Emma pulled back, looking down into Georgia's face, gorgeously flushed and framed by her thick hair where it had been loosed from her braid by Emma's tugging, eyes heavy-lidded and glazed.

How Georgia's eyes widened, pupils flaring, and she gasped when Emma rubbed her palms against her nipples, feeling them harden beneath her touch.

"You are so fucking beautiful," Emma panted, voice like steel wool, echoing Georgia's words from days ago back to her.

Georgia groaned as her hips kept moving. "You feel so good, Em. Make me feel so good."

Taking one hand from inside Emma's shorts, Georgia gripped the back of Emma's neck to bring Emma's face to hers again. Rather than kiss her, though, she pushed their foreheads together, her hips picking up tempo against the pressure of Emma's leg, breaths coming more heavily.

Emma's back was beginning to cramp from the angle, her thigh burning slightly, but there was no way, *no way*, she was going to move.

She planted one hand on the wall above Georgia's head for leverage and slid the other one around her hip, her hand splaying out against the bare skin of Georgia's back beneath her pajama top, pressing her body closer, down harder against Emma's leg.

Nothing existed for her beyond this, the need to keep Georgia close to her, to drive her further and further to that point of no return, to feel the way Georgia's legs were beginning to shake and clamp around her thigh.

Georgia tilted her head back against the wall again, eyes squeezed closed, mouth agape, and Emma ducked down to bite at the soft flesh where her neck met her shoulder. She felt small shudders race through Georgia's body, her grip on Emma tightening as she edged closer to that peak.

Then a door slammed open in the distance, feet stumbled across the carpet on the upstairs landing, and the sound of retching came from the bathroom.

Emma and Georgia jumped apart, staring at each other, chests heaving.

"I should go check on her," Georgia said after a moment, and her dazed eyes moved to stare in the direction of where Cora now puked her guts up.

"Right," Emma panted, mind whirling.

Their eyes locked again, and both of them seemed reluctant to let the other go. Slowly, Georgia disentangled their limbs, tugged her shorts down, and fastened the buttons on her top where they'd come loose from Emma's insistent movements.

"Um," Emma said, throwing her hair into a fresh ponytail, feeling awkward and unsure of what to do. Half her mind was focused on the parts of her body that were still glaringly awake and begging for Georgia to *come back now* and give them attention. That part told her to go up to Georgia's room and lie naked in her bed until Cora was done puking and they could get back to sex.

The other, nonhorny part of her brain was worried about Cora, confused about what was happening between her and Georgia, and wondering if it would—incredibly, wonderfully—keep happening.

If it even should.

"Not now, Em," Georgia said. She pushed her wild hair back from her face, not meeting Emma's eyes as she peeled away from the wall on shaky legs and headed toward the stairs. "I swear we'll talk about this, just…not now."

Emma nodded and watched Georgia tread up the stairs to take care of Cora, body still buzzing with the feel of her.

Georgia turned at the top of the stairs and looked down at Emma. Their gazes locked like magnets, and Emma was struck all over again by how stunningly, familiarly beautiful she was. How aloof she seemed up there, like a maiden kept atop a tower.

"Night, Em," she said, voice gentle now, so different from when she'd stormed down the stairs ten minutes ago. "And…I'm sorry."

Before she could ask what she was apologizing for, Georgia gave her a small smile and turned to attend to the sick girl in her bathroom.

Emma felt her heart sink down to her toes, but she opened the door and walked across the street to her own home and her sleeping father.

Chapter Sixteen

The next morning, Emma woke early and lay in her bed thinking over everything that happened the previous night. Cora's stumbling home drunk, Georgia's anger, their fight.

Georgia's words echoed in her head.

Sometimes it feels like all you can see is Henry, and that makes you oblivious to everything else going on around you.

The disappointment that had been so clear in her voice, as if Emma's devotion to her father was a bad thing.

What they'd done in the living room, the feel of Georgia's voluptuous curves pressed against her, the way her bare skin had felt under Emma's fingers, had tasted on Emma's tongue, the way she'd shivered and gripped Emma's body like it was the only thing keeping her from drowning. How good, how right, how proud she'd been to be the one to make Georgia feel pleasure. How sad she was that she hadn't gotten to take her that final distance to the finish line.

It all felt too big, too confusing to face.

Dangerously all-consuming, too, the realization of a childhood crush turned adult fantasy come true. Like Emma could replay last night and that night in her own home over and over in her head until she got lost in them, forgetting to eat or sleep or breathe. Forgetting everything else that existed around her.

She kept recalling the image of Georgia pinned between her body and the wall, the flush on her cheeks as she'd gazed heavy-lidded up at her. Just that memory alone had Emma pressing her thighs together and shifting in bed as she stared unseeingly at the ceiling of her bedroom.

She imagined unbuttoning Georgia's pajama top and letting it fall to the floor, sliding her shorts down those sumptuous thighs until she was bared before her. Imagined that it was her hand between Georgia's legs that made her gasp and groan. Imagined sinking to her knees on the hardwood floor and burying her face there instead, Georgia squeezing her between thick thighs and tugging on her hair to bring her closer.

Just as she felt the ache that hadn't really gone away reawaken between her legs, she remembered Georgia's parting words.

I'm sorry.

Sorry for what? For kissing her? For telling her to leave rather than ravishing her? For the interruption? For letting herself get pulled into that moment? That she shouldn't have let it get that far, like Emma was a sheet cake she'd eaten too much of, an indulgence.

What would it mean for her, for her father, for their friendship if she kept sleeping with Georgia? And did Georgia even want that? Or were these some fever-dream encounters never to be spoken about again? Perfect soap bubble moments to pull out and remember but not repeat for fear of bursting everything?

Their lives were all so enmeshed. Endangering that by what they were doing was a terrible idea. She needed Georgia in a way that went beyond the demands and desires of her body, beyond what her feelings might dictate.

Besides, her father needed Georgia, too, and nothing could come before his needs.

It would be really nice if I could talk this through with my mom, Emma thought and felt her heart pinch.

She'd have to make do with the next best thing.

"Morning, sugar," Hattie sang out when Emma returned from her run, a green smoothie already waiting for her on the counter as she panted and sweated her way into the kitchen, where Hattie was finishing a crossword at the counter.

"Morning, Hattie," Emma said.

She plopped onto a stool at the island and inspected the smoothie.

"Kale, banana, spinach, almond butter, protein powder, oat milk, and honey," Hattie said before Emma could open her mouth. She was still staring down at the crossword in front of her on the marble island. Emma grinned at her profile.

"Henry is drinking one, too. He's in the sitting room reading the paper," Hattie said, giving Emma the full report.

"How's he looking this morning?" Emma inquired, taking a big pull on the metal straw in her smoothie.

"Told me the same supreme court joke twice," Hattie said. "Wasn't particularly funny either time, but otherwise he's in a good mood."

Thank God for that, Emma thought. If she had to puzzle out Georgia and navigate her father's distress at the same time, her head might just explode.

Thinking of Georgia brought up the memory of her kiss again and then the whole spiral began anew.

"What's eating you, kid?" Hattie asked, peering at her over the top of her red reading glasses. She swatted Emma with her crossword to bring her back to earth.

"Hmm?" Emma replied distractedly. "Nothing, I'm fine."

"Uh-huh," Hattie said skeptically, leaning her round hip against the counter, today's turquoise gauzy tunic brushing against the marble.

"Seriously, I'm good," Emma said.

Hattie raised her eyebrow and Emma crumbled like feta.

"Okay, here's what happened," she said in a rush and divulged the whole story of the night before in one breath. She closed her eyes to keep from seeing Hattie's reactions.

Hattie whistled. "Damn, you have as much going on as those Korean drama things my granddaughter watches."

Emma grimaced at her, and Hattie smiled.

"The worst part is that she said *I'm sorry* before going to see to Cora," Emma continued. "I mean, what does that mean? I'm sorry I kissed you? I'm sorry I'm not into you that way? I'm sorry, you're too young for me? I'm sorry I yelled at you and then groped you in my foyer?"

Hattie chimed in, cutting off Emma's increasingly manic rant. "You know who would be great to ask these questions to?"

She leaned onto her forearms, her jumble of necklaces bouncing against her ample bosom as she swayed forward.

"A therapist?" Emma replied and Hattie laughed.

"Always a good answer, kid. But no. Georgia. You need to talk to Georgia," she said, pushing herself off the counter.

Emma stared moodily into the dregs of her smoothie.

"That's probably the mature, adult thing to do," she agreed.

"Mm-hmm," Hattie replied, leaning her chin on her hands, elbow resting on the counter. "Now tell me about the tennis hottie."

"Oh my God, you and Cora are the worst, I swear." Emma rolled her eyes. "Her name is Bridget, we talked for, like, ten minutes max at the yacht club pool party, she gave me her number, the end."

"Look at you, fending off gorgeous women left and right," Hattie teased, swatting Emma on the forearm. "Must be your Saturn return."

"I'm pretty sure that's not for another few years," Emma replied. She crossed her own sweaty arms on the cool marble surface of the counter, smoothie finished.

"God, I forget how young you are sometimes," Hattie said fondly. "You act all mature and woman-of-the-house-ish, but you're not much more than a babe in the woods."

"Do you think Georgia thinks I'm too young?" Emma chewed on her lower lip. She shook her head, halting the spiral before it could begin again. "No, you know what? I'm taking your advice, Hattie," Emma said, sitting up.

"Uh-oh," Hattie said, "I don't think I like the sound of that."

"I'm going to get out and meet new people," Emma declared, snatching up her phone and scrolling for the short text thread from the night before. "I need to kiss someone who hasn't known me all her life, doesn't live across the street, and isn't instrumental in my father's medical care."

"Shouldn't be too hard to find," Hattie quipped, and Emma shot her a glare.

She was just lonely and horny and had been spending too much time with Georgia, Emma decided. She was just projecting her long ignored libido onto her.

That was it.

And if Georgia was going to be sorry about kissing her, then Emma was going to kiss someone else.

Hey, she texted Bridget. *What are you doing tonight?*

Triumphantly, she pressed send and then placed her phone face down on the counter.

"I'm not sure who you just texted, but I hope you have fun with them," Hattie said.

"Me too," Emma replied.

She went over the grocery list with Hattie and chatted for a few more minutes about Hattie's kids' and grandkids' summer plans.

Then Emma headed upstairs to shower.

Where she definitely didn't spend the whole time reliving every minute detail from the night before, pretending her hands were Georgia's as they skimmed across her slick skin until she had to touch herself.

Absolutely *didn't* press her head against the tiled wall and bite her lip to keep her moans in as her fingers worked between her legs until her stomach clenched and her breath came in gasps.

She certainly did not.

CHAPTER SEVENTEEN

Emma met Bridget at the lighthouse a half hour before sunset, having seen her father safely to dinner at the club with his friends first, making sure they each had her number stored in their phone in case of emergencies.

She was lounging on a red checked Turkish cotton blanket positioned perfectly to have a view over where the harbor met the wilder waves of the open ocean, a woven picnic basket by her side, when Bridget found her.

She looked just as cute as she had the night before, dressed in a blue romper with a thin beige and black striped sweater on top and Birkenstock sandals on her feet. Her curly hair was piled in a high bun on the top of her head, tendrils falling to frame her face, a million silver rings on all her fingers, and five different silver chains tangling around her neck. Where Georgia was all bright patterns and simple yet elegant silhouettes, Bridget seemed to be a maximalist. Not that Emma was comparing them.

"This is quite the setup you've got going on here," Bridget said, taking a seat by Emma's side and leaning over to give her a friendly, if lingering, hug.

Emma started to pull food from the basket. Mozzarella, pesto, and tomato sandwiches on baguettes from a local bakery wrapped in beeswax cloth wraps. A bag of potato chips, a can of seltzer each, a bottle of white wine in a travel chiller, plates, and cloth napkins all emerged from its depths.

"Shit, girl"—Bridget laughed—"you were serious when you said you liked to prepare."

Emma's face grew warm. "Is it too much?"

Bridget smiled and rested her hand on top of Emma's.

"I think it's sweet," she said brightly.

Emma's flush grew when Bridget's hand lingered a beat before she reached for her sandwich.

They ate their food and chatted about life. Emma noticed that Bridget liked to speak more than listen and that her sense of humor leaned a bit sharp and biting. People from the yacht club stopped to say hi to both Emma and Bridget as they filtered past.

Emma wasn't sure whether this was a date or not, as Bridget seemed to like to flirt with everyone around her—resting her hand on a forearm or shoulder or tossing her head back to laugh at jokes—from middle aged men, to mothers with kids, to a group of teen girls and boys who all seemed obviously enamored with her.

Emma didn't mind it, though.

Bridget didn't seem like someone looking for anything serious. Besides, there was an automatic end date to her time on the Neck, and she'd just gotten out of what Emma had learned was a five-year relationship.

"We met in high school and just clicked immediately," Bridget said as they dug into their sandwiches. "We were on and off in college, doing long distance. But I guess graduation made her realize that just because we've been together forever doesn't mean we necessarily need to stay together, you know?"

Bridget's eyes looked sad as she spoke, and Emma could tell that she wasn't over her ex, no matter how much she flirted.

"I'm sorry," Emma said, thinking back to Sam, a lifetime ago. "My college girlfriend and I broke up soon after graduation, too."

"What happened?" Bridget asked, tilting her head inquisitively. "You seem like someone you'd want to hold on to."

She gestured at the spread.

Emma smiled and shrugged, feeling reluctant to divulge the whole truth.

"We just…grew apart," she hedged. "She moved to New York, and I couldn't come down to see her as often as she wanted, and it just sort of fizzled as our lives got more crowded. Nothing too dramatic or sad."

"And nothing since?" Bridget asked.

Hungry mouths in the quiet of the dark, hands roaming up her stomach, tracing her ribs. Pressure and warmth grinding against her thigh, moans muffled in her neck, sweet fingers between her thighs, Georgia's laughing smile framed by the sun and waves and—

"Nope," Emma said with a tight smile.

"I find that hard to believe. With that hair and those sculpted shoulders, you're too beautiful to be single," Bridget said, a glint in her eye, running one hand up Emma's bicep and squeezing the defined muscle of Emma's deltoid revealed by the tight-fitting black tank she wore with her loose summer weight jeans. Bridget's fingers were warm and slightly rough from her tennis calluses, scratching pleasantly against Emma's skin.

Emma waited for goose bumps or a chill to erupt in their wake, but her skin remained resolutely flat and untingly.

Emma rolled her eyes. "Wow, does that usually work for you?"

Bridget threw her head back and laughed. She had a nice laugh, big and boisterous and easy.

"You're not an easy nut to crack, are you, Wilson?" Bridget remarked.

She squeezed Emma's arm again and let go.

The conversation drifted back toward Bridget, Emma happy just to listen to a life she wasn't intimately familiar with or responsible for.

Bridget liked to stick to amusing anecdotes and TV shows she'd been watching, nothing too deep or intense or emotional, skating along the surface of life.

An image of one of those water skimmer bugs you saw on Lake Winnipesaukee appeared in Emma's mind as Bridget talked about some spy thriller she'd watched recently with her cousin.

She really is very cute, Emma thought as she watched her speak. The curves of her lips, bottom slightly fuller than the top, the way her groomed eyebrows moved as she talked, her expressive face dotted every inch with freckles. The curve of her breasts beneath her sweater, more on Emma's end of the spectrum than Georgia's. Her body was lanky and toned in that way of tennis players and dancers, more curving than solid Emma's rower's build. Her freckled legs stretched in front of her on the blanket, her feet bare and toes painted hot Barbie pink.

Emma noted these things in a sort of clinical way, like she was evaluating a painting for purchase, feeling nothing of that pull she felt around Georgia, that feeling that they were planets on decaying orbits bound to crash into each other.

Everything about Bridget felt light and airy. Emma wondered if she'd ever known grief, if she'd ever lain awake at night gripped with anxiety and jumping at even the slightest noise in the house as she had those first weeks after her father's diagnosis.

Emma pulled out the cookies she'd had Hattie make, to Bridget's amusement, and they sipped their wine, laughing and chatting and nibbling on snickerdoodles as the sun began to set. Families gathered around them, kids doing cartwheels in the grass, dogs chasing each other, couples cuddling, all there to watch the everyday magic of the sunset over the water.

When it really got going, pinks and purples and a little splash of orange spilling across the darkening blue and reflecting in the calm surface of the water below, a hush fell over the gathered people.

"Wow," Bridget said softly from beside her.

"Told you." Emma smirked, and Bridget snorted. "My mom used to call it a cotton candy sky." Emma smiled to herself.

"She's right about that. Reminds me of the cotton candy ice cream I used to get when I was a kid. I'd have, like, three bites and then immediately feel sick," Bridget replied, but Emma wasn't really listening.

She was lost in a memory of being in the same scene, her mom's blond hair, the exact shade of Emma's, blowing in the breeze off the water, her knees tucked up to her chest, her head resting against Emma's father's shoulder, his arm braced behind her back. Emma, nine or ten at the time, sat in his lap, full of the simple happiness of being safe and surrounded by the people she loved, and sure it would always be that way.

An ache formed in her chest, a longing to get back to that place so fierce she felt like she couldn't breathe.

She turned to tell Georgia about the memory, only to find Bridget at her side, still prattling on.

"You know those foods you loved as a kid that now you can't stomach? Like Zebra Cakes or Twinkies, just pure unadulterated sugar that hurts your teeth," Bridget continued, oblivious to the shift in Emma's mood, eyes on the sunset.

Emma took a long sip of her seltzer and tucked that tender memory away in mental tissue paper for protection.

They lingered by the lighthouse as the night deepened and the bugs came out. The families left, and groups of teens clumped together, the smell of weed thick in the air.

"I better head back home. Got to be up for a tennis clinic at eight tomorrow," Bridget said, grimacing.

"Yikes, that's early," Emma said, remembering her years of waking up at five for frigid crew practice on the river.

They packed up all of Emma's picnic gear, and Emma walked her back to her bike where it was locked at the rack by the parking lot.

"I had a great time tonight," Bridget said, flipping her helmet around in her hands. "Thanks for suggesting we hang."

"Yeah, I had a great time, too," Emma said, which wasn't a lie. Bridget was easy to be around, low maintenance.

"I know this wasn't really a date and you seem weirdly resistant to my charm, but I do think you're just incredibly beautiful and I'd be kicking myself if I didn't ask…Can I kiss you?" Bridget said, taking Emma a bit off guard, eyes dropping to Emma's lips.

What the hell, Emma thought.

After all, this was exactly what she'd wanted, wasn't it?

"Yes, you can kiss me," Emma said with a smile, and Bridget grinned back at her.

She took a step forward and pulled Emma in by the waist, looping her fingers into the belt loops of Emma's jeans. She was only an inch or two shorter than Emma, so Emma didn't have to crane her neck too far down.

It was…nice. Not fueled by panic and lust and fraught with desperation to feel good. Not some kiss at the witching hour that set her whole body on fire and confused the hell out of her and made her feel more alive than she had in years.

Just an everyday, ordinary kiss between two people who were getting to know each other and had had a fun time together on a sort of date.

Bridget pulled away, smiling up at Emma, the flush on her cheeks tinging her freckles a deeper copper.

"We should definitely do that again," Bridget said as she put her helmet on and wheeled her bike around. "I'll text you when I know my schedule later this week."

"Sure, sounds good," Emma replied, a sense of almost disappointment sweeping through her.

"Bye, Emma." Bridget mounted her bike and swung her leg over the seat, then headed off into the distance.

"Bye," Emma called after her.

On the walk home, Emma realized Bridget had never asked her where she worked.

CHAPTER EIGHTEEN

"And where are you coming from?" Cora called to Emma as she turned down Highbury Lane, swinging her picnic basket at her side.

Cora, Johnny, and Georgia sat out on the front porch of Georgia's house, sprawled on the outdoor couch to the right of the front door.

"I was just watching the sunset at the lighthouse," Emma said as she opened the gate and walked up the path to them. Johnny came to greet her when she drew near, before he curled back up on the outdoor rug in front of the couch. Emma sat down on the wicker rocking chair facing where Cora and Georgia sat and slipped her feet out of her sandals to rest on Johnny's fluffy side, rubbing him back and forth with her soles.

She hadn't seen Georgia since the night before and found it difficult to stop the sound of her gasping into Emma's neck from playing in her mind.

Now was so *not* the time for sex flashbacks.

"How are you feeling, Cora?" she asked, trying to keep her mind clear and on innocent thoughts.

Cora waved her question away. "I'm fine, I'm seventeen, my liver is in tip-top shape. Were you at the lighthouse alone, though?"

There was a pause as Emma narrowed her eyes at the twinkle in Cora's expression.

"I…no," Emma said, swallowing and glancing at Georgia, who flipped through a magazine with studied attention.

"Who were you with?" Cora prompted, a knowing smile now spreading across her face.

Emma squinted at her. "What do you know?"

Cora smirked.

"Oh, nothing. Only one of the girls I met last night was also down at the lighthouse and just so happened to capture this"—she whipped out her phone and thrust it in Emma's face dramatically, like she was a TV lawyer trying to rattle a suspect—"little gem and sent it to me."

Emma took the phone from her warily and looked down at her screen. It was a picture of her kissing Bridget, her hand resting behind Bridget's head tilting Bridget's neck up to her face, her other hand on Bridget's slim waist, Bridget's hands tangled in the loop of her jeans.

"Your friend sent you that?" Emma said, handing the phone back to Cora. "That's some stalker shit."

"What is it?" Georgia asked, putting her magazine down on the coffee table and reaching for Cora's phone.

Before Emma could react, Georgia looked down at that picture, her face going carefully blank.

"Good for you, girl," Cora said, waggling her eyebrows. "Getting out there and spreading your wild oats. How was it?"

"Okay, one, you are too horny for your own good," Emma said, lifting her index finger and glaring at Cora. Cora just rolled her eyes and kicked Emma in the thigh.

"Ow. Two, the kiss was…nice. Unexpected, but nice." Emma shrugged.

"That's it?" Cora said. "In other words, it was boring and gross."

Georgia, who had tossed Cora's phone onto her lap, went back to flipping through her magazine.

"You should delete that, Cor," she said, eyes glued to the glossy pages before her. "It's weird to have pictures of other people kissing on your phone."

"That's your response? You're not interested in Emma's date?" Cora turned to Georgia, an incredulous look on her face. "Or did she text you about it on her walk home since you guys seem to be, like, embedded in each other's lives."

"Emma's allowed to have a private life, she's an adult," Georgia replied sternly, still not looking at Emma.

"Ugh, you guys are so old and annoying," Cora said. "I'm going inside since it's the only place I'm allowed to go on house arrest."

"You got drunk with strange children on a public beach last night," Georgia called to her retreating back. "Be glad I'm not telling your mom. You'd be locked in your room until orientation."

Cora made some teenage sounds of angst and dismissal and let the door slam behind her.

Then Emma and Georgia were left alone, Georgia still pretending to be engrossed in her magazine.

Emma knew it was an act because Georgia's eyes didn't seem to move around the pages, and her shoulders were stiff.

"So," Georgia said finally, "you went on a date with the tennis instructor."

A statement, not a question.

"It wasn't, like, a *date* date," Emma hedged. "It was just one woman asking another woman to watch a sunset with her over a picnic dinner."

"So not just a date, but an incredibly romantic one," Georgia said, and she finally tossed the magazine aside and looked at Emma, a steely fire in her eyes. "One that ended in kissing."

Georgia arched her brow at Emma.

"What's that fucking look for?" Emma huffed. "You're the one that apologized for kissing me last night."

Emma sat back in her chair and folded her arms, trying her best not to pout like a five-year-old.

"What?" Georgia said. "Is that what you think I was apologizing for?"

"I mean, you did say it literally minutes after we stopped," Emma replied, glaring down at her toes.

"Yeah, but I meant I was sorry for yelling at you," Georgia said as she leaned forward, elbows on her knees, her loose hair falling over her shoulders. "I meant I was sorry for taking out my concern for Cora on you."

Emma waved her hand dismissively. "I already knew you weren't only angry with me. That you were really afraid of what could have happened to Cora because you act all exasperated with her but you love her, and you were worried about letting Eleni down because you pride yourself on being someone people can depend on."

Georgia looked at her, a bit stunned.

"You did?" she asked softly, eyes on Emma's face.

"Yeah, plus you weren't wrong about me," Emma said. She looked down at her toes in Johnny's fur again, unable to witness the tender look Georgia was sending her without it going straight to her foolish heart. "I did rush to judge Chris and his friends as safe because they belonged to the yacht club, and I was distracted by my dad and should have kept a closer eye on Cora. At the very least I should have checked that she made it home at the end of the night," she said.

"You're so incredibly thoughtful, sometimes, you know that?" Georgia said. She sounded almost annoyed. "It's making it very hard not to kiss you right now."

Emma felt her heart kick up and bit her lip.

"Fuck," Georgia groaned, burying her head in her hands, as if the sight of Emma was too much to bear, "this is bad, Em."

"I know," Emma said quietly.

"Maybe it's good you went out with Bridget." Georgia scrubbed her hands through her hair as she sat up and let them fall back between her cotton clad legs. "She's more your speed."

"What's that supposed to mean?" Emma demanded.

"She's around your age, for one," Georgia answered. "She's an athlete."

"And I'm just some jock meathead?" Emma crossed her arms over her chest.

"Of course not, Em. I just meant, you guys have things in common in a simple way. An easy way, something you could handle right now. Isn't that what you're afraid of, not being there for your dad? Isn't that why you've walled yourself off over there?"

She gestured across the street at Heartfield.

Emma scoffed, offended and hurt. Even if she had thought nearly those same things about Bridget only an hour before.

"You make it sound like I'm using my dad's dementia as an excuse not to live my life," Emma said and sat back, legs crossed angrily.

"Aren't you?" Georgia challenged, her eyes fierce as they met Emma's.

Emma stood up.

"You know what, I don't need to sit here and be lectured at by a woman who's making out with me one minute and then acting like I'm five the next. Which is it, Georgia? Am I an adult you want or a child you need to lecture?"

"I don't know!" Georgia shot back, practically yelling now.

"You don't know," Emma repeated flatly, not sitting down but not walking away either.

Georgia just stared at her for a moment and then laughed ruefully, looking up at the roof of the porch.

"I don't know what the fuck I'm doing with you, Em," she said quietly.

Emma stood in silence waiting for her to gather her thoughts.

"I…I wasn't expecting you to kiss me the other night," Georgia began hesitantly, looking at Emma where she stood on the porch.

Emma sighed, the wind leaving the sails of her anger. So, they were finally talking about this.

She sat back down on the couch, bracing herself for this conversation.

"I know," Emma said. "I'm sorry. I was in such a crazy frame of mind that night that I'm not really sure I knew what I was doing."

It was mostly true, if not the whole truth.

The whole truth was that she'd wanted to kiss Georgia very badly for a long time, a lot longer than she'd let herself admit, but never imagined that Georgia would return those feelings.

"I was surprised," Georgia continued. "I'll admit I'd…thought about you, like that, before."

Emma could feel her eyes going wide with shock. Georgia'd been thinking about her before that night? Thinking sexy thoughts about her?

Georgia cleared her throat and closed her eyes in a grimace, before she took a deep breath and continued.

"And then," she said slowly, "that night, I just really, really wanted to make you feel good, to take care of you in any way I could think to."

She swallowed.

Emma remembered every detail of how Georgia had taken care of her.

"I never thought I'd feel this way about you, Em. Never," she continued. "But the last couple of years have been…intense. For you. For me, watching you go through this. You've grown so much, had to grow. I realized you're not the little girl I used to babysit anymore, and in her place was this"—she gestured to Emma, eyes lingering on her shoulders, her breasts, her face—"this absolutely gorgeous and strong as fuck woman who sometimes drives me crazy with her stubbornness, but who I care about so fiercely."

Emma swallowed thickly, her heart beating so fast she thought it might hammer out of her chest, her thoughts and body buzzing.

"And last night?" she asked quietly.

Georgia blushed, looking down.

"I was so angry at the situation with Cora, sure. But…uh, I didn't like the idea of you flirting with someone else," Georgia said, looking off to the left, like she was ashamed of her behavior.

"You were jealous," Emma said slowly.

Georgia scratched her head in embarrassment.

"I'm not proud of that. But I had been reliving that moment in your foyer so much, trying to figure out how to talk to you about it, and then to hear you were meeting cute, age-appropriate women? It kind of drove me wild."

"I'd been thinking about that part of the night a lot, too," Emma said, and Georgia looked up sharply to meet her gaze.

"Yeah?" She felt Georgia's hand slide up her ankle and calf, stroking the skin under the hem of her jeans. For a moment, she wanted nothing more than to sink into Georgia's kiss, her touch, to surrender her body to Georgia, mature conversation be damned.

"Oh no, no, no," Emma said, drawing her leg up under her and away from Georgia's touch.

Something fell in Georgia's face, and Emma couldn't help but smile at the sad puppy eyes she was giving her.

"We need to talk, to figure out whatever this is," Emma said, part of her hating every syllable of it. But she knew if she let Georgia kiss her now, let her touch her, they'd fall into bed together, and that wouldn't be fair to either of them.

"You're right, you're right," Georgia said, shaking her head and leaning back into the couch cushion. "I feel like Cora right now, too horny to think straight."

Emma laughed and squirmed in her seat, thighs pressed together in a way she knew Georgia noticed.

Emma said, "So, we both admit we want each other."

"Yeah," Georgia said, eyes flicking down to Emma's lips and away, "but God, this is too confusing. I mean, I held you when you were born. I've known you literally your whole life."

"I know," Emma said gently. She wanted to reach out to touch Georgia so strongly she could feel her fingers practically vibrating.

"I had such a crush on you in high school," Emma admitted.

Georgia smiled. "Yeah?"

Emma shook her head wryly at the expression on Georgia's face.

"And," she went on, "you're my dad's neurologist. He needs you."

"And he comes before everything," Georgia said, nodding in understanding.

Emma nodded in return.

"Yeah," she breathed.

Georgia sighed.

"So we pretend nothing happened. You date the tennis instructor, and I go on as I've always been, the kindly older neighbor you lean on for support," Georgia proposed, a sour note in her tone.

"You make it sound like you're Mr. Rogers," Emma joked, even as a part of her heart was breaking into tiny, icy slivers.

"I bet Mr. Rogers never fingered any of his neighbors in their entryways," Georgia said, and Emma spat out a laugh.

"You never know. They say it's always the most buttoned-up that are the freakiest," Emma quipped back, and Georgia grinned, broad and beautiful.

Maybe we can do this, Emma thought. Be like we've been for the past few years.

But then Georgia licked her lips, and Emma's attention zeroed in on her mouth, and Georgia absolutely noticed, the air growing thick with tension.

Shit, she thought, this is going to be hard.

Chapter Nineteen

Like she'd committed to torturing them both, Georgia was in her space almost every day for the next few days.

She came over for coffee and Hattie's famous omelets before work on Monday. Emma didn't know she was there until after she'd barged into the kitchen in just a sports bra and tight running shorts, sweat glistening on her skin post run.

Georgia's eyes went wide at the sight of her, and Emma definitely didn't preen, didn't put a strut in her step, stick her ass out a bit as she bent to grab a coconut water from the fridge, flex her arms and back and abs as she moved around the kitchen, knowing Georgia watched her.

"It's hot out there today," Emma said.

She gulped down her water and saw Georgia note every motion, track the beads of sweat as they dripped down her chest, and grinned to herself. Who knew teasing Georgia would be so fun?

"Why are you guys being so weird?" Cora said, spearing a spare piece of broccoli and plonking it into her mouth.

Georgia blinked, seeming to realize that other people were in the kitchen besides her and Emma, and took a long sip of her coffee.

"Finish eating, we have to get to the office," she snapped at Cora, but her eyes flitted back to Emma once more before she picked up her phone and buried herself in it.

Emma smirked to herself as she finished her coconut water and turned to Hattie, who just shook her head at her ruefully.

Tuesday, Emma lounged in her backyard with her father and Anne, and texted Bridget. They'd made tentative plans to see a movie together this week at the tiny theater in town.

Emma decided if she and Georgia were going to go back to normal, hanging out with Bridget could be the distraction she needed.

Just like every conversation, Bridget kept it light. She described her recent trip to Boston because there was a boutique athletic wear store on Newbury Street that carried the specific shade of white she preferred all her tennis gear to be.

Emma, who found it to be a bit ridiculous but endearing Bridget would travel that whole way just for a specific shade of white, was smiling down at her phone.

"What's got you grinning like that at your phone?" her dad asked her, leaning over to peer at her screen.

"Ooh, Anne, look, she's texting a girl," he said in a singsong that would make any middle school boy proud.

"Good for you, Emma dear," Anne replied blandly, barely looking up from the tiny cardigan she was knitting, "you deserve to have a bit of fun."

Emma rolled her eyes at her father just as his look grew serious.

"You certainly do," he said.

"I have tons of fun hanging out with you," Emma said, hooking her arm around his and leaning into his shoulder. He kissed the top of her head, and she rested there for a minute.

"What's for dinner?" he asked, and Emma met Anne's eyes.

They'd eaten half an hour before.

Wednesday, Georgia and Cora came over for dinner and a game night, and Emma played hostess. She kept busy to avoid glancing over at Georgia too much. She grilled chicken and corn and served the potato salad Hattie had made, refilling wineglasses and making sure her dad ate enough. He'd been more agitated with the heat this week, something Emma felt acutely.

After dinner, they played Taboo. Her dad, to everyone's surprise, cleaned up. Emma and Georgia shared a look when he got a particularly tricky word, Emma's heart swelling.

When they got tired of the game, Emma brought out ice cream, and Cora and her dad sat out in the yard with bowls in their laps.

She could hear him telling Cora about the constellations, throwing in made-up ones every once in a while like he used to do with Emma when she was little, while Georgia helped her wash up.

Emma smiled as she listened to Cora calling out her father's fakes, both of them laughing.

She looked over at Georgia to see her watching Emma, a tender expression on her face.

Georgia reached over and squeezed Emma's hand.

They gazed at each other for a few seconds longer, Emma opening her hand so Georgia could entwine her fingers with Emma's soapy ones. The slow slide of her sudsy fingers against the skin of Georgia's palm sent tingles all the way up her arm.

But Georgia pulled away abruptly and looked down at her dishrag.

They both went back to washing in silence after that.

The next night, Emma went to meet Bridget at the movies, Georgia and Cora coming over to hang out with her dad.

"Is this weird?" Emma asked Georgia in an undertone as she grabbed her car keys from the table in the front hall, her father and Cora already squabbling over what to watch.

"A little," Georgia admitted, her eyebrows drawing together slightly. "I—we're going to miss you. But I think it's good, you going out and doing things for yourself."

Emma smiled and leaned down to give Georgia a quick kiss on her cheek, a habitual gesture that, until recently, would have meant nothing. She accidentally took in a deep breath of Georgia's scent, cedar and citrus and a hint of salt. Georgia grabbed her wrist as she pulled away and Emma looked into her eyes.

They just stood there for a moment, gazes locked, Georgia's thumb stroked gently at the inside of her wrist. It seemed to take Georgia effort, but she finally let Emma go.

"Have a good time," Georgia said, tucking her hand into the pocket of her wide-leg linen pants.

"Bye, Em," Cora called from the couch where she and her father had settled on *The Godfather*, one of his favorites.

"Bye, sweetheart," he called, too, not looking away from the TV screen.

Emma felt a pang in her chest, suddenly reluctant to leave them.

"Go," Georgia insisted, ushering her out of the house, and Emma nodded, turning to leave.

She looked back to see Georgia and Johnny watching her from the door.

CHAPTER TWENTY

Her movie definitely-a-date with Bridget was fun, Emma had to admit to herself.

They shared a bucket of popcorn, hands brushing as they each took handfuls. They saw the summer blockbuster, some movie about a guy who had to save the world from an incoming asteroid. It wasn't quite Emma's taste, but there were worse ways to spend two hours than in an air-conditioned room holding hands with a beautiful woman and eating salty snacks.

After the movie, they went to the bar attached to the theater and got drinks, Bridget chattering away about the improbability of the ending.

"I mean, you can't just move the moon like that!" she said emphatically, and Emma laughed as she sipped her Aperol Spritz. Bridget rested her hand on Emma's knee as she spoke. Their legs faced each other on their bar stools.

This all feels nice, Emma thought, easy.

Everything about tonight felt sweet in a change-of-pace kind of way.

And Bridget *was* gorgeous, with her freckles and wiry body and wild curly hair. Her flirtatious smile and manner made Emma feel warm inside from all the attention, her skin alive from Bridget's constant light caresses.

But part of Emma's brain was back on Highbury Lane, curled on the couch with her dad and Georgia and Cora, resting her head on Georgia's shoulder as they watched a movie, Johnny sprawled and snoring at their feet.

"My ex would have hated that movie. She's an engineer, and when things defy the laws of physics in movies it just totally pisses her off," Bridget said with a smile just a bit too tender for thinking about someone you were supposedly over, in Emma's opinion.

She'd clocked the number of times Bridget's ex had made it into the conversation during the course of the night. It gave her the impression that part of Bridget's brain wasn't fully here, either.

When their drinks were done, they walked back to the parking lot, and Bridget turned to Emma.

"Here's the part where I ask you if you want to go make out somewhere in your car like we're teenagers because we're both living with our families," Bridget joked.

Emma smiled and took a moment to check in with herself.

Did she want to do that?

On one hand it sounded fun. Bridget was adorable and her usual type, tall and fit like Sam had been. Her hair was pulled back in a ponytail tonight, glossy red curls spilling down her slender back, her face free of makeup and yet still glowing with a young, carefree light Emma wanted to taste again. And part of her reason for asking Bridget out in the first place had been to do just that.

But on the other hand, the yearning to be home was overpowering.

"As fun as trying to figure out how to fit two adult ladies over five foot eight comfortably in the back seat of a car is, I think I've got to say no," Emma said, and Bridget nodded good-naturedly. "Maybe just a kiss good night?"

"That, I can definitely do," Bridget said, a grin stretching across her face, causing the freckles on her cheeks to crinkle.

She would be so easy to fall into, Emma thought as Bridget reached for her, placing both her hands lightly behind Emma's head, her blunt nails scratching just behind Emma's ears as her lips brushed against Emma's. They were soft, not quite as plush as Georgia's, her mouth tasting of popcorn and the beer she'd had after the movie.

The salt and hops reminded Emma of a baseball game on a hot summer afternoon, slow, sultry, and sedate. Emma placed her hands on her hips and pulled Bridget in just enough so their stomachs brushed through their tops, flat abs to flat abs.

But her head was too busy, cataloging and comparing. She never quite lost herself to it the way she hoped she would. When Bridget pulled back less than a minute after the kiss began, Emma didn't chase her, didn't lean in for one last kiss. She let Bridget drift to her bike with a final squeeze of her hand.

"See you around, Emma Wilson," Bridget said, hand on the handlebar of her bike as she wheeled it toward the street, light blue helmet strapped to her head. She winked and swung her leg up onto the bike before pushing off and coasting out of the parking lot, flirtatious charm coating her every action.

"Bye," Emma called to her retreating back.

Her stomach churned with a slightly nauseating mix of disappointment and popcorn as she got into her car.

Her heart lifted, though, when she pulled into the driveway and saw the reflection of the little group in the sitting room backlit against the summer dark.

"How was your date, honey?" her dad asked when she came into the room and leaned against the molding of the doorway.

The three of them were spread out on the various couches and armchairs of the room. Cora scrolled on her phone, Georgia worked on her laptop, and her father read a paperback mystery. Cora and Georgia had looked up when her father spoke, though, their eyes intense on Emma.

"It was nice," Emma said, coming to sit next to her dad on the couch, taking Anne's usual spot. "The movie was absurd, but Bridget seemed to like it."

"What did you see?" Cora asked.

Georgia raised her eyebrows when she said the title.

"Not your usual taste," she said. "What do you call those types of movies? A hundred and twenty minutes of explosions and bullshit?"

Emma snorted, "Yeah, that sounds right. This one didn't have too many explosions, though, just using nukes to move the moon. We got drinks after the movie, too."

"So, why aren't you out smooching somewhere?" Cora asked. "Isn't that how these types of nights usually end?"

"Yeah, Em, why aren't you parked somewhere like you used to do with that *friend* of yours in high school, when you used to tell me you guys were *stargazing*, but you'd come home with hickeys," her dad said, a teasing glint in his eyes.

"Oh my God, Dad," Emma said, cheeks heating. "Why is it that's what you remember?"

"Christine!" he shouted victoriously, slapping his hand against his knee. "Christine Debenidetto, your cocaptain on the field hockey team."

Emma looked at the proud expression in his face and couldn't even feel annoyed with him for bringing up that memory.

She felt Georgia's gaze and looked up, expecting to exchange one of their usual glances, but her gaze was on Emma's neck where her T-shirt collar met her collarbone, as if imagining what a hickey would look like there. What giving her a hickey there would be like.

Emma swallowed, feeling heat flick through her, knowing she should look away, but not quite being able to. Georgia seemed to realize what she was doing, though, and her eyes went back to her computer again without meeting Emma's.

"Wow, Emma, who knew you had it in you?" Cora laughed, smiling at her father, both of them oblivious to the tension between her and Georgia.

"Should we be expecting Miss Bridget over for dinner anytime soon?" her dad asked.

"Maybe," Emma said coyly, half just to see how Georgia would react. She seemed to be staring at her computer with extra focus, but her shoulders tensed slightly.

"I'm glad you're getting out more, gives me a break from that little furrowed spot between your eyebrows when you look at me. If you don't loosen up, you'll need to start getting Botox, darling," her dad said, sounding eerily like Connie Brightley, as he got up and stretched.

Emma felt her own shoulders tighten a notch.

"Cora, Georgia, it was lovely spending the evening with such elegant and refined young ladies. Or sorry, young lady and just lady," her father quipped.

Georgia shot him a good-natured glare.

"But it's time for this feebleminded old man to go to bed," he finished. Emma noticed a hint of despair beneath the joke.

"Night, Dad," Emma said as he bent down to kiss her cheek, his chin scratchy. He'd forgotten to shave this morning, Emma realized with a small jolt.

"Yeah, I'm going to go to bed, too. It's exhausting being a working woman," Cora said, getting up and pocketing her phone.

"You spent an hour texting Martin instead of doing the filing and then played Roblox for the rest of the afternoon today," Georgia called after her, looking up from her computer.

"And it was exhausting," Cora said. She flipped her ponytail over her shoulder dramatically before she headed to the back door, Johnny hot on her heels.

"Brat," Georgia called to her retreating back. "And make sure my dog doesn't fall asleep in your bed."

Emma snickered. "Johnny's got no loyalty?"

"She lets him sleep in the bed—I make him sleep on the floor. He clearly has a new favorite," Georgia said. She watched Cora's retreating form until she was out of the house before she turned back to Emma.

Then it was just the two of them.

"*So*," Georgia said, drawing out the syllable. She finally met Emma's eyes, something tense and dark in their gray depths. "You had fun with Bridget?"

"Yeah," Emma said simply, scratching her left shoulder nervously.

Georgia nodded. "Good, that's good."

"She did ask me to go somewhere to make out," Emma blurted into the silence that stretched between them, an unfamiliar tension filling the air.

Georgia paused in the middle of setting her laptop on the coffee table. "Oh?"

"But I figured I should probably relieve you guys from Henry duty," she went on.

She wasn't sure why she didn't tell Georgia the truth, that she just wanted to be home with her dad, with her. That she *had* kissed Bridget again, and it had felt fine, nice in the way kissing a pretty girl always felt nice, but not hungry, consuming, necessary, like if she didn't taste her lips she'd suffocate, the way it did with Georgia.

But Georgia had drawn a line in the sand and was keeping Emma on the other side of it. They were supposed to be pretending they didn't know what it felt like to kiss each other's mouths, didn't know how their bodies felt pressed together.

Georgia gave her a small, tight smile.

"How generous of you," she said, shifting in her seat.

"You okay? You seem weird," Emma asked, trying to dispel the tension, to get them to where they'd been before, confidants and friends.

She wanted to point out that Georgia had been the one to encourage her to go out, had encouraged her to branch out, had said they should pretend that nothing had happened between them. Emma was just doing what Georgia had said she'd wanted her to.

"I'm just tired, Em. Some of us have to work all day, you know," she said with a sigh. "Not that you'd know."

"Wow, what a good one, so original," Emma said. She rolled her eyes and crossed her arms and legs, one sandal dangling from the end of her foot. "Aren't you tired of having this argument?"

"What I'm tired of is watching such a smart person living the life of a fifties housewife when it isn't what she wants to be doing," Georgia said, resting her feet flat on the ground and leaning forward, elbows on her knees and hands clasped between her legs, eyes intense on Emma's face. "I'm tired of waiting for you to do something to change that."

"What am I supposed to do, huh? Just leave my dad here alone all day?" Emma said, voice tight with irritation. Why did they keep fighting now?

"He isn't alone, Em. He's got Anne and Hattie and me"—she jabbed a finger into her chest—"watching out for him. You could hire a night nurse if you wanted to, it's not like money is holding you back. You can't tell me you're not bored out of your mind sitting here day after day. How many times have you redone rooms that were perfectly fine just so you'd have something to do? How many runs can you go on a day, huh?"

"Is that all you think I do all day?" Emma snarled back, hackles raised like a cornered animal. Her life sounded so petty and small when laid out like that. It made her feel petty and small. "That I'm just frittering away my time, day in and day out. Do you think I don't want to become a psychologist like I planned to? Or live in New York with Wesley and my other friends? Have a girlfriend? A social life beyond this tiny fucking town? My dad has dementia, Georgia."

Emma fought to keep her voice level, to keep all the emotion she'd been shoving down for years from spewing out.

"I think you're just scared," Georgia said sharply, almost cruelly, her eyes glittering like cold steel.

"Of course I'm scared," Emma scoffed back. "I'm scared all the time that he'll forget something big and hurt himself or someone else. That he'll freak out when he's with his friends at the club or on a walk or in the middle of the night, or just any fucking time. I lie awake in bed every night petrified that when I wake up he won't be him anymore."

She was practically shouting now, Georgia's hard gaze never wavering as her words came out faster, tasting like hot ash on her tongue. It felt like betrayal to let this out, to acknowledge how fearful she was beneath the facade of their placid life by the water.

"Tell me the rest of it, Em," Georgia said, cool and even, using her doctor voice, like she was trying to get a patient to admit that they did in fact still smoke a pack a day even though they'd recently had a stroke.

"The rest of it?" Emma looked at her scornfully. "You want there to be more than me being a horrible daughter who resents her father for being sick?"

"I know there is. Tell me why you and Sam really broke up. Why you haven't gone to visit any of your friends from college, barely left the Neck, in three years. Tell me."

Emma laughed bitterly but stared her down, noting how she didn't contradict her about being a bad daughter. "Fuck you, Georgia. You think you're so much better, why aren't you dating, huh? Why don't you have a family of your own, or a partner? I think it's because *you're* scared that if you let someone close they'll see beyond your perfect exterior to the truth of you. That you're so desperate to please other people because you're afraid, really, that if you're not doing things for them, there's no reason for them to stick around. You let your family walk all over you, pay for their shit, take in their wayward kids, because you think that's all you're good for," Emma said in a rush, the words pouring from her.

She didn't tell her what she also thought, that Georgia's selfless heart was one of her best qualities, that she was so much more than just what she did for other people. A molten need to wound the way she was wounded filled her chest, and she couldn't seem to stop.

Georgia closed her eyes and flinched like Emma physically punched her but said nothing. Emma watched her, breathing heavily.

"Get it all out, Em," Georgia said finally, voice low and a bit scratchy, like she was holding back tears.

Emma tossed up her hands in exasperation.

Georgia said, "If you really resented him that much, you wouldn't do all this"—she gestured at the puzzles and books and memory exercises, at the reminder notes she'd started putting up around the house—"for him. You'd hire people to do it for you."

"What do you want me to say?" Emma practically shouted, standing up and pacing, needing to move, feeling that kernel of truth stuck in her chest making its way up like heartburn, Emma's ability to keep it in waning rapidly. "That *he* has people, you, Cora, Hattie, Anne, his friends, looking after him, but who do I have? My mother is dead. I have no other close family. I barely speak to Wesley or my high school friends. If he forgets, there'll be no one who remembers my first steps, my graduations, running with me on weekend mornings. What happens if I leave, and he forgets who I am, then who do I have? It'll be like I stop existing."

She took a great gulp of air in, realizing she was crying as tears were already streaming down her cheeks.

"Can you imagine," she said, voice watery, "what it would be like if I went to work or grad school, if I moved away, if I went away even for a weekend, and I came home and he greeted me like a stranger. My own father, not knowing who I am. I don't think I could bear it, to be that alone."

She tossed the words out of her mouth like they were a poison her body needed to expel, angry tears streaming down her face. She was furious with Georgia for making her confront this truth, furious that this was her fate, that despite her money and connections and privilege she'd still end up losing her father, just like she'd lost her mother thirteen years ago.

"You have me," Georgia said tenderly, her eyes finally softening, like she had known this was the truth all along. She stood from her chair and reached for Emma.

"No," Emma said, shoving her hands away. "I don't really, do I. Because you can leave, at any moment, you could leave. You're so beautiful and amazing and caring, Georgie, and if you let someone, they would fall so hard for you," Emma said, tears still streaming down her face.

I already have, she thought, knowing it to be true down to her very bones.

"I know you're going to fall in love with some beautiful doctor or lawyer or businessperson, and they're going to whisk you away, and I'll just be here, stuck in this house with a father who forgets me a little more every day," Emma finished, slumping over in on herself.

"Oh," Georgia said in a small voice, as if she'd just realized something. "Oh shit."

But Emma wasn't listening, she was stuck imagining her father turning to her and introducing himself like he sometimes did to Anne when she came in the morning. He'd reach out those large hands that had held hers since she learned to walk, that had clapped for her on the sidelines of high school field hockey games and cheered for her during college regattas, for her to shake.

She was sobbing now, breath coming out in gasps, her lungs working like she just couldn't draw enough air into them. A dam in her soul burst, and grief for someone who was sleeping upstairs poured through. Grief for a life that already seemed to be slipping through her fingers.

"Come sit down," Georgia said, using that calm and soothing tone Emma remembered from the other night, reaching an arm out to guide Emma to the couch. Georgia sat down next to Emma, going to wrap her arm around Emma's back, but Emma flinched away.

"Don't touch me," she gasped out again.

Georgia dropped her arm into her lap, but she didn't move away, her heat warming Emma's suddenly shaking body, but not close enough to touch.

And God, even though Emma was furious at her, was confused by her, needed her and wanted her gone, she still reached over and grabbed Georgia's hand in hers. She took comfort in Georgia's presence and grounded herself as her sobs slowed to a trickle. Georgia flipped her palm to lace their fingers together, swiping her thumb across the back of Emma's hand soothingly until Emma's tears quieted.

"Your father knows how much you love him. You show him every day. Even when he might forget the here and now, he will still feel that. And I will always, always be here for you, Em," Georgia said quietly, stroking Emma's hair out of her eyes and guiding her head to rest on her shoulder, rocking her gently. "No matter what happens or who comes into our lives."

Emma sniffled, hated how small and pathetic she sounded, her tears and snot wetting the material of Georgia's soft T-shirt. She was always so soft.

"You give so much to other people, Georgie," she said, sniffling. "I don't want to be someone else who takes from you without giving back."

Georgia was quiet for a moment.

"You don't think that you give anything back to me," Georgia said, more a statement than a question. "That I'm not yours, your family, like your dad is, like your mom was."

Emma looked at her, knowing her face was a mess of tears and snot and blotchy as hell, her hair a snarl from running her fingers through it.

"You're my neighbor, my friend," Emma said, and Georgia looked like she'd slapped her.

"Oh," Georgia breathed, again. After a moment, she shifted. "I need to go."

Emma nodded dejectedly and took her hand back from Georgia, lifting her head from her shoulder.

It was only right that she leave now, when Emma had bared the squishiest, ugliest bits of her soul to her.

Georgia stood up, gathered her laptop, and left Emma sitting there staring after her, tears drying on her cheeks.

CHAPTER TWENTY-ONE

Emma woke up feeling like shit that Friday morning. Like the worst hangover mixed with a stomach flu and the body aches of a 4,000-meter sprint.

She'd cried and cried, and now she felt as dried out as a husk.

For the first time in years, she didn't go for a run that morning. In fact, she didn't leave bed until that afternoon, when Anne came to tell her she was leaving.

Emma pried herself out of her covers to make sure her dad ate dinner. She sat with him after, watching something mindless on the TV and avoiding his anxious looks at her silence. When he went to bed, she made sure he took his meds, locked the front door, and then collapsed back into bed, spending most of the night gazing unseeingly at her ceiling and, inexplicably, missing her mom.

Saturday, she felt more alive, so she and her dad went to the beach, just the two of them. They waded into the surprisingly mild water. Emma led her father past the big rocks and out to where the bottom became sandy. She dove under the water and resurfaced, turning to float on her back. Her dad floated by her side, and for a moment, they were just a father and daughter suspended in time, weightless and waterlogged and soaking up the sun.

That night, when only Cora showed up for dinner, Emma felt something sink into her stomach and settle, like an anchor thrown overboard embedded in the sea floor.

By Monday, when she came back from her run and Georgia wasn't in the kitchen gossiping with Hattie, when no texts from Georgia explaining her sudden departure Thursday night had appeared on her phone, Emma was sure of two things.

"What's that amazing smell?" Cora said, coming into the kitchen dressed in a pair of old black slacks of Emma's and a blue top, her caramel hair hanging loose around her face.

"Lemon poppyseed muffins, kiddo," Hattie said as she pointed to the tray that sat on the kitchen island.

Emma drank a protein shake at the kitchen table and scrolled on her phone, not really absorbing any of what passed in front of her eyes.

Cora came and sat opposite her.

"No Georgia today?" Hattie asked.

"Nah, didn't she tell you? She has a breakfast date," Cora said, wiggling her eyebrows, mouth full of muffin.

Those words registered, and Emma swallowed, coughed, and blinked up from her phone. "What?" she wheezed.

Hattie's eyes flicked over to her, but Emma ignored her as she gulped down some water.

"Yeah, looks like you inspired her," Cora said, oblivious to the tension ratcheting up in Emma's body. "She's meeting up with some chick from med school, Jane something or other. Here, this is her Instagram."

Cora pushed her phone across the table to Emma, finished her muffin, and went back for seconds.

Emma picked up the phone and saw a gorgeous brunette woman about Georgia's age with tanned skin in a slinky black dress smiling up at her from the screen. She was tall and thin, like Emma, but unlike Emma, her body curved where it should, her chest and hips full.

She clicked on the profile. *Jane Fairfield, MD/PsyD* turned out to be a pediatric psychiatrist with a specialty in oncology patients. She appeared to love to travel, have an adorable mini goldendoodle named French Toast, and be Georgia's perfect match.

Emma felt her shake coming back up her throat.

"Isn't she totally hot? Georgia's got mad rizz apparently," Cora said, mouth full of muffin again.

Emma was too focused on the gorgeous woman currently wooing Georgia to ask what the fuck that meant.

"Man, I'm happy for her. She works so hard—she deserves to have a little fun with a pretty girl." Cora sighed, voice full of affection for her older cousin.

Emma discreetly messaged the profile to her own account.

Just then, a text from Chris Elton appeared at the top of Cora's screen.

"You're still talking to Chris?" Emma asked, handing the phone back to Cora, trying to pretend she hadn't just been rocked to her fucking core.

"Not really," Cora said with a shrug. "He keeps hitting me up to hang out again, but the way Georgia grounded my ass after the last time, I think I'm done with him."

"How's Martin doing?" Emma asked, trying to take her mind off Jane, whom she instantly disliked immensely.

Stupid child cancer doctor with her perfect face and body. How dare she be smart, caring, and beautiful and love dogs. Emma could picture their Christmas cards now. Two gorgeous doctors posed on the beach in matching elegantly understated cashmere sweaters, their dogs playing at their feet. It made Emma want to punch something.

A soft, sweet smile spread across Cora's face at the mention of Martin.

"He's amazing." She practically swooned. "He calls me every day right before bed and asks me about my day and tells me about his. Isn't that so sweet?"

To Emma, who was pulling herself out of even more painful imaginings of Georgia and Jane, that sounded like basic conversation, but she knew straight women's bars were basically on the ground.

"That's so great of him. And what exactly does he do all day?" she asked.

"Well, he's currently doing an AmeriCorps fellowship helping maintain some of the trails in the Green Belt properties," Cora recited.

"The hiking paths and shit in state parks?" Emma asked, surprised.

"Yeah. What did you think he was doing, getting high and playing video games?" Cora said, voice a giant eye roll.

Honestly, yes.

Cora rolled her eyes for real at Emma's silence.

"You're such a snob sometimes, Em," Cora scolded. "Yeah, he's interested in doing something in the parks. He just doesn't like sitting still—that's why he dropped out of school. But we love to go on hikes around the marshes up in Ipswich."

"That's…surprisingly wholesome," Emma said.

Everything she learned about Martin made her wonder what Eleni's real objection was to him. And, sure, made her realize how harshly she had judged him herself.

"Mm-hmm," Cora replied.

"I better go, Georgia told me if I'm late today, she's making me cook dinner," Cora said, standing up from the table and taking the sandwich Hattie held out for her on her way. "Although that honestly sounds like more of a punishment for her than me."

"Hmm," Hattie said, plopping her wide frame down in the chair Cora had just vacated when the teen girl departed, usual jewelry chiming. "No Georgia for breakfast or dinner recently."

"Looks like it," Emma said, looking down into the dregs of her shake.

"And now she's out on a breakfast date with someone else," Hattie went on.

"*Apparently*," Emma said, enunciating each syllable.

"Did you two break up?" Hattie asked.

Emma shrugged. "We were never together, really. We just kissed a few times."

It was such a reductive way to talk about it, the feel of Georgia's mouth on hers, her hands on her skin. That sense of safety and wild desire all at once. But Emma had opened up to her, and Georgia had run. Had wanted to pretend and keep pretending that nothing had gone on between them.

"Uh-huh, so the reason you look like someone just told you you could never erg again is…?" Hattie said, voice trailing off.

"I need to go cool down," Emma said. She stood abruptly and left the kitchen, feeling Hattie's eyes following her as she went.

As she stretched on a yoga mat in the gym room, Emma reflected on those two things she now felt down in her bones.

First, she was utterly in love with Georgia and had been for a good while now. Her date with Bridget and the lack of sparks between them and her yearning to be on the couch just sitting next to Georgia rather than hooking up with Bridget had solidified this fact for her.

Second, she should never have kissed Georgia, because it had thrown the careful order of her world wildly out of balance. All she wanted now was to forget those nights had happened, to have Georgia smiling at her in the kitchen and teasing her over dinner, not out on dates with women like Jane Fairfield.

Emma slumped her head against the mat, collapsed onto her back, and closed her eyes, letting the truth beat down on her like the midsummer sun.

Later that afternoon, she sat in her mother's study, absolutely not looking through Dr. Jane Fairfield's latest article on the use of art therapy versus antidepressants alone in influencing the outcomes of children who were experiencing trauma, a begrudgingly interesting read, when she got a call from Connie.

"Hey, Connie," she answered, injecting what little pep she could into her voice.

She was immediately greeted by Connie's excited voice exclaiming, "I have news!"

"What's up?" Emma asked, leaning back in the leather desk chair.

"I was seeing Georgia about my migraines, you know how I get those awful splitting headaches and need to lie down in a cool dark room? That woman is an incredible doctor, by the way, really such a gentle touch—"

Unbidden, a memory of that gentle touch between her thighs popped into Emma's mind, and she shook her head to clear it.

Connie was still speaking. "And that cousin of hers is shaping up nicely, her eye makeup is much more tasteful these days, you know? I could actually see the upper lid of her eye today."

That's because I had Georgia confiscate all her eyeliner, Emma thought, as she relived how upset Cora was those weeks ago when she'd discovered it. How she and Georgia had exchanged mischievous glances, that intoxicating glint in Georgia's eye, when Cora had stormed out of the bathroom looking bereft.

"You were at the doctor's…" Emma prompted, not wanting this conversation to get too off the rails.

"Yes! Yes, I was at the office waiting to see Georgia when this gorgeous woman came in looking for her, saying how she'd left her sunglasses at breakfast and she wanted to return them to her. Breakfast, Emma! A *before*-work meal means there might have been a nighttime meal before that!"

Emma could practically hear the eyebrow wiggle in her voice.

The thought that Georgia might have slept with this woman, who was obviously Jane, made the urge to puke feel even stronger.

"So?" Connie was practically squealing from excitement.

"So what?" Emma said in a daze.

"What do you know about the sunglasses goddess?"

Emma did *not* care for that nickname.

"Nothing, Connie, I'm just hearing about this from you," Emma said, resting her head in her hands and willing herself not to cry.

"How strange, I thought you two told each other everything. You're practically joined at the hip these days," Connie mused. "Anyway, you should have seen this woman, Emma, so polished, and she had the most lovely Coach tote bag, that quilted black one I've been begging Gerald to get me for years. And the outfit she was wearing, this gorgeous little pastel purple sheath dress, I swear it was something I'd seen on Georgia, although their bodies are very different types, to be sure. Oh, and when Georgia came out, they greeted each other with a kiss on the cheek, how cute is that! They made such a darling couple, Emma dear. Oh, I do so hope this turns into something for our Georgie. I know she's been so lonely since her parents moved away."

Listening to Connie chatter away about how gorgeous and suave and elegant and smart Jane was, how good she and Georgia looked together, felt like tiny knives digging into her heart over and over again. Emma gripped her phone so tightly she half thought she'd crush it.

"Anyway, Emma darling, the real reason I called is because I have an event invitation for you and your father and his lovely companion, Anne," Connie said.

Emma nearly laughed at Connie describing Anne as her father's *companion.*

"Oh, really?" Emma said, feigning interest, expecting an invite to a silent auction raising money for repairs to the main club building or a stuffy dinner celebrating one of her sons' various accomplishments.

"Remember Rachel Whiteman's fiancé who cheated on her?" Connie asked.

Emma was starting to see why Georgia had objected to her gossiping about another woman's broken heart. How draining to be known for the worst moment in your life.

"I remember," she said.

"She couldn't get any refunds because it was so close to the date, so she's still throwing a reception at the club, and since her fiancé told her he'd cover her dream wedding—I think someone had a guilty conscience—it's a party on his dime. Isn't that a hoot?"

She kept speaking before Emma could reply.

"Marian, Rachel's mom, she's in my book club and she just hates every book we choose, isn't that hilarious? I always say, Marian, if you hate the books, why do you come to the club? And you know what she says? *I hate the books, but I love the wine!* I mean, what a firecracker she is. Well, she told me to invite as many people as I want, club members and non, friends, strangers, literally anyone I could think of who might like a party, can you believe it? They have room for three hundred! I've already invited Georgia and Cora, and of course I told Georgia to bring that beautiful woman who came into her office today, and I want you and your father and Anne and, hell, bring anyone else you feel like. Your housekeeper, your dog walker, the pool boy, bring them all. Marian says they added a whole clambake onto the caterer's tab, and it's an open bar with top shelf liquor. Ha!" She let out a booming guffaw. "I hope that fiancé feels good about his life decisions when he gets that bill. Oh, and don't worry about inviting Bridget. I already told her all about it at tennis this morning."

Emma was sure she had. She pictured Bridget impatiently waiting for Connie to serve the ball while she chattered away. The thought almost brought a smile to her face, but then she remembered that Georgia was probably going to bring Jane to this event, and it dissolved before it could even form.

"It's just formal, not black tie, FYI," Connie went on. "Oh, honey, I need to run, but I'll see you on Saturday at seven thirty."

Connie hung up before Emma could say good-bye.

Emma recovered from her conversation with Connie, then slunk down in the desk chair and rested her head on its back, legs spread out before her, feeling the picture of dejection.

Chapter Twenty-two

"Why don't you have anything sexier?" Cora asked on Thursday, standing in Emma's closet and flipping through her rack of fancy dresses.

"I'm not really a sexy dresser," Emma said, lying on the carpeted floor and staring up at the ceiling of her closet. She'd been wallowing for the last few days, talking to no one and casting vacant stares into the middle distance like a waifish Regency lady whose betrothed had died in some far-off battle before they could consummate their love. She'd gone punishingly hard on the erg and taken extra-long runs, and now her whole body ached to match the aching in her heart.

Even her dad had noticed her mood. He cast her concerned glances all through dinner last night when there was still no sight of Georgia. Emma could only assume it was because she was out with Jane, drinking wine at her luxury condo in Boston and then having passionate sex all night long with no interruptions from puking teens or dads with dementia.

That thought had kept Emma up half the night as she glared into the dark, imagining Georgia's face between Jane's legs while Jane spouted off medical terms.

She'd still hung out with Johnny when Georgia was at work. Georgia now communicated by leaving her notes on Post-its attached to Johnny's leash about his stomach being upset, or to remember to bring his bottle because it was hot out, or to rinse him off if she took him swimming. Somehow, Georgia still managed to boss her around even when they weren't speaking.

It made Emma furious and frustrated. Made her want to cry, want to pin Georgia against the wall again, only this time so she'd have to look at her, speak to her.

Beyond being heartbroken, Emma missed her friend, her daily companion and confidant. There was no one else she wanted to talk with about what was going on more than Georgia.

"I've seen those tiny shorts you run in. I'd say those are definitely sexy. I bet Bridget would love to see you in those," Cora said suggestively, waggling her eyebrows and bringing Emma back into the room.

Emma rolled her eyes and said, "That's just athletic wear, you pervy child."

"So it can't be sexy? How about this one?" Cora said, pulling out another dress from Emma's rack.

"That'll look great on you," Emma said flatly.

"You're fully not looking at me right now, Emma," Cora said, annoyed.

"I fully am," Emma retorted half-heartedly, absolutely not looking at her.

It seemed pointless anyway. Cora's month in Marblehead was almost up. Her mom, none the wiser about the Chris Elton experience, was ready to have her come home after her month of working for Georgia.

Georgia was basically married now to her hot doctor lady and would never speak to Emma again, and soon her dad would forget her existence. Who cared what she or anyone else wore to some stupid non-wedding party?

"Okay, what's the deal?" Cora said, flopping down on the floor next to Emma.

"What do you mean?" Emma asked. She peered over at Cora without sitting up.

"You've been in this funk since last weekend," Cora replied. "Since you and Georgia had that fight after you thought I left to go to sleep."

"You were eavesdropping on us?" Emma said and sat up, feeling a ping of outrage pierce her funereal fog.

"That's not the point," Cora said, waving her hand as if to shoo the invasion of privacy she'd just admitted to away. "For the record, I think Georgia was being a real dick to you. But I do think she was right."

"Wow," Emma said, flopping back down onto the carpet. "You can go now. Maybe Georgia happens to have some size six dresses lying around her house you can borrow."

Cora grabbed Emma's arm, shaking her. "Bro"—Emma

immediately resented being called this—"I think you're cool, even if you are an annoyingly fit rich girl who is kind of judgmental and needs to loosen up a bit."

"Thanks, I guess?" Emma said, closing her eyes.

"You're dealing with this huge shit, and from the outside it looks like you've got it all figured out. I admit, I was a bit intimidated by you at the beginning. I mean"—she snorted—"I know better now."

Emma reached over and pinched her calf.

"Ow, fuck off, I'm trying to say something meaningful and profound here." Cora crouched down into a squat so she was more level with Emma's face. "You've got a huge support system, even if you don't see it, Em. All those people you said your dad has—me, Hattie, Anne, Connie even—you have them in your corner, too. I know you like to be Miss, like, perfectly prepared or whatever, but you can rely on us, too, if you ever need to. I know I'm going off to school, but Henry and I are tight now. I'm definitely coming back to watch movies with that guy whenever I can. I'd be more than happy to hang with him if you ever needed a night off, or want to go on a date or something."

Emma felt tears pricking her eyes and squeezed them tight. She was not going to cry right now.

"Thanks, Cor, that's really nice of you," she said.

"See, I'm not just a horny teen," Cora replied, standing back up and returning to her closet shopping. "I'm actually, like, wicked mature for my age and shit."

Emma laughed.

"I mean it," Cora cried indignantly, dropping a silk scarf that had belonged to her mother on Emma's face. "Martin says that's why we get along so well, because I'm an old soul."

Emma felt the urge to say something cutting like *Did he say that before or after you blew him?*, but she actually liked Martin, so she refrained.

"Try that blue one," Emma said, sitting up and pointing to a strapless blue satin dress she'd worn to Sam's sorority formal eons ago.

Cora pulled the dress from the rack and assessed it.

"How about a bet?" Cora said. "If I can guess what's really bugging you, I get to style you for this weird not-wedding rich people party."

"What do I get if you guess wrong?" Emma inquired, looking through her shoes for the nude block heeled sandals she'd worn with the dress.

"To choose your own outfit," Cora said simply, shimmying out of her jean shorts and tank and slipping into the dress. It was fitted up top, showing off more cleavage than it had on Emma and hugging Cora's curvier ass.

Cora reviewed her reflection in the full-length mirror in the closet before announcing, "I look hot."

Cora smoothed her hands down her hips and took the heels from Emma, bending over to buckle the strap over the front of her ankle.

"So, what's your guess?" Emma asked, giving Cora room to turn and twist and strut to her heart's content. Cora let her caramel-colored waves down and tousled them, turning this way and that, lips pouted at her reflection.

"You and Georgia hooked up, and now it's weird, and you're really fighting about that because she wants to be with you but you're pushing her away," Cora stated matter-of-factly. "Can you hand me those earrings?"

Emma stared at her, openmouthed.

Cora gestured for the gold teardrop earrings again, unfazed by Emma's shocked expression.

"What?" Cora replied.

"How did you know?" Emma asked quietly.

"Um, I can sense a vibe like that a mile off. And I have eyes," Cora said, rolling them. "Plus, Georgia's living room is visible from the landing on the second floor that leads to the bathroom and you guys were making out *right there*. Nice, by the way."

She held out her hand for a fist bump, but Emma just stared at it.

"But…" Emma trailed off, remembering the sound of a slamming door, running feet, vomiting. "You were drunk. And asleep."

"I woke up and had to pee"—Cora shrugged—"you know, before the puking. I opened my door and saw you guys going at it and then closed it immediately. I was debating how long I needed to wait before peeing, but then the nausea hit, and I just had to go for it."

"Oh my God," Emma said, burying her face in her hands.

Cora patted her on the head like she was a small child.

"But you were teasing me about Bridget in front of Georgia," Emma recalled.

"Nothing like a bit of jealousy to get people going." Cora smirked, flipping her hair behind her shoulder sassily and turning back to the mirror to see how the earrings went with the dress. "The same thing happened with my friends Kayla and Erin. They'd had crushes on each other forever and wouldn't make a move, so I decided to make Erin jealous by setting Kayla up with Melanie's brother. They didn't hit it off, but Erin *did* get super jealous. It totally worked. They hooked up at the next party we had."

Emma, still stuck on the fact that Cora had witnessed Georgia grinding on her in the living room, asked, "So, what happened between Kayla and Erin?"

"Well now *Erin's* dating Melanie's brother, but totally still hooking up with Kayla, like, multiple times a week when she tells her boyfriend they're just hanging out. She says it's because she's poly, but I'm all like, if you're poly, then just date both of them out in public," Cora concluded, now playing around with Emma's lipsticks.

"So, she chose to do the most unhealthy thing she could possibly do," Emma summarized. Cora's own love life looked practically conventional in comparison. "And Kayla knows about her boyfriend? You have a wicked messy friend group."

"Pretty much, yeah," Cora agreed. "But it sure is fun. Moral of the story is: Don't be Erin, Emma."

Emma scoffed, "*I* am not being Erin."

Cora gave her a look. "Bridget," she said, raising her eyebrow.

"Jane!" Emma burst out. "If anything, Georgia is Erin. She's the one who told me it was too confusing if we kept making out and then she goes and dates the hottest child psychiatrist she could find literally like an hour after I spilled my secrets to her. I'm not the one who doesn't want to be with her. *She* doesn't want *me*."

"Duh, Jane is obviously just a reaction to Bridget. Georgia is probably convinced she's too old for you, or you only think of her as a friend or you're just looking for an escape from your trauma or something else delulu, and she's trying to let you go. But I can tell you she has been just as miserable this past week as you've been. She's eaten frozen mac 'n' cheese in her pj's for three dinners in a row," Cora confided. "Didn't you major in psychology? Aren't you supposed to be, like, good at reading people? She's missing you like crazy, Em."

Emma just shook her head.

Cora tossed up her hands.

"Fine, don't believe me. But," she said, grinning evilly at Emma through the mirror, "I still get to style you."

Chapter Twenty-three

Emma and her dad strolled arm in arm into the tent that had been erected by the tennis courts, a life-size image of Rachel Whiteman with what could only be the man she was supposed to marry standing at the entrance. His eyes had been crossed out with marker and devil horns and a mustache had been drawn on him. A sign that said *Please deface me* was posted over his head, and multiple colored Sharpies were attached to it by a string.

"This is by far the strangest event I can remember going to," her dad said. He looked dapper tonight in a tan linen suit with a pale green dress shirt unbuttoned at the neck, his face clean-shaven and his hair neatly combed. Emma had picked out a paisley silk pocket square and the silver cufflinks her mother had given him for their tenth anniversary to finish the outfit. "And while that might not be saying something, this is leaving a lasting impression."

Emma laughed, squeezing his arm with her own.

"You look stunning, my dear Emma," he said, turning to her and giving her a kiss on the cheek. "A touch different than your usual look."

"I lost a bet to Cora," she said ruefully, smoothing her hand down the skirt of her dress.

It was a slinky black column gown with a high neckline that left her shoulders and arms bare, highlighting their definition. The back plunged to below her waist, revealing the muscular column of her spine and the delicate bones of her shoulder blades. The skirt ended two inches or so above the tops of the slim ankle straps of her low-heeled gold sandals.

Cora had smoothed Emma's hair and twisted it up into a chignon, curling one piece to frame the left side of her face. To her relief, Cora hadn't done more than add a thin swipe of shimmery gold liner over her lids and black mascara on her lashes, highlighting the golden tones in her brown eyes, and just a touch of makeup to make her skin look dewy, her lips full and rosy.

She had forgotten about this dress, bought for an event she'd never ended up attending when she was younger, and buried behind her other formal wear. Cora had pulled it out for herself but rejected it because she couldn't wear a bra with it and Emma had no such issues. She'd paired it with the gold sandals and dangling gold earrings studded with tiny diamonds that had once belonged to her mother.

She felt elegant and, yes, sexy, but comfortable in her skin in a way she didn't think was possible. Emma was starting to think Cora was the one mentoring her.

Speaking of Cora, she was waving to them from the table she sat at accompanied by a young man in a dark blue summer suit. He had a tie on that complemented, but didn't exactly match, the blue of the strapless satin gown Cora had settled on. They would look fabulous in pictures, Emma thought.

Cora had lined her lids geometrically with shimmering white liner and painted her lips in bright red, her hair parted neatly down the middle and slicked into a bun at the nap of her neck. Trendy but sophisticated, she was a far cry from the girl in ripped jeans and heavy eyeliner Emma had met a month ago, but still very much herself.

"Cora!" Emma said, hugging the girl and holding her arms out to her sides so she could take her in. "You look fabulous!"

"What can I say, I contain multitudes," Cora said with a cheeky shrug.

She leaned forward to hug Emma's father.

"Stunning, Cora, simply stunning," her father said, giving her a kiss on the cheek. "And nice work on this one," he motioned with his thumb to Emma.

"It was a tough job, but I'm satisfied with the results," Cora quipped.

"I'm literally standing right here," Emma grumbled.

The boy at the table stood up to shake their hands.

"Martin?" Emma said when he leaned across Cora to shake her hand. "Wow, you clean up well."

"Thanks," he said proudly. "It's all thanks to my girl."

He pressed a kiss to Cora's temple, making her positively glow with happiness.

"It was my brother's old suit," Cora said. "Georgia bought it for him for prom, but he's gotten way into lifting since then so it doesn't fit him. When Martin told me he'd been invited tonight, I thought it would look great on him, and I was right. I bought him the tie, too."

Her heart twisted slightly at the mention of Georgia's name, but she pushed on.

"You didn't invite him?" Emma shot a sneaky smile at Martin.

"No, it was a total surprise. Why are you smirking at each other like that?" Cora asked, looking between Emma and Martin.

Emma opened her mouth to ask where Georgia was, but just then, the band leader said into the mic, "Ladies and gentlemen, put your hands together for the woman of the hour, Miss Rachel Whiteman!"

A spotlight swept to the entrance to the tent, and there was Rachel in a floor-length strapless red dress, wobbly striking a pose.

"So fucking weird," Emma heard Cora mutter. She looked back over her shoulder, caught Martin's eye, and grinned to see he'd wound his arm around Cora's waist.

Emma clapped her hands as Rachel strutted into the tent and up onto the band stage, grabbing up a glass of champagne.

Emma grabbed her glass and glanced at Cora's, who mouthed, "It's sparkling water, you narc," at her.

"Friends, family, random people who live nearby, thank you so much for coming out tonight to eat the fancy food and drink the nice liquor my ex-fiancé paid for. James, if someone is recording this to send to you, I hope you get syphilis and your dick falls off," the obviously drunk woman onstage said.

"Goodness," her father muttered.

Emma saw some of the older guests quite literally clutch their pearls.

"Fuck him, let's party!" Rachel yelled into the microphone and downed the glass of champagne.

"Oh, she's sloshed. Let's join her," her father said, lifting his champagne up to toast Emma's and taking a delicate sip. Emma smiled at him and drank her own champagne, the bubbles filling her mouth, crisp and cold and lovely.

The music struck up and Martin whirled Cora out onto the dance floor. Emma watched them with a smile, her eyes scanning the room, looking for…something. With a jolt, she realized she was looking for Georgia. She was probably cozied up with Dr. Jane in a dark corner.

"Want to dance?" a voice said to Emma's right, and she turned over her shoulder to find Bridget. She looked beautiful in a seafoam-green silk slip dress with a bold floral pattern printed on it, her curls hanging loosely down her back. Strappy silver heeled sandals on her feet, and thick silver hoops in her ears and rings on her fingers completed the look. The nails on the hand she held out to Emma were painted magenta.

Her dad nodded to her.

"Go," he said. "I'll be fine."

"Just come find me if you're ready to head home," Emma said, taking Bridget's hand as she stood from the table.

"You look incredible," Bridget said, holding Emma's arms out from her body to survey her head to toe. She twirled Emma around and whistled.

"Thanks," Emma said, and she felt her face go warm.

She and Bridget had exchanged some texts since their date a week ago, mostly idle chatter about the club and TV shows and memes, but there had been no firm mention of trying to meet up again, and Emma was fine with that.

She thought of something to say, but then the band struck up a pop hit from the early aughts, and there was no need to talk as they sang the lyrics to each other and moved to the beat.

They danced for two full songs before a willowy woman with light brown hair pinned up in a braided crown, wearing a magenta jumpsuit nearly the same color as Bridget's nails, approached them. Her outfit had a deep, cleavage-exposing neckline that showed off the many thin gold chains she wore around her neck.

"Hey, babe," the woman said to Bridget, handing her one of the glasses. "I got you a G and T. It's the bride's drink."

"Thanks, honey," Bridget replied.

Emma clocked the pet names, her suspicions confirmed as they smiled at each other with swoony expressions, locked in their own little world.

"What's the groom's drink?" Emma asked and they both blinked and looked around like they'd forgotten Emma was there.

"The dirty bucket they dump the remains of the drinks in," the woman said, and they all laughed.

"Emma, this is Sydney, my sort of ex, sort of current girlfriend," Bridget said, and Sydney snorted.

She held out a slender hand for Emma to shake, an amber resin cuff sliding down her wrist.

"It's nice to meet you," Emma said, meaning it. She raised her eyebrows at Bridget, who shrugged.

"After our date last Saturday, I realized I don't want to be with anyone else and reached out to Syd. Turns out she was feeling the same way, so we've been talking and hanging out again," Bridget supplied.

Bridget wrapped her arm around Sydney, and Sydney smiled at her. They kissed, drawn together like magnets. Emma felt her heart thud painfully.

"That's great, I'm really happy for you guys," Emma said enthusiastically, although her smile was suddenly hard to maintain.

"Would you mind if I stole her?" Sydney said, pointing to Bridget.

"Bye, Em," Bridget said before Emma could respond, tumbling after Sydney into the crush of bodies in the middle of the floor.

Emma smiled after them and turned to go back to the table but saw Connie and her husband Gerald talking with her father and didn't quite feel up to a verbal barrage. She searched the sea of bodies and found Cora and Martin wrapped around each other and swaying, even though the music wasn't slow. They both leaned in for a kiss and pulled back grinning.

It seemed like everyone around her had found happiness tonight.

Well, besides Rachel Whiteman.

She got in line to get a gin martini—straight up with a twist, the classy way—and made her way around the dance floor, saying hello to people she knew, all glittering in their finery, as she passed.

She sipped her cocktail, watching the sea of couples dancing, and suddenly felt drained. Was this her destiny, to watch everyone else's happiness while she stood on the sidelines? Had she ruined one of her most essential relationships when she'd muddied the waters with Georgia? Was Georgia right? Was she going to miss out on living her life while she sat by and watched her dad fade, too scared to let go?

And where was Georgia? Would she ever speak to Emma again?

Deciding she needed a break, she filled a plate with food from the buffet—coconut shrimp and oysters on the half shell, platters of puff pastry wrapped cheese and bacon wrapped scallops and lamb sliders and mini lobster rolls—and took it down to the dock. She walked past couples canoodling on the sloping lawn, tween girls holding hands and spinning in a circle, their shoes kicked off and hair coming undone.

After she'd climbed down the walkway, Emma kicked off her own heels and let her feet dangle over the edge of the old wooden dock, the skirt of her dress bunched around her knees. She stared out at the darkened harbor and watched the boats bob, their swaying lights creating a mini galaxy on the water.

She rubbed against the ache in her sternum, thinking of all the happy couples in the tent behind her, the smile on her father's face when he saw her all dolled up.

"Care for some company?" said a familiar voice that sent her heart pounding. Emma closed her eyes, braced herself, and turned.

Georgia stood there, looking like a literal Greek goddess who had descended from Olympus to seduce a mortal before leaving them to some tragic end. She was backlit by the floodlight on the flagpole, the stars rolled out above her. Standing at the top of the gangway down to the dock, Emma couldn't get a good look at her face, but she peered behind her, looking for Jane in the shadows.

"Who are you looking for?" Georgia asked, walking down the gangway, the flowing skirt of her patterned wrap dress fanning about her legs, her high heeled mule sandals smacking against the wood with every step.

"I thought you might have a date with you," Emma replied.

Georgia's steps faltered for a moment, but then she walked the rest of the way onto the dock, slipping out of her sandals and padding over to sit next to Emma.

"Why would you think I had a date with me?" Georgia asked. She leaned back on her hands, and the clear crystal cocktail ring on her middle finger winked as it reflected the floodlight. They both looked out at the harbor and not at each other.

A soft wind picked up and set the bells on the buoys ringing.

"Cora told me about Jane," Emma answered.

"Ah," Georgia said in a flat voice.

"I'm happy for you, she seems absolutely perfect. I mean, a doctor who also looks like a swimsuit model and who seems to be a genuinely kind person? What else could you want?" Emma said, unable to keep a note of bitterness from her voice.

Especially when compared to a twenty-five-year-old who just read and did puzzles all day and was fueled by the selfish desire to keep everything the way it was, she thought.

Georgia let out a little laugh.

"I see someone did a bit of Instagram stalking. Jealous, Emma?" she said smugly.

That is just not fair, Emma thought.

She sprang to her feet, needing to be away from this moment, from the note of satisfaction in Georgia's voice.

"Gloating doesn't suit you," Emma said. She bent to pick up her shoes and plate.

Was this how it was going to be now? Every interaction prickly and loaded until they got so uncomfortable they stopped speaking?

"Wait, Em," Georgia said, grabbing her wrist to keep her from leaving. Emma paused, bent at the waist.

Georgia let out a long sigh and said, "Jane is just an old friend from med school who happened to move back to town recently. There's nothing going on between us. I'm sorry for misleading you, that wasn't fair."

Relief swept through Emma at that news, immediately followed by anger.

"Why did Cora think you guys went on a date?" she demanded.

Georgia tucked some hair behind her ear and looked down. She was embarrassed, Emma realized.

"I, uh, may have wanted her to think it was a date, so she would tell you about it," Georgia replied, looking down into the water below them.

"Why?" Emma prodded.

"Because," Georgia said on an outward breath, "you were dating Bridget, and I wanted you to think I didn't care, that I was dating someone else, too."

"Why?" Emma asked again, sitting back down on the dock next to her. Her legs hung down above the water next to Georgia's.

"Fuck, Emma, you know why," Georgia said, turning toward her, a look of desperation on her gorgeous face. "And I know you're dating Bridget, but I just need to say this because it's been absolute torture not talking to you this last week, but I needed space to sort through what I was feeling."

She took a deep breath and squeezed Emma's hand, and Emma's heart dropped into her stomach.

"You don't need to tell me," Emma said, feeling Georgia's pain in her own chest. "And I'm not dating Bridget. She's actually back with her ex, even brought her tonight."

"She…what?" Georgia said, stunned. "I'm so sorry, I can't believe she'd do that to you."

Emma waved her words away and said, "We only went on, like, two dates. I never really felt that way about her. I…I mostly dated her because of you."

It was Emma's turn to be embarrassed, to feel her cheeks flame.

Georgia's shoulders tensed as if she was stealing herself.

"I guess I'm glad to hear that," she said, "but I need to tell you this. I just need to get it out."

Georgia paused, taking a deep breath before she turned to Emma.

"Last weekend, when you told me that you were worried I wouldn't be around because I'd find someone, I realized something," she began, "the reason I haven't been dating these past few years. I told myself that it was just because I needed to get my practice off the ground, that I was too busy to date. But the truth is, I tried. I went on a date about six months ago with a perfectly nice man. And you know what I thought about the whole time, Em?"

Emma shook her head and Georgia smiled that soft smile at her, the one that sent her heart into overdrive.

"How I would much rather be sitting in your dining room hearing Henry rib you and bickering with you over the right way for toilet paper to face." She reached out and took one of Emma's hands in hers. "I realized that I would rather be doing that than almost anything else. I figured it was just because we're all comfortable with each other. But when you told me that I was just your neighbor and your friend, it hurt me so badly I knew," Georgia paused and looked down at the hand she was holding, tracing over the knuckle of Emma's index finger with her thumb.

"Knew what?" Emma prompted, chest feeling tight with anticipation and disbelief.

"That I love you, Em," Georgia said, voice hushed, a bit wondering at her own emotions. "I'm *in love* with you. I think I've been falling in love with you for the last three years."

Emma's heart stopped altogether, the words ringing through her head like the sweetest music.

"You have?" She gasped, voice barely above a whisper.

Georgia closed her eyes, almost grimacing. "I think…" She paused, took a breath.

Georgia started over. "I think I hadn't realized it because it came on so slowly. You were just there, in my space, not the little kid I remembered anymore. Taking on this big, difficult, monumental thing, sacrificing so much of yourself and your future and I just…wanted to support you, make you happy. I know I've been a hard-ass sometimes. I've lectured you and pushed you, and you, somehow, kept putting up with me." She gave a little laugh and swallowed thickly. "I'm not one for making big speeches. I'm a doctor, Em, not a poet. I think, though, if I loved you less, I could probably talk about it more."

Emma's heart was now hammering in her chest so hard it felt like it was trying to get out so it could leap into Georgia's palms. She felt too overwhelmed for words.

"Say something, Emma," Georgia said quietly. "Tell me I've fucked up, that you don't feel the same. Don't spare my feelings, love."

That was too much for Emma, and she had to reach for Georgia. She put her hand on Georgia's shoulder so she'd look at her and then gripped the back of Georgia's hair and crushed their mouths together in a searing kiss.

Emma wanted to crawl into Georgia, to hold her as close as she could get, intertwine their souls inseparably. Instead, she flicked her tongue into Georgia's mouth and tugged her closer, trying to lick those words from her mouth to taste them.

She pushed all the feelings she wasn't yet able to voice into the kiss, gasping against Georgia's lips when Georgia's hand met the bare skin of her back exposed by her dress, her fingers gliding against her skin.

"What does this mean, Em?" Georgia said. She pulled back, put space between them so they could breathe. She gripped Emma's wrist where her hand was buried in her hair. "I need you to use your words."

"I'm in love with you, too, obviously," Emma panted.

"Oh, thank God," Georgia said, and then they were kissing again, hot and fierce and unrestrained.

Both of Georgia's hands ran up and down the warm skin of Emma's back, sending shivers across Emma's body. Emma let her mouth wander to Georgia's neck, gathered all her thick hair into her hands so she could get better access to that sensitive skin.

Emma's hands itched to unwrap Georgia's dress, to untie that tie that kept it together and kiss every inch of her body, feel Georgia against her own bare skin. Instead, her hands reached up to cup Georgia's breasts through the thin chiffon of the dress, to slide into the slit of the skirt and glide up her thigh, skimming over the fabric of the shapewear she wore under it.

"I want you naked," Georgia groaned as Emma grazed the sensitive skin of her neck with her teeth.

"Okay," Emma said, blindly reaching for the zipper of her dress under her left armpit.

"Wait, wait, wait," Georgia said, pulling Emma's hands away from the zipper. "We're basically in public."

"No one's over here," Emma said, her body confused why they'd stopped touching. "It's nighttime, there aren't any lights on this dock."

She leaned forward, her hands still in Georgia's grasp, and kissed her slowly, lips nudging Georgia's apart with delicate motions, tongue licking into her mouth. Georgia whimpered just a little.

Got her, Emma thought victoriously, as she pulled her own wrists behind her back. She used her strength to drag against Georgia's hold on her, pushed them chest to chest, leaning farther back so Georgia had to inch forward to maintain contact. Basically, she forced Georgia to crawl into her lap and straddle her hips with her knees if she wanted to keep kissing her.

"Menace," Georgia muttered against her lips. She let go of Emma's wrists and gripped her face, rubbing her thumb along Emma's lower lip. "Fuck, you are so beautiful," Georgia groaned. "How are you so beautiful?"

Emma shrugged, beyond words. She used her thighs to lift her hips and drag her body between Georgia's legs, rubbing against that spot she'd found Georgia liked.

Satisfaction flooded Emma as she heard Georgia gasp at the contact. All Emma could think about was making her make that sound again. Emma ran her hands up Georgia's legs until she grabbed Georgia's perfect ass in her hands, gripped into the fabric of her dress, and pressed Georgia's body to hers more firmly, using her abs to support them.

They looked at each other, lipstick smudged and hair mussed.

"I want you so badly, Georgie," Emma whined, and Georgia grinned.

She rocked her hips against Emma slightly, testing, teasing. Emma leaned in, kissing at the exposed skin of Georgia's cleavage as Georgia gripped the back of her head and pulled her closer.

Emma groaned, frustrated by the angle and the clothing they both still wore.

Georgia started shaking, and Emma pulled back to see her laughing at her, beaming so brightly that Emma couldn't help but arch her neck to taste her smile.

"Okay," Georgia said between kisses. "Here's what we're going to do. Are you listening, Emma?"

Emma nodded her head and swallowed.

"Yes, yup. Totally, totally listening, not thinking about peeling your shapewear off you and licking every inch of your body at all," Emma said in a rush, eyes planted on the slope of Georgia's breasts as they heaved against the line of the dress.

Georgia tilted her head back to the sky and let out a long breath.

"*Fuck*, Emma, you are killing me right now," Georgia groaned to the sky. "Okay…" Georgia tried again. Emma took advantage of her position and trailed her lips up Georgia's neck. "We're going to go back to the party. We're going to get another drink and talk to our friends and"—Georgia's breath hitched as Emma sucked hard at her skin and then scraped her teeth across. Georgia's hips pushed into Emma's stomach involuntarily in response—"and maybe dance a little. Then we'll bring Henry home and make sure his door is firmly locked, and then I'm going to fuck you until you collapse."

"Okay," Emma said, kissing under the hinge of Georgia's jaw, speaking into her skin.

"Okay," Georgia said. She guided Emma's mouth back to her lips and stole one last deep kiss that left them both breathless, before Georgia pried herself out of Emma's arms.

Emma's body immediately missed her warmth, her scent, the weight of her.

Georgia offered Emma her hand, helped her stand, and then kept it twined with her own fingers.

Emma felt dazed and needy, her body humming with *Georgia Georgia Georgia*. Her legs were shaky as a sailor on land after a months-long voyage. She must have looked like she felt because Georgia surveyed her and then burst out laughing.

"What?" Emma said, unable to keep the smile from her lips.

"You just"—Georgia started, reaching out to try to smooth Emma's hair and rubbing at her lips to fix her lipstick. Emma took the opportunity to take Georgia's hand and place a kiss on her palm—"you look like you've been ravished."

"Unfortunately, not as ravished as I would like to be," Emma replied, a bit grumpily.

"Brat," Georgia said affectionately.

Emma sighed, taking in Georgia's own appearance. The loose

curls she'd styled her hair into were gone, replaced by a tangled snarl from Emma's hands. Georgia's neck, chest, and cleavage were peppered with dark smudges Emma could only suspect were from her lipstick.

"I think our first stop might have to be to the bathroom, Georgie," Emma remarked with her own laugh. "You have my lipstick all over your boobs."

Georgia looked down at her cleavage and swore.

"I was a little too overeager, I think," Emma said as she scratched sheepishly at the back of her head.

Georgia's hands gripped her cheeks. "I loved every minute of it, baby."

Emma preened, both at the praise and the pet name, and kissed Georgia. Her plan was to keep going until Georgia forgot being reasonable and she could drag Georgia home.

"No," Georgia said, letting go of her cheeks and stepping away to gather both of their shoes. "We have a plan, and we are sticking to it."

Emma relented, put her shoes on, and turned back to the party.

They headed up the gangway, hand in hand.

There was more to talk about, more to figure out, about their futures, what this all meant. But it could wait until tomorrow.

Tonight, they knew they loved each other, and that was enough.

CHAPTER TWENTY-FOUR

After a quick trip to the bathroom where she fixed her hair and makeup to the best of her ability, Emma walked back into the party, with Georgia a careful distance away from her.

What a difference twenty minutes could make. When she'd left the party, she had been sure she was doomed to spend her days alone, watching from the sideline as the people around her moved through their lives. But now, Georgia had told her she *loved* her, was *in love* with her, wanted to be with her in a romantic and sexual way, and Emma could barely comprehend being this happy.

The evening felt interminable to Emma as they danced and drank and chatted with their friends. All Emma could think about was after the party when she and Georgia could be alone together.

It didn't help that Georgia kept shooting her glances that set her skin tingling with the promise of Georgia's touch.

Eventually, Emma noticed that her father looked like he was about to fall asleep at the table and, from a purely selfless need to make sure he was taken care of and for no other reason, decided it was time they called it a night.

So she and Georgia walked him home, just the three of them. Georgia had allowed Cora to stay out until midnight with Martin and said he could stay over, so long as he stayed on the couch in the living room.

As they trod home, the sounds of laughter and music faded behind them, lost to the summer night. Emma's father walked a few paces in front of them through the quiet, sparsely lit streets, and Emma couldn't help herself from tracing the tired sag of his shoulders in his suit jacket. Georgia reached over and slid her fingers through Emma's, the metal of her cocktail ring cool against Emma's skin in the humid night, as if Georgia sensed her worry and wanted to let her know that she was there for her.

"Emma, darling," her father said, looking down at himself when they made it home, the door securely shut behind them, "why exactly am I in a suit?"

Emma swallowed, but Georgia swooped in, taking her father's hand and leading him to the stairs.

"We just went to a party, Henry," she said, voice even and patient. "Do you remember? You spent most of the night talking to Connie and Gerald."

"Where's Giselle, Georgia? She always loves a party," her father replied, his voice a bit groggy.

"She was there," Georgia replied, their voices growing faint as they climbed the stairs. "You danced, and everyone said how beautiful you looked together."

"Ah, that's all her," Emma heard her father say, fondness limning his voice, before the bedroom door snicked shut behind him.

Emma sat on the bottom stairs, strappy heeled sandals kicked off and lined up neatly by the door next to Georgia's own heeled mules, and closed her eyes, needing a moment to collect herself.

She took five deep breaths, then got up and went to the kitchen and filled two glasses with water from the fridge. She took them upstairs, where she found Georgia at the window in her bedroom looking at the dark churning ocean. Her hands and wrists and ears were free of jewelry, hair shaken out to hang thick and wild and wavy around her shoulders and down her back.

Emma leaned on the doorjamb and took a moment just to watch, to admire her outline.

"Here," she said, stepping into the room, and Georgia turned to smile at her. She handed Georgia the glass, and their fingers brushed gently.

"Thanks, love," Georgia said. "I got him changed into pj's and tucked into bed. He took his pills and was asleep before I turned the light out. The party must have worn him out."

Emma leaned down and pressed a soft, sweet kiss to Georgia's mouth. She nuzzled her face into Georgia's neck when she pulled back and wrapped her arms around Georgia's waist, just breathing her in.

"Thank you," Emma whispered, body relaxing against Georgia's hold as Georgia's arms wrapped around her waist and held her steady.

Georgia backed away to put her water on the bookshelf by the window, reaching for Emma's glass and placing it next to hers.

She came back to Emma's embrace and kissed her as she slowly slid her hands up Emma's hips and around to the bare skin of Emma's back. She trailed her fingers along the groove of Emma's spine with light fingertips, Emma's body melting incrementally with every touch.

"We don't have to do anything more tonight," Georgia said, pulling back to look at Emma's face. "I'm happy just to hold you if that's what you need."

Emma felt her heart swell. But that was not what she needed, not what she wanted, not right now, anyway.

"I want you to make me feel alive tonight," Emma said, bending down to nip at Georgia's lower lip, luxuriating in the gasp that she drew from Georgia's throat, the tenor of their touches changing instantly. "I want you to make me forget about anything outside this room."

"Yes," Georgia said, nodding her head emphatically, as she lunged upward for Emma's mouth, "I certainly can do that."

They kissed, and their passion built with each press of lips until they were both breathless. Emma had her hands buried in Georgia's hair, while Georgia's were pressed flat against the skin of Emma's back.

"This dress," Georgia said in a low voice, "has been driving me to distraction all night, Em."

"Yeah?" Emma grinned, and Georgia's hands slipped to her slim hips, gripping her and turning so she was backing Emma in the direction of Emma's bed.

Georgia nodded. "I was watching you dance with Bridget—"

"Creeper," Emma interrupted, and Georgia slapped her ass.

"Hey!" Emma replied indignantly, but it was short lived when Georgia continued speaking.

"I was trying to say something sexy to you about how hot you looked dancing, but I guess I won't," Georgia teased, a sly grin on her lips.

Her hands gripped Emma's waist again and turned Emma around so Emma's back faced her. Emma closed her eyes as she felt Georgia's lips land on her bare skin, starting at the top of her spine and working down, taking her sweet time.

Emma had to grasp the knob at the corner of her footboard to steady herself, knees gone wobbly, as Georgia's hands skimmed along the material of her dress and Georgia's lips worked their way back up the column of her spine. They slipped under the satin to glide along the smooth skin of Emma's stomach and higher, running up her ribs and to her breasts under the loose fabric.

Emma moaned at the feel of Georgia's fingers softly brushing against her nipples, the quick sensation making her crave more touch. Her back arched when Georgia pinched one, breath hitching when she did it to the other.

"Now the dress comes off," Georgia whispered in her ear, sucking at Emma's earlobe as she pressed her warmth against Emma's back. Georgia unfastened the buttons behind Emma's neck, and Emma reached for the zipper, fingers shaking slightly as she dragged it down the teeth. The top flopped off her shoulders, and the skirt pooled at her feet until she was only wearing a pair of black lace bikini cut underwear.

Emma felt Georgia's warmth move away and heard Georgia groan at the sight of Emma's nearly naked back. She felt hands roam over her ass, her hips, fingers trace the outline of her underwear and up the expanse of her naked torso. Felt them return to her breasts as Georgia pushed her chest against Emma's midback. Felt Georgia's lips place kisses along her shoulder blade, each touch a little swipe of fire lighting up her body.

One of Georgia's hands drifted down over the front of Emma's underwear, brushing lightly between her legs, and Emma's hands tightened on the bedpost, her hips bucking up into the touch.

"Ah," she whimpered, "Georgia!"

"Yes?" Georgia asked archly, pinching at Emma's nipple again as her fingers passed over the front of her.

"Stop teasing me," Emma demanded breathlessly, the authority in her voice undercut by the way she was turning to a puddle under Georgia's hands. She heard Georgia laugh low, making Emma's stomach clench.

"Not yet, Em," she murmured into Emma's skin.

Emma let out a sound of disappointment, but Georgia continued to touch her through the fabric of her underwear, strokes tantalizing and light.

Her hips were shifting, trying to chase Georgia's fingers, her knees getting weaker, legs trembling with the effort to keep herself standing.

Emma craned her head back over her shoulder, seeking Georgia's mouth, but with their height difference it didn't quite work. Georgia was just out of reach. Emma let out another frustrated noise, and Georgia, finally, took pity on her.

"Bed," she said firmly.

Georgia's hands drew back from Emma's body and gave her a light push in that direction. Emma nodded emphatically, climbing eagerly onto the bed and scooting until she was leaning back on the pillows, legs parted slightly.

Emma watched as Georgia looked at her, eyes scanning the length of her body. Georgia took Emma in from her long well-muscled legs to her flat stomach and small breasts, all the way up to her biceps and shoulders stretched across the pillows. Emma shifted under her gaze, pressed against that pressing ache between her thighs. Her eyes dipped to the tie of Georgia's wrap dress expectantly, and Georgia huffed a laugh.

"You're so impatient," Georgia said, running her hands across the knot but not untying it.

Emma shrugged, so turned on she could barely speak. She watched Georgia's eyes flick down to her breasts with the movement and decided two could play this game.

"You're the one that's standing all the way over there," Emma managed to say as she spread her thighs and ran her fingers over her lower stomach, stroked right above the waistband of her underwear.

Georgia smiled and bit her lip, eyes glued to Emma's fingers, "Now who's the tease?"

But she finally gave Emma what she wanted, untying and unwrapping her dress and tossing it over the armchair by the window.

"This part, not so sexy," Georgia said, gesturing at the full bodysuit shapewear she wore. "Some of us don't look like former college rowers."

Emma stretched out on her side, still softly touching her own skin, and watched, rapt, as each glorious inch of Georgia was revealed. Her chest, her soft stomach and hips and thighs, and that dark thatch of hair between her legs had Emma's already frantic heartbeat racing in her chest. How Georgia could believe anything she did wasn't unbelievably sexy was beyond Emma.

She was practically panting by the time Georgia had slipped the shapewear to the floor and kicked it in the direction of her dress, heavy breasts swaying with the motion.

"Fuck, you are so hot," Emma murmured reverently on an out breath as Georgia walked toward her. Her eyes flitted over the expanse of olive skin, the summer tan lines, the little silvery stretch marks on Georgia's hips and inner thighs and lower belly.

All Georgia, wonderfully Georgia.

Emma couldn't stop her fingers as they slipped into her underwear and rubbed to relieve some of the pressure building there. Georgia's eyes went wide as she tracked the movement of Emma's hands, teeth sinking into her plump lower lip.

"Let me see," she said, voice husky and rough.

Emma swallowed.

She used her other hand to pull her panties to the side, revealing her fingers gently circling there.

Georgia let out a low sound, and growled, "*Fuck*, Em."

Emma felt it reverberate in her chest, sending pleasure zipping right to where her fingers pressed.

Georgia came closer, brushing her hand against Emma's leg as Emma touched herself. A whine left Emma's throat at the sensation of Georgia's fingers gliding up her inner thigh.

"Enough," Georgia said.

She grabbed Emma's wrist and pulled it away, pinned to the bed at Emma's side. Emma lay back as Georgia crawled over her, looked up at her as she sat straddling Emma's hips. Georgia released her hold on Emma's hand to let Emma explore her thighs, her stomach, palm her large breasts. She closed her eyes and tilted her head back, long hair cascading down her shoulders, clearly enjoying the feel of Emma's touch.

"I love your tits," Emma said.

She would have been embarrassed by the nearly worshipful tenor of her voice if she could feel anything but overwhelming desire for the woman before her. She leaned up on her elbows to kiss one of her breasts and sucked a nipple into her mouth, felt Georgia's stomach clench at the contact. Georgia leaned forward over her, bracing herself on one arm among the pillows. Emma followed and lay back down to prevent her lips from losing contact with Georgia's body.

"Your whole body is so amazingly soft, Georgie," she whispered into Georgia's skin, hands gripped into Georgia's hips.

"*Ohhh*," Georgia breathed and her hand fisted into Emma's hair as Emma continued to lavish attention on Georgia's chest, pulling her closer, "that feels so good, Em."

"Kiss me," Georgia demanded a moment later as she tugged Emma back from her breasts.

Emma complied eagerly, exhilarated by the way Georgia was handling her body. She surged up, so their bodies were flush from hip to chest. The arm Georgia had been supporting herself with gave out, and she collapsed onto Emma. Then they both were *moaning moaning moaning* at that delicious first touch of skin on skin, warmth and pleasure spreading out in all directions.

Emma was in absolute heaven as their kisses deepened, Georgia slotting their legs so Emma could grind down on her thigh as Georgia ground down on hers. They were both too wound up to wait for anything more than hot slick movements against the other.

Emma arched her back, rubbed her sensitive nipples against Georgia's sternum, the sensation electric. She twitched against Georgia's thigh and moaned into Georgia's mouth and felt Georgia's body go taut in response. Georgia's hips thrust wildly against Emma's leg and stomach as Emma rode out the cresting wave of her own pleasure.

Georgia had hardly caught her breath before she moved down Emma's torso, stopping to kiss and lick at her small breasts, her own heavy ones trailing against Emma's flat stomach. The touch stoked the barely snuffed fire in Emma's lower belly to an inferno once more.

Emma reached for Georgia, hands stroking and touching any spare inch of skin she could reach, feeling desperate.

Georgia pulled back and guided Emma's hands off her body and onto the duvet, squeezing her wrists in silent command.

In answer to Emma's growl of complaint, Georgia said, "You'll have a turn, I swear. Right now, though, I just need to focus on you. Just let me make you feel good, baby, please."

Georgia sounded a bit desperate herself.

Emma swallowed, hands twisting into the fabric of the duvet beneath her, back arched slightly in response to the plea in Georgia's voice, the dominance in her touch, and said breathily, "Okay."

What else could she say?

Georgia grinned.

She began by sliding Emma's ruined panties off her long legs, lingering on her muscular thighs with her mouth as she made her way back up. Then she pulled Emma with surprising strength down flat on her back and settled between her legs.

The sight of Georgia lying between her spread thighs nearly tipped her over, so she squeezed her eyes shut. But this proved to be a mistake because it amplified all other sensations. At the first swipe of Georgia's tongue, wet and warm and *perfect* against her, Emma grabbed for a pillow to muffle her sounds, unable to stay quiet any longer.

She felt Georgia's low chuckle in response, a hot puff of air against her skin.

Then it was all sensation as Georgia focused on her with her mouth and hands and lips and teeth. Georgia brought her to the edge over and over until Emma didn't think there was any more pleasure left in her body, every nerve ending wrung out. And yet somehow Georgia found just an ounce more for her to give.

Sex had been good before, Emma thought when she could think again. Her partners had always been considerate with her body and attentive to her needs. But this was something else.

How could even the sight of Georgia's dark hair spread out against the summer freckled skin of Emma's thigh, her eyes sparkling up at Emma as she rested there and licked her lips, satisfaction gleaming on her face, have Emma on the verge again?

Georgia came to lie beside her, finally, cradling and soothing her body through the last of her shudders. Emma peered at her through bleary eyes, too wrung out to do more than bury her head in Georgia's chest as Georgia traced light circles into her sweat damp skin.

"Georgie," she managed to croak, once her head had stopped spinning.

"Yeah, Em?" Georgia replied, fingers tracing the grooves of her abs, the shape of her arm muscles, the outside of her thighs in comforting touches.

"I think you killed me," Emma said, eyes closing again of their own accord.

Georgia laughed and brushed Emma's tousled hair off her face, pressed soft kisses to her forehead and cheeks.

"Go to sleep, Em," she murmured, low and soothing.

"I can't just pass out and leave you horny. I'm not a guy," Emma muttered, mustering what energy she had left to stare indignantly up at Georgia through half-lidded eyes.

Georgia just grinned down at her.

"Seeing you like this, knowing it's because of me? That's all I need. Trust me, Emma, I am beyond good right now," Georgia said, fingers trailing down Emma's face, up her ribs, over her nipple. Emma squinted at her and scrunched up her nose, and Georgia kissed the tip of it.

"Do you not want me to touch you?" she asked, confused.

"Oh my God, Emma, *of course* I want you to touch me. It's all I've been thinking about for weeks now," Georgia responded with her usual fond exasperation evident in her tone. "But making you feel good makes *me* feel good. So good I, uh, had to take care of myself while I was going down on you."

Emma stared at her face. Georgia, calm, confident, collected Georgia, was blushing as she watched her own tanned fingers trail across the pale expanse of Emma's stomach.

"You made yourself come and I missed it?" Emma asked.

"To be fair," Georgia replied, finger tracing the curve where Emma's breast met her chest, "you were a bit preoccupied."

"Still," Emma said stubbornly, hoisting herself up on one elbow to look her eye to eye.

Georgia sighed. "I promise you can make me come later," she said.

"That's all I wanted to hear," Emma said and flopped back down, letting Georgia gather her back to her chest and position them against the pillows.

"Ridiculous woman," she breathed against Emma's hair.

"Mmm, but you love me," Emma said, the buzzing in her body turning to a relaxation so deep her eyes drifted shut.

Georgia chuckled. "God, I really do."

"Stay?" Emma asked sleepily, rolling to her side and wrapping Georgia's arm around her middle.

"Always," Georgia whispered, pressing her front to Emma's back and tangling their legs beneath the covers.

Sleep, easy and deep, came quickly for Emma and didn't let her go all night.

CHAPTER TWENTY-FIVE

Emma woke to the blissful sight of Georgia's sleeping face inches from her own. The panicked thoughts that waited to swarm on the edges of her mind were blown apart by the vision.

Georgia had stayed.

What they had shared the night before was real and true.

She grinned into the pillow and then flicked her eyes down, and her smile grew.

The blankets were tangled around Georgia's waist, right arm thrown over her head, left hand resting on Emma's hip, her glorious breasts bared to the morning light filtering through Emma's windows. Emma couldn't stop herself from reaching out to trail her fingers over them, to lean down and nuzzle them with her cheek.

"Good morning to you, too," Georgia croaked, hips shifting as she woke to find Emma's attention locked in on her breasts. Georgia's hand buried itself in Emma's hair and combed through the strands sleepily. Then, to Emma's delight, her fingers tugged at the strands, seemingly involuntarily, as Emma scraped her teeth along the sensitive flesh of her nipple. Georgia arched and moaned quietly at the touch, so Emma did it again.

"Morning." She smiled up at Georgia from her spot by her chest. She shifted onto all fours over Georgia's body and then moved leisurely down Georgia's stomach, lavishing kisses on her ribs, her belly, her hips. She spread Georgia's legs and smoothed her fingers up Georgia's silken inner thighs, flecked here and there with silvery stretch marks.

"Shit," Emma heard Georgia call, high and breathy, as she ran her tongue over Georgia for the first time. "Oh God, Em, that's so good."

Emma had to agree.

It was unbelievable, the feel of Georgia beneath Emma's hands as Georgia quivered with need. The taste of her on Emma's tongue, all sweet heat and spice.

She understood why Georgia couldn't wait for Emma to touch her the night before. As Georgia gave her body over to pleasure, Emma felt her own desire building, pressure growing insistently between her legs. She couldn't help but lose herself completely in the thrill of bringing someone she loved so intensely to the height of desire.

Georgia's hands twined in her hair, guided her with touch and words to the spots that she liked most, and Emma followed her lead willingly.

When Emma had made Georgia's body clench and twitch and shake twice, sweet little sounds pouring from her throat like music to Emma's ears, Georgia hauled her up and kissed her fiercely. She panted against Emma's lips as Emma trailed her fingers gently along Georgia's stomach and down the outside of her thighs, unable to stop touching her.

Emma pulled back, and they gazed at each other, Georgia's face flushed and her hair a wild tangle on the pillow, her eyes a bit glossy from sleep and lingering pleasure.

"Wow," she said, and Emma smiled as she rested her head on her hand, looking down at the wonderful mess she'd made of this woman, so put together in every other moment of her life.

"I knew you'd be bossing me around, even in bed. I *am* a bit out of practice," Emma admitted shyly. "It was good, though?"

"Em, it was incredible," Georgia said, leaning up on her elbow to look Emma eye to eye.

Emma pressed her forehead against Georgia's, relishing the feeling of being just the two of them in this little bubble for the moment as they breathed together.

Eventually, Georgia placed a gentle kiss on her lips and sighed.

"I should probably go before Henry wakes up," she said. "Might be disorienting for him to see me here."

Emma's body relaxed before she could feel anxious about Georgia wanting to sneak out.

"So thoughtful," Emma said, leaning forward to kiss her again, long and lingering. She dripped her emotion, honey-like, into her touch.

After a slow moment, Georgia rolled on top of her with a grunt. It wasn't long before Emma gripped Georgia's back, nails digging in as Georgia's skilled fingers circled and pressed between her legs. She wound Emma tighter and tighter until Emma cried out, unable to keep quiet. She bit Georgia's shoulder where it met her neck in an attempt to muffle her noise as her body shook.

"I'm sorry," Emma said when she could talk again, running her fingers lightly over the red spot that was sure to bruise on Georgia's collarbone. "I didn't mean to hurt you."

"Don't be," Georgia whispered, voice husky. She captured Emma's fretting fingers and pressed tender kisses to the tips of them. "And trust me, you didn't. But I really should go, or Cora will be insufferable, and poor Johnny must be a nervous wreck."

Emma lolled naked in the bed as she watched Georgia gather up her dress and shapewear.

"You can borrow something to wear," Emma proposed as she glanced at the clinging shapewear in Georgia's hands.

Georgia cast Emma a skeptical look over her shoulder.

"I've got some big crew T-shirts in that bottom drawer," Emma said, gesturing with a flick of her foot.

Georgia bent over, giving Emma an excellent view, and opened the drawer.

"Em, this is all jeans," she said, rummaging through the drawer.

"I know." Emma smiled, and Georgia raised her eyebrow at her over her shoulder.

"Did you tell me that just to see me bend over?" Georgia asked, hands on her plump hips.

Emma grinned, delighted with herself.

"Who knew you were such a horny menace," Georgia replied with a shake of her head, but a smile on her lips. She opened the dresser drawers one by one until she found the T-shirts and pulled out an old forest-green Dartmouth Crew tee, yanking it over her head.

"Only for you," Emma said, pouting a little now that Georgia's body was concealed. The shirt was a snug fit on Georgia but hit her midthigh and covered all the necessary bits.

It was true, though, Emma thought as Georgia grabbed a hair tie from Emma's vanity and tied her hair up in a messy bun. Even with streaks of makeup under her eyes, her morning breath, and the orgasms they'd already given each other, Emma wanted nothing more than for Georgia to crawl back into bed with her, to hold her close and press gentle kisses on her lips.

It wasn't even a lust thing, although there was plenty of that. She just wanted to be close to her, to look over and know Georgia existed and be comforted by that fact.

Something possessive thrummed in her as she watched Georgia approach the bed clad in only Emma's shirt.

"Alright," Georgia said, leaning over to plant a good-bye kiss on Emma. "I'm going to leave now before you do something sexy like sit up and then I get dragged back into bed with you. Plus, there's this glint in your eye right now that's dangerous. I'll be over again in"—she glanced at the clock which read seven fifteen—"two hours and fifteen minutes for breakfast with Cora."

One second Emma admired the way her T-shirt hugged Georgia's curves, and the next, "I don't think we should tell anyone yet" burst out of her mouth at the reminder of the world beyond her bedroom door.

Georgia nodded, but Emma could see something shutter in her gaze.

"Want to tell me why?" she asked patiently.

Emma closed her eyes, trying to think through the blissful haze clouding her mind.

"I just..." She swallowed, puzzling out the right words in her mind. "Once everyone knows, *they'll all know*, you know?"

"Use more words, love," Georgia replied, brushing some hair back from Emma's face.

"If my dad and Cora know, then Anne and Hattie will know, and once Hattie knows, Connie will know and then—"

"Everyone in the world will know," Georgia concluded for her with a nod, her bun bobbing with the motion. "So? What's your real worry?"

"We don't know what we are yet," Emma said, sitting up and taking Georgia's hand. "I mean, I know I'm so deeply, deeply in love with you, Georgie, and I know I *need* to never stop kissing and touching you as much as I can."

Georgia smiled and prompted, "But?"

"But...my dad," Emma said, voice quieting. "I mean, how are we supposed to have a relationship?"

The idea of even trying scared her. Could they go on dates? Have sleepovers at Georgia's house? Go away for the weekend?

She wanted a full life with Georgia. *God*, how she wanted it. But just admitting she wanted it was one thing, seeing how it could become a reality was another.

"I thought we had been over this," Georgia said, putting her hands on her hips as her stern expression appeared on her face, little crinkle between her brows and all.

Okay, Emma thought, that look was actually pretty cute.

"You can get more help," Georgia went on. "Didn't Cora give you the speech about relying on your friends more?"

"Did you coach her to give that speech?" Emma asked in mock outrage.

Georgia shrugged and simply said, "Of course."

Emma knelt in bed and smacked Georgia's shoulder, exclaiming, "Georgia!"

Georgia grinned, eyes flicking down Emma's bare body, before coming to take a seat on the edge of Emma's bed.

"We weren't speaking," she said, patting the bed so Emma settled next to her, "and I wanted you to see how it could work if you wanted to keep seeing Bridget. That there were people to take up the slack. I didn't want you to cut off something good before it started because you were afraid to let go a little."

"Coming from someone who needs to be so in control they manipulated a teen into doing their dirty work," Emma muttered with no real heat.

Georgia squeezed Emma's hand tightly, eye contact direct and serious.

"Listen, Em. Don't cut me off, this off, because you're scared of what might happen with your dad. He wants you to live a full life, and your mom would want you to, too," Georgia finished, voice tender, eyes fierce.

"Wow, low blow, pulling the dead parent card," Emma said, eyes going a bit watery as they gazed into Georgia's. "I do wish we'd saved the emotional chat until I was wearing clothes."

Georgia stroked her hair, tucking some of the blond strands behind her ear.

"We can keep talking," Georgia said, "because I'm serious about this, us. I want to build a future with you, Em. But for today, around our friends and family, we can pretend we didn't spend the night having world changing sex."

Emma's heart swooped and soared at Georgia's declaration that she wanted them to build a future together, something Emma had never thought possible.

"You're the best and I love you, Georgie," Emma said simply, leaning forward to kiss her.

"I know," Georgia replied against her lips, and Emma pushed her away, rolling her eyes.

Georgia laughed and got up to leave, for now.

Emma lay back in bed with a smile in her eye and a laugh on her lips, Georgia's heart tucked in her pocket.

Chapter Twenty-six

Emma barely paid attention to where she ran that morning, her mind full of *Georgia Georgia Georgia.* Georgia as she walked to her backlit by the stars. The way she looked as she danced with Emma's father and Cora the night before. The feel of her kiss, her body, the taste and smell of her. Waking to her sleeping face. The sound of her saying *I love you.* The sounds she made as Emma made her come.

Her chest felt too full of emotion, happiness, fear, lust, love, and worry, all jumbling together as her feet pounded the pavement. Before she knew it, she was turning down Highbury Lane, her watch telling her she'd run over ten miles.

"You were out early this morning, Em," her father greeted her as she entered the kitchen and went for her coconut water.

"I woke up energized and decided to go for a long run," Emma replied, turning to survey the kitchen. She nearly spat her water out at the sight of the breakfast table.

Cora, Martin, and her dad were all seated around a big white box full of enormous muffins, scones, and croissants. The addition of Martin this morning was a bit of a surprise, but her dad seemed to be tolerating it well.

"Cora, did you bring all this over?" Emma asked, plopping down in the chair next to her dad and perusing the pastry options.

"You think I got up early enough to go out and get muffins from that amazing place in Old Town before they ran out of triple berry and apple cinnamon?" Cora said.

She gave Emma a look that said she was delusional.

"Are you delusional?" she added.

"I brought it," said a voice entering the kitchen, and then Georgia was there, and everything else vanished from Emma's surroundings.

She looked so beautiful, hair tied back in a long loose braid and dressed in a black cotton V-neck jumpsuit that flowed around her ankles, simple and summery. Emma wanted to kiss her so badly she had to grip the tabletop to restrain herself.

Her eyes noted how the edge of a red mark peeked out of Georgia's neckline near her collarbone, and her mouth was suddenly parched, heart skittering around in her chest.

Uh-oh, Emma thought as she averted her gaze and chugged the rest of her coconut water. That's not good.

Georgia strode over to them, a smile on her plump lips.

"Yes, we were all just marveling at our dear Georgia's good mood this morning," her dad said. "And it's nice to see your face at our table again. We missed you all last week."

He cast a reproachful look at Emma.

"Why are you giving me that look?" she shot back.

"I'm just glad you guys aren't fighting anymore," Cora said. "Did the non-wedding remind you about what is truly important in this cruel, cruel world?"

"Something like that," Georgia said, winking at Emma, her foot caressing Emma's under the table.

Emma smiled back, hoping her face didn't look too moony.

"Georgie, what's that on your collarbone?" Cora asked, pointing at the spot on her own neck. "It looks like a bruise."

Emma resisted the urge to let her forehead fall to the kitchen table. Fucking Cora!

"Oh, uh, must just be heat rash," Georgie hedged, scratching at the mark absently as a red flush crept up her neck.

The situation was getting away from them, Emma thought frantically, trying to shoot Georgia a look without being too conspicuous.

"I had an interesting dream last night," her dad said after a pause, as he took a blueberry scone and applied butter to it with a flourish.

"Oh, do tell," Emma said mimicking his formal accent, grateful to shift attention away from her and Georgia. She cut a triple berry muffin into quarters and took one.

"I dreamed that I went downstairs to get water around three in the morning last night, and I saw two pairs of women's shoes and two purses by the door. One set was Emma's and the other looked a lot like the ones you had with you last night, Georgia."

He took a bite of his scone and chewed thoughtfully.

Oh no, Emma thought. This was the opposite of the attention moving away from them.

Her heart rate picked up, but she focused on eating her muffin and not on looking at Georgia.

Okay, so he'd spotted Georgia's shoes. That didn't necessarily mean that he knew Georgia was in her bed, Emma reasoned with herself. Maybe Georgia took them off when she came over and forgot to get them when she left. That's plausible, right?

"Of course," her dad went on, "I thought I was awake, and the glass was next to my bed when I woke up this morning, but when I came down today, there were only Emma's heels and bag by the front door, so I must have been dreaming."

"What an *interesting* dream, Henry," Cora remarked, drawing out the syllables of the word *interesting*.

"And coincidentally, when we got home last night around one, yes after curfew," Cora said when Georgia opened her mouth and then frowned, "but when we came in, Johnny was sleeping on the couch, and there was no sign that you'd come back from the party. Even though you left around ten with Henry. And Emma."

Georgia shot her a look, eyebrows raised.

But, Emma thought, unwilling to give in to the mounting evidence being laid out before her, there was nothing unusual with Georgia's stuff being here late. They could have fallen asleep watching a movie together.

"We fell asleep watching TV together," Emma blurted.

"Really?" her dad said, "because I distinctly remember that there was no one in the TV room when I passed it on my way back to bed."

Emma gaped at him.

"I may be losing my memory, honey, but my vision is fine," he said, popping the last of his scone into his mouth and high-fiving Cora across the table.

Martin smiled at Emma apologetically.

"Busted!" Cora crowed obnoxiously, and Emma felt her sweaty face turning even redder.

"How long have the two of you been…involved?" her dad asked.

"Gross, Dad, don't ask that," Emma whined, hiding her head in her hands, and Cora whooped.

"Spill, spill, spill," she chanted, hitting the table.

"Not if you keep doing that," Georgia said, moving her coffee cup away from Cora's enthusiastic hands, gripping Emma's knee in support under the table.

"I need to go take a shower," Emma said, springing up from the table and practically running toward the stairs.

"Fine, we'll just pester Georgia for deets, then," Cora shouted after her.

Emma heard Georgia say, "This is the thanks I get for providing you all with pastries? I think it's time for Johnny's walk, anyway," then the scrape of a chair pushed back.

She had just closed the door behind her when Georgia flung it open.

"Looks like we've been found out," she said, coming close to wrap Emma in her arms.

"I was hoping it would take them a little longer," Emma pouted, wrapping her own arms around Georgia's upper back and sighing as she nuzzled into her neck. "I'm all sweaty, Georgie."

"I know, I like it," Georgia said, breathing in her scent, even licking some dried sweat off Emma's jaw.

Emma laughed and pushed her away. "You weirdo."

But Georgia grabbed her from behind, pulling Emma in her sports bra and spandex running shorts into her as Emma shrieked and giggled.

"God, these things are such a tease," Georgia said, running her hands over the shorts where they stretched over the muscles of Emma's thighs, and back up over her ass.

"Yeah?" Emma said, enjoying Georgia's attention.

"Your body is so fucking unreal," Georgia murmured, her index finger running down the groove on the side of her stomach, then tracing the line of her bicep as Emma's arm reached behind her to bury her hand in Georgia's hair. "So strong and sexy."

"You don't think I'm too muscular and square?" Emma asked self-consciously. It was a secret fear of hers, that she wasn't feminine enough, wasn't attractive in that way, society poking its head into her mind and whispering that she wasn't right for being shaped like this.

"You have these amazing curves and you're just so *soft*"—Emma almost moaned the word—"your skin, your thighs, your boobs."

"Someone's getting themselves a little worked up." Georgia chuckled, her hands trailing up and down Emma's sides, running along the band of her sports bra. "I think you are one of the most beautiful women I've ever seen, Em."

Emma turned in her arms, needing to kiss her.

Just before their lips met, though, the door flew open.

"I *knew* you'd be up here together," Cora crowed triumphantly from the doorway.

"You fucking snoop," Emma said, picking up a pillow from her bed and tossing it at Cora, who closed the door with a yelp to block the pillow from hitting her. "And stay out!"

She turned back to Georgia, who was grinning from ear to ear.

"What?"

"I'm just really happy right now." Georgia shrugged, and Emma kissed her because how could she not?

"Me too." Emma grinned.

CHAPTER TWENTY-SEVEN

I wanted to talk to you about something," Georgia said a few days later.

It was the last Thursday night in July, the summer flying by, and Emma was curled on a lounge chair on the deck of Georgia's pool, having been reluctantly persuaded to hang out by it, at least until Anne left for the day.

Cora had taken a postgraduation vacation with her friends to the Winnipesaukee house for the week, having made up with her mom and gotten back into her good graces. She had decided to spend the rest of the summer with Georgia and said the job would look great on her résumé. Martin was now allowed to visit, but not to spend the night, as often as he liked after Emma had written a reference letter on his behalf. Turned out that he was actually a very sweet, thoughtful, and caring young man who supported Cora's dreams, even if Emma wasn't entirely sure she approved of his life choices.

Emma hummed distractedly and looked up from the book she had been reading as Georgia took a seat at the end of her chair. She was wearing the flowy blue dress with the embroidered neckline and ruffled shoulders she loved to lounge in on hot days, feet bare and hair twisted up in a clip. She looked summery and sweet.

How Emma ever could have thought she wasn't in love with Georgia was beyond her comprehension. She loved her so deeply it felt like a vital organ she'd just recently discovered was now working in overdrive. It hit her all over every time Georgia entered a room, every time she smiled affectionately at Emma, every time she kissed or touched Emma's body.

Georgia lifted Emma's feet to make room for herself at the end of Emma's chair, then deposited them on her lap. She wasn't disturbed by the callouses on Emma's hands and feet the way Sam had been, squealing every time they scratched her.

"Remember Jane?" Georgia said, running her thumb up the arch of Emma's left foot.

"If you're going to suggest a threesome this early into our relationship, I might break up with you," Emma quipped.

Georgia shook her head in fond exasperation and dug her nails playfully into Emma's sole.

"She runs a clinic in Boston," Georgia continued, her thumb digging into Emma's arch a bit harder.

"Okay?" Emma said, suspicion creeping into her mind.

"It's a clinic that specializes in providing support to kids whose parents or siblings are going through cancer treatment. Mental health support," she added at Emma's blank look.

Emma sat up, and Georgia let go of her foot. She crossed her legs under her and took a deep breath.

"We've had four amazing days together, Georgie," Emma said cautiously. Georgia just looked at her. They'd slept together in Emma's bed, Johnny curled at their feet, the last three nights so Emma could be close to her dad, but they could still be together. "Don't ruin it by making us have a fight."

"I'm not making us have a fight, Em. You're the one that's being wicked stubborn about this," Georgia said, scooting closer and resting her hand on her knee. "At least hear what I have to say."

Emma could feel her hackles and defenses rising, but the pleading look in the eyes of the woman she loved was too much for her to withstand.

"Fine," she said, defeated. "Let's hear your pitch."

Georgia smiled and rewarded her with a kiss, pulling back before they could get too carried away.

"Okay," Georgia said. "The reason I met up with Jane was because I had read about her clinic on an alumni news blast. I didn't know she was in Boston until that point, and I remember that you volunteered with children in crisis in college."

Emma was touched that she'd remembered that. She'd spent a semester interning for credit at a free clinic in Hanover run by the Dartmouth psychology department, filing documents, entering data, chatting with parents while their kids were in sessions, writing up reports for the counselors, and sitting in on meetings as they discussed their caseloads. It had been fascinating and at times heavy, but she had loved every minute of it.

"So the reason you met up with Jane…" she began, putting pieces together in her mind.

"Was to talk about you, yeah," Georgia finished with a slight blush.

Not for the first time, Emma cussed Cora out in her mind for making her doubt Georgia's intentions, causing them both unnecessary pain.

"So," Emma said tentatively, "what did she say?"

"She's looking for interns," Georgia said immediately. "It pays minimum wage, will probably end up just covering your gas and tolls into and out of the city, but you're not really hurting for money. It could look really good for a résumé, too, if you decide to ultimately go back to school. But it would also get you out of the house, get your mind working again."

Emma's heart thumped with excitement at the idea, but her stomach clenched with anxiety.

"At a clinic, in Boston."

Her emotional uncertainty seeped into her voice.

"Em, listen, this could be an amazing opportunity for you. And you could be home with your dad every night." Georgia reached for Emma's hand, grasping it hard so she'd look at her. "And with me. At least think about it, love."

Emma sighed. Trust Georgia to find the perfect opportunity that refuted every one of her objections.

"Okay, I'll think about it."

Georgia smiled triumphantly and stood up.

"Great," she said, "because she's coming over for dinner tomorrow, and I told her you'd be so excited to talk to her about the position."

"What the fuck, Georgia," Emma shrieked, and the only response she could think of was to get up and push her girlfriend into the pool, fully clothed.

Georgia shot up, staring at her in shock, water dripping off every inch of her, and then burst out into laughter.

"I'm sorry, I'm sorry," Emma said, hands over her mouth. "It was just the first reaction that popped into my head."

"Help me out," Georgia whined, her waterlogged dress swirling around her as she swam to the edge.

Emma crouched down and reached for her.

"Do you have your phone on you?" Georgia asked, a twinkle in her eye.

"No, I left it on the chair," Emma responded without thinking and then Georgia grasped her hand and tugged, sending Emma toppling headfirst into the deep end of the pool, soaking her jean shorts and tank top.

She surfaced to find Georgia cackling and gripping the edge of the pool.

"I can't believe you fell for that," she gasped, fighting for breath.

Emma swiped water in her direction.

"Hey," Georgia shouted.

It devolved into a splash fight, water flying all over the tiled deck of the pool. Johnny got up and trotted over to the grass to escape the spray.

Georgia swam away from Emma, but Emma grabbed her around the waist as she swam past, hauling her up out of the water and dunking them under together.

They both bobbed to the surface, laughing, and Emma used Georgia's dress to reel her in for a kiss.

"See," Georgia said as she pushed back and wriggled out of her wet dress, tossing it onto the tiles, followed by her bra and underwear. "There are perks to a private pool."

Emma surveyed Georgia swimming before her, her beautiful body blurred by the water from the shoulders down, and swallowed.

"I'm beginning to see your point," she said as Georgia drew nearer, Emma tracking her every movement.

"Your turn," Georgia said, standing in the water in front of Emma and pulling on the submerged waistband of her shorts.

Emma's clothes quickly followed Georgia's, landing with a slap against the pool deck.

Thank God Cora wasn't home, Emma thought as Georgia crowded her against the side of the pool, slick bodies pressed against each other in the water, kisses turning heated as hands roamed and tongues flicked into mouths.

But she stopped thinking about Cora or Jane Fairfield and her clinic as Georgia's lips sucked at her neck, and Emma had her hands on Georgia's breasts. Not as Georgia's legs wrapped around Emma's hips, pressed close. Not as they took each other apart with their hands, water sloshing with the movement of their bodies.

"That's one for the pro pool column," Georgia whispered later as she rested her head against Emma's shoulder, recovering.

Emma laughed, her head lolling back on the edge of the pool, sun beating down on them, gilding them in light.

The next night found them seated on Emma and her father's patio, Emma once again playing hostess, serving small cups of gazpacho and refilling wineglasses as Georgia and Jane chatted about mutual friends and reminisced about their med school days. Her father was withdrawn, which Emma knew meant he was having a hard day, and ate his dinner quietly before excusing himself early.

"He's tired today," Emma said, taking the seat to the left of Georgia across the table from Jane, trying not to show her concern. "The heat gets to him."

"It's okay," Jane said, her voice musical and light. "I understand from Georgia he has early onset dementia."

Emma cast Georgia a look and Georgia shoved her with her shoulder.

"Uh, yeah. He was diagnosed about three years ago. It's not bad enough that he needs around the clock care yet, but he had to stop working shortly after the diagnosis, and he mistakes me for my mom who passed away thirteen years ago sometimes and forgets where he is or who he's with suddenly," Emma said, feeling an itch under her skin at divulging this information to a stranger.

"That must be quite stressful for you," Jane said, cocking her head to the side as Georgia reached for Emma's hand under the table and intertwined their fingers.

"Yeah, it's not a fun time," Emma admitted, looking at Georgia for reassurance. She gave her a small smile, and Emma squeezed her hand.

"You're lucky you have someone as solid as Georgia to lean back on," Jane said, smiling sweetly at her.

Jane was actually very nice once you got to know her, Emma thought.

"I really am," Emma agreed, and Georgia leaned in to kiss her cheek.

"I didn't know you two were a couple when Georgia asked me if I knew of any connections to help you out," Jane said.

"We weren't," Georgia replied. "It's a bit new."

Jane looked surprised but didn't say anything further about it, turning to Emma instead and asking her about her volunteering and other things she did in college, inquiring about what she'd done since.

"I know I haven't done much career-wise for the last three years," Emma said, surprised by her own urge to impress Jane, almost as if she might actually be interested in the job.

"On the contrary, what you've been doing shows a tremendous amount of empathy that might make you uniquely qualified to help us out. The kids we deal with are processing a huge trauma that some of them don't even know how to begin to talk about. It sounds like you have some personal experience with that—that's something you can't learn in training," Jane responded.

Emma felt the urge to cry but swallowed it down.

"Thank you," she said solemnly.

"I can't guarantee anything, obviously, but I do think you should come in for an interview next week. Meet the clinic staff and see what we're all about."

"That would be amazing," Emma said and meant it.

"Excellent, I'll have my assistant email you to set it up." Jane smiled.

They spent the rest of the evening with Jane and Georgia trading med school horror stories, Emma laughing at the image of Georgia as a petrified twenty-three-year-old staying up until dawn to cram because she was worried a mean professor would cold-call her, or falling asleep on her cadaver with his brain exposed.

"This has been a lovely night. Thanks so much for inviting me, Georgia," Jane said after Emma had broken out the ice cream.

"Yeah, thanks for inviting her to my home without telling me," Emma said, swatting Georgia on the arm. Georgia captured her hand and pressed a kiss to the back of it in apology.

"I should get going, though. My wife just texted that my five-year-old is refusing to go to bed until I get home," she said with a long-suffering parental sigh.

They walked Jane to the door.

"I'll see you next week, Emma?" she said in parting.

"Yes, definitely," Emma said with a confidence that surprised her.

She found, as she stuck her hand out for a shake, that while part of her brain was whirring over her father's schedule of appointments and care, another part was really looking forward to checking out the lab.

Jane ignored her hand and leaned in for a hug.

"It was really wonderful to meet you as Georgia's girlfriend," Jane said as she pulled back. "You two obviously make each other very happy."

"Oh, thanks," Emma said, feeling herself blush as she remembered her furious jealousy-fueled social media stalking of this very kind and warm woman, and apparently mother, and the nasty thoughts she'd had about her.

Jane waved to them as she walked to her car down the circular driveway.

Emma turned to Georgia after they closed the door.

"Don't start," Emma said, holding up a hand.

"I didn't say anything," Georgia exclaimed, trailing after Emma as she made her way into the kitchen to start loading the dishwasher. Georgia took her usual position at the sink, rinsing and handing dishes to Emma.

"But I know what you're thinking," Emma said, taking a plate from Georgia and putting it in the washer, their movements in sync, able to argue and do dishes at the same time from years of practice. "That you always know what's best for me and without you pushing me I'd never face my fears."

"You said it," Georgia muttered, and Emma stood up, hands on her hips as she glared at her girlfriend. Georgia smirked down at the wineglass in her hand, amused by Emma's exasperation.

"Why I ever let you kiss me when you are so aggravating is beyond me," Emma said, undercutting her words by wrapping Georgia in a hug from behind and bending to place a kiss on the nape of her neck. Georgia leaned back into her, resting her head against Emma's cheek. They stood like that for an extended pause.

"Thank you," Emma said after a moment.

"For infuriating you into loving me?" Georgia joked.

Emma laughed quietly.

"No," she said a beat later. "For not being afraid to make me mad. For telling me hard truths I need to hear when I don't want to hear them. For pushing me to be better."

Georgia slowly spun in her arms, wrapping hers around Emma's neck and rising on her toes to kiss her.

"Now *you* say something sweet and loving about *me*," Emma said when they broke apart.

Georgia smiled and shook her head.

"You are such a brat," she said, kissing her again.

"That's the spirit," Emma replied. "You're staying over, right?" Emma asked, gripping Georgia's waist when they pulled away from each other.

"Of course," Georgia replied. "If only because I love scandalizing Hattie when I come down in my pajamas in the morning."

Emma rolled her eyes and went back to loading the dishwasher.

Chapter Twenty-eight

Later that night, as Emma lay in her bed with Georgia breathing deeply beside her and Johnny snoring from his bed on the floor, she stared at the ceiling, contemplating everything Jane had said.

Was it possible she could have everything? A relationship with Georgia, the beginnings of the career she'd planned for, and to be there for her dad every day?

The possibility was almost as terrifying as the idea that none of it would ever happen.

She sat up in bed, thinking she'd just take a few hits and that would help her relax, but Georgia stirred beside her.

"Em," she said groggily, "where are you going? Is everything okay?"

She looked so adorably sleep rumpled, squinting up at her with red sheet creases on her round cheek, her hair thrown up in a messy bun, that Emma couldn't help climbing back into bed and cuddling close to her.

"It's nothing, just couldn't sleep," Emma whispered to her as Georgia curled into her side.

"Want to talk about it?" Georgia murmured, eyes already closing.

Emma planted a kiss on her forehead and settled down into the pillows, letting the sound of Georgia's breath evening out soothe her.

She rubbed idle circles into the soft skin of Georgia's low back beneath her sleep shirt, and Georgia made a little sound in her sleep. Emma felt her heart tug, tears inexplicably leaking from the corners of her eyes.

This future was daunting. Her dad's health would decline, and his care would become more complicated. She knew she could open up more to her community: Georgia, Cora, even Connie.

And maybe she wouldn't get the internship or would decide that psychology wasn't for her. But she wanted to try to move forward, not just tread water to stay afloat like she'd been doing for the last three years. You couldn't prepare for everything in this life, no matter how hard you tried.

In this moment, her dad asleep and safe in the room down the hall, the woman she loved most tucked into her side, the world felt sweet and simple, that future she wanted possible. All she had to do was reach for it.

And she *would* reach for it, just as she'd reached for Georgia, just as Georgia had reached for her.

She hoped, somewhere, somehow, her mother knew it and was proud.

EPILOGUE

Connie Brightley has never been known for her subtlety, Emma thought as she, Georgia, her father, and Anne walked up the drive to her red brick home.

On this blustery December night, it was bedecked with about ten thousand yards of white Christmas lights. Every shrub and tree and inch of brick had a light strung from it. A steady stream of people bundled into wool and down coats made their way through the white front door, passing under the golden cod affixed above the lintel.

"Welcome!" Connie squealed enthusiastically when she saw Emma and her companions enter the house.

A worker in a white shirt and black pants with a sequined bow tie was there to take their coats. Connie came gliding over to them in her long one-shouldered silver sequined gown, her highlighted hair elegantly curled around her face, understated diamonds glittering at her ears and wrists and on her finger.

"Emma, my dear, you look stunning as usual," Connie said as she leaned up to kiss Emma on her cheek. "Henry, so dapper, my God, you don't look a day over forty-five, I swear. Oh," she went on, swooping in to greet all of them in turn, but giving none of them the chance to greet her back, "Georgia! So lovely to see you, and what a gorgeous couple the two of you make, I must say."

Emma smiled and tangled her hand with Georgia's. She opened her mouth to respond, but Connie was on a roll.

"Trevor brought his latest girlfriend, an absolutely lovely girl who wore a suit to the party, can you imagine. It's silver! You must meet her. Oh, Daniella, there you are!"

Connie swooped off in a swirl of sequins, leaving them all a bit dazed.

"Such a mellow, easygoing woman," Anne said.

"Low energy," Emma's dad agreed. "She really should try some coffee."

They all laughed.

Anne threaded her arm through her dad's, and they walked into the bustle of the party together. She had become something more than just a caregiver to Henry in the last few months as Emma spent increasing amounts of time with Georgia and at her internship at the clinic. Anne sometimes stayed until nine or later, playing games and reading with him or just sitting and knitting beside him, occasionally helping him when he made a mistake. Emma had a lavender scarf and matching hat he had made her for Christmas sitting in the coat closet, and they weren't even too knobbly.

She watched as he said something to Anne, easy to spot as she had the only brown skin in the crowd, and she threw her head back and laughed. Their companionship made Emma's heart easy.

"I think Henry might have a bit of a crush," Georgia murmured in her ear, and Emma raised her eyebrows at her girlfriend.

"On Anne?"

"Look at them, he can't stop staring at her," Georgia said. She motioned her head toward them as they wove their way to the appetizer table.

Emma looked at Georgia instead, the sleek fall of her dark hair, blown straight with a slight curl at the end for the night. In her dark green off the shoulder dress with a tulip skirt that flowed over her curves like water, red on her lips and a light line of black on her upper lids, she looked like a 40s movie star.

"I can't stop staring at you," Emma murmured, sliding her arm around Georgia's waist and pulling her into her side. "Have I told you how gorgeous you look tonight?"

Georgia grinned up at her.

"Yes, but tell me again. And you don't look too bad yourself," she replied. Georgia pulled back so her eyes could survey the plunging neckline of Emma's long-sleeved red velvet jumpsuit, her hair parted in the middle and pinned back in a slick bun at the nape of her neck.

"Does my hair look okay? Cora sent me a video, but I feel like I look like I'm on my way to a dance recital rather than a New Year's Eve party," Emma said, patting her hair nervously.

Georgia slid her hand over the exposed nape of her neck.

"Your hair looks beautiful, Em. I like being able to see this part of your neck." To emphasize her point, she leaned forward and pressed a kiss to Emma's nape, making Emma shiver. "Speaking of Cora, I hope she and Martin don't get the cops called on their party for a noise complaint tonight. Eleni's still on the fence about him."

"Even after I wrote such a glowing recommendation?" Emma said, eyes wide and hand pressed to her chest in mock outrage.

Georgia smirked and said, "I still can't believe you wrote an actual reference letter for him."

Emma shrugged as they made their way through the crowd of familiar faces and strangers. "I like the guy. He's a good influence on Cora."

She recognized many of her neighbors and fellow club members, and they had to stop and chat with people every few feet, Georgia never far from her side. People were curious about her new internship—amazing!—and how her father was doing—about as well as could be expected. But she knew what they were really curious about was her and Georgia's relationship.

After Connie had found out the Saturday a week after they'd gotten together when she'd caught them kissing on Georgia's front porch, post trip to the beach, the news quickly spread around their community.

To Emma's surprise, the fact that they were now together seemed to fascinate people as much as Rachel Whiteman's broken engagement had. Maybe it was because they were two women, maybe it was the thirteen-year age gap, Emma didn't know, but she certainly didn't care.

Let people gossip about them. She was happier than she'd been since she'd lost her mother.

"Should we give the vultures something to chew on?" Georgia whispered in Emma's ear, coming up behind where she'd been sitting, chatting with one of Connie's tennis friends.

"What did you have in mind?" Emma said. She turned to face Georgia as she handed Emma a glass of champagne.

Georgia grinned and placed a lingering kiss on her lips, cupping Emma's face gently, and angling her so she could get deeper. It never ceased to amaze Emma how just the brush of Georgia's lips against hers made the rest of the world disappear. Georgia pulled away, leaving Emma panting slightly.

"Want to go find a closet or even a very dark corner?" Emma said, getting a great look down Georgia's dress from this angle.

"How about a dance instead," Georgia said. She stood up and offered Emma her hand.

Emma took it, downed her champagne in one gulp, and let Georgia tug her to the room where a few couples were dancing to some jazz streaming from the sound system. Georgia spun her out and, with a gentle tug on her hand, reeled her back in, wrapping her arm around Emma's waist, Emma's hand clasped loosely in Georgia's.

She rested her hand on Georgia's low back as they swayed together, cheek to cheek.

Emma spun Georgia out and then dipped her, both of them giggling like little kids when she righted her.

They passed the hours to midnight wrapped up in each other, dancing and kissing and laughing, paying no attention to the whispers of others around them.

"Let's get some fresh air," Emma said eventually. She took Georgia's hand to pull her from the room, which had grown more crowded as midnight drew nearer.

Emma led her to the patio where their breath fogged in the cold air. The winter harbor, empty and dark beneath the cloudy sky, spread out below their feet. There were blankets piled in a wicker basket by the door, and Emma, appreciating the forethought, grabbed one and draped it over her shoulders before draping her arms over Georgia and tucking her in tight, Georgia's back to her chest.

Behind them, they heard the voices of their friends and neighbors as they counted down the end of the year. When the sound of "Happy New Year!" filled the air, Emma leaned forward over Georgia's shoulder, and Georgia turned to face her, peering at Emma over her exposed shoulder, her gray eyes piercing into Emma's.

They kissed, soft and slow and languid, taking their time tasting each other as the party raged on behind them, tucked safely into their own little bubble. Emma's hands ran down Georgia's sides, feeling her ribs expand and contract as she breathed into the kiss. Georgia's hands came up to cover her own, pressing Emma's palms against her waist.

"Happy New Year, Georgie," Emma murmured against her lips.

"Happy New Year, my love," Georgia echoed.

They turned back to the water, snuggled together as a new year began. Snow fell softly in the world beyond their little pocket of warmth, dancing down in fat white flakes that coated the Brightleys' sloping lawn. A light bobbed on a buoy out in the harbor as the tide turned.

Emma rested her chin on Georgia's shoulder and wrapped her

arms around her waist, letting Georgia hold her weight up, if only for this moment.

Happy New Year, Mom, Emma thought as she tipped her head to the sky. I think, this year, your girl's going to be okay.

"Ready to go back inside, babe?" Georgia murmured to her. "It's getting frosty out here."

"Yeah, let's go in," Emma replied softly, placing a light kiss on Georgia's cheek and wiping the imprint of her lipstick away when she pulled back.

They turned and simultaneously reached for each other's hands as they strode through the door, fingers tangled and hearts beating in time.

About the Author

Sarah Levine is a writer and teacher originally from a small seaside town in Massachusetts. She now lives in Brooklyn, NY, with her partner Jasmine and many houseplants. This is her first novel.

Books Available From Bold Strokes Books

Discovering Gold by Sam Ledel. In 1920s Colorado, a single mother and a rowdy cowgirl must set aside their fears and initial reservations about one another if they want to find love in the mining town each of them calls home. (978-1-63679-786-1)

Dream a Little Dream by Melissa Brayden. Savanna can't believe it when Dr. Kyle Remington, the woman who left her feeling like a fool, shows up in Dreamer's Bay. Life is too complicated for second chances. Or is it? (978-1-63679-839-4)

Emma by the Sea by Sarah G. Levine. A delightful modern-day romance inspired by *Emma*, one of Jane Austen's most beloved novels. (978-1-63679-879-0)

Goodbye Hello by Heather K O'Malley. With so much time apart and the challenges of a long-distance relationship, Kelly and Teresa's second chance at love may end just as awkwardly as the first. (978-1-63679-790-8)

One Measure of Love by Annie McDonald. Vancouver's hit competitive cooking show *Recipe for Success* has begun filming its second season, and two talented young chefs are desperate for more than a winning dish. (978-1-63679-827-1)

The Smallest Day by J.M. Redmann. The first bullet missed—can Micky Knight stop the second bullet from finding its target? (978-1-63679-854-7)

To Please Her by Elena Abbott. A spilled coffee leads Sabrina into a world of erotic BDSM that may just land her the love of her life. (978-1-63679-849-3)

Two Weddings and a Funeral by Claudia Parr. Stella and Theo have spent the last thirteen years pretending they can be just friends, but surely "just friends" don't make out every chance they get. (978-1-63679-820-2)

Firecamp by Jaycie Morrison. Going their separate ways seemed inevitable for two people as different as Fallon and Nora, while meeting up again is strictly coincidental. (978-1-63679-753-3)

Coming Up Clutch by Anna Gram. College softball star Kelly "Razor" Mitchell hung up her cleats early, but when former crush, now coach Ashton Sharpe shows up on her doorstep seven years later, beautiful as ever, Razor hopes the longing in her gaze has nothing to do with softball. (978-1-63679-817-2)

Fixed Up by Aurora Rey. When electrician Jack Barrow and artist Ellie Lancaster get stuck on a job site during a blizzard, close quarters send all sorts of sparks flying. (978-1-63679-788-5)

Stranded by Ronica Black. Can Abigail and Whitley overcome their personal hang-ups and stubbornness to survive not only Alaska but a dangerous stalker as well? (978-1-63679-761-8)

Whisk Me Away by Georgia Beers. Regan's a gorgeous flake. Ava, a beautiful untouchable ice queen. When they meet again at a retreat for up-and-coming pastry chefs, the competition, and the ovens, heat up. (978-1-63679-796-0)

Across the Enchanted Border by Crin Claxton. Magic, telepathy, swordsmanship, tyranny, and tenderness abound in a tale of two lands separated by the enchanted border. (978-1-63679-804-2)

Deep Cover by Kara A. McLeod. Running from your problems by pretending to be someone else only works if the person you're pretending to be doesn't have even bigger problems. (978-1-63679-808-0)

Good Game by Suzanne Lenoir. Even though Lauren has sworn off dating gamers, it's becoming hard to resist the multifaceted Sam. An opposites attract lesbian romance. (978-1-63679-764-9)

Innocence of the Maiden by Ileandra Young. Three powerful women. Two covens at war. One horrifying murder. When mighty and powerful witches begin to butt heads, who out there is strong enough to mediate? (978-1-63679-765-6)

Protection in Paradise by Julia Underwood. When arson forces them together, the flames between chief of police Eve Maguire and librarian Shaye Hayden aren't that easy to extinguish. (978-1-63679-847-9)

Too Forward by Krystina Rivers. Just as professional basketball player Jane May's career finally starts heating up, a new relationship with her team's brand consultant could derail the success and happiness she's struggled so long to find. (978-1-63679-717-5)

Worth Waiting For by Kristin Keppler. For Peyton and Hanna, reliving the past is painful, but looking back might be the only way to move forward. (978-1-63679-773-1)

All For Her: Forbidden Romance Novellas by Gun Brooke, J.J. Hale & Aurora Rey. Explore the angst and excitement of forbidden love few would dare in this heart-stopping novella collection. (978-1-63679-713-7)

Finding Harmony by CF Frizzell. Rock star Harper Cushing has to rearrange her grandmother's future and sell the family store out from under her, but she reassesses everything because Gram's helper, Frankie, could be offering the harmony her heart has been missing. (978-1-63679-741-0)

Gaze by Kris Bryant. Love at first sight is for dreamers, but the more time Lucky and Brianna spend together, the more they realize the chemistry of a gaze can make anything possible. (978-1-63679-711-3)

Laying of Hands by Patricia Evans. The mysterious new writing instructor at camp makes Grace Waters brave enough to wonder what would happen if she dared to write her own story. (978-1-63679-782-3)

The Naked Truth by Sandy Lowe. How far are Rowan and Genevieve willing to go and how much will they risk to make their most captivating and forbidden fantasies a reality? (978-1-63679-426-6)

The Roommate by Claire Forsythe. Jess Black's boyfriend is handsome and successful. That's why it comes as a shock when she meets a woman on the train who makes her pulse race. (978-1-63679-757-1)

The Blessed by Anne Shade. Layla and Suri are brought together by fate to defeat the darkness threatening to tear their world apart. What they don't expect to discover is a love that might set them free. (978-1-63679-715-1)

Seducing the Widow by Jane Walsh. Former rival debutantes have a second chance at love after fifteen years apart when a spinster persuades her ex-lover to help save her family business. (978-1-63679-747-2)